# The Killing Sands

## An

## Anthology

Short stories by
these crime-story novelists:

Gary Ponzo
Dani Amore
Rick Murcer
Traci Hohenstein
Tim Ellis
Lawrence Kelter
Rebecca Stroud

CREATESPACE EDITION
PUBLISHED BY
Murcer Press, LLC

Cover by
Katy Whipple Group

Edited by
Jan Green of The Wordverve

Interior book design by
Bob Houston eBook Formatting
http://about.me/BobHouston

ISBN:9780615665740

# The Killing Sands

## An

## Anthology

# Contents

# A Lethal Connection

## by Gary Ponzo

A dead body never looks like it does on TV. There's nothing natural about the position a person takes once they're no longer a person. This is what Detective Mike Barton thought as he approached the lifeless frame hugging the collection of rocks along the beach in La Jolla. The man's head faced straight down as if he'd attempted an ill-advised belly flop from cliffs above the California shoreline. The only problem with that notion was the round hole just beneath the base of his skull. Professional. One bullet. Small caliber. The bullet was still inside the man's brain, a casualty of inertia taking hold after several ricochets.

The sun had just set, and the tide was still moving in, raising the noise level as the waves slapped at the lone group of rocks amidst a quiet stretch of sandy beach. Barton straddled a couple of large boulders, avoiding the ocean water, as his partner Nate Jenson crouched down next to the victim for a closer look.

Jenson clicked on his penlight and said, "I see the problem right here." He illuminated the small, round entrance wound oozing red and white fluid. "He seems to have sprung a leak."

"You're a sick bastard," Barton said.

"Yeah, but I'm *your* sick bastard," Jenson said, flashing his brilliant-white smile against his chocolate-brown skin.

Barton examined the crime scene to assure its integrity. Yellow police tape provided an appropriate perimeter, while a forensic team unloaded equipment from a white van parked on Coast Boulevard. They would soon begin the rudimentary process of collecting evidence. A half dozen uniforms canvassed the area, asking questions to the small gathering outside the tape line; most of them were tourists taking an evening stroll along the beach and discovering a bit of excitement to spice up their vacation.

Barton stretched on a pair of nitrile gloves and sighed. This was the worst part of the process. He had to determine the man's name and assign him an identity. This made it more personal and, therefore, more real. He reached into the man's back pocket and removed his wallet. The man's name was Elliot Sinclair. Barton didn't notice anything extraordinary: credit cards, insurance card, and fitness club identification. It was only when Barton probed further that he came upon the item he dreaded most. A picture of a small girl, maybe four, smiling at the camera with the unabated zest that only the purely innocent can provide. He turned over the photo and saw writing on the back. In crayon, it read, "I luv you Daddy."

"Why do you go and do that to every corpse you see?" Jenson said, looking over his shoulder. "You're fifty-two, never been married, never had kids, and yet the first thing you do is look for the children left behind."

Barton held up the photo for his partner. "You're too guilty to smile like that. Something happens to a human being when they age that prevents them from exuding that kind of sincerity."

"It's called naïveté," Jenson said. "They don't know enough about the world yet to settle into a good old-fashioned sneer."

"You were probably six months old when that sneer first reared its ugly head, huh?"

"Hey, I came out of the womb with street smarts."

Barton frowned. Another cold night, another dead body. Another fatherless child. He made eye contact with a uniform canvassing the crowd along the beach. "Anything?"

The officer shook his head.

"Of course not," Barton murmured. He didn't expect much. This part of the cove was tucked under the cliffs and barely visible from the street. A clever spot to make a kill.

"You know what your problem is?" Jenson said.

"I didn't know I had a problem."

"You're too suspicious. You treat every date like it's an interrogation. I've seen you at work. You dig and dig until you find the flaw. It's a classic case of bringing your work home with you. Next time you go on a date, give it a rest. Just shut down that investigative mind and let it happen."

"Let what happen?"

"Love, man. Let love happen."

"I'll get right on it." Barton grinned. It was all he could do to combat the truths that Jenson was throwing at him. He looked back to the photo. The fatherless girl would not be smiling tonight. Her life had just taken a terrible turn that she didn't deserve. When he looked up, he saw Jenson shaking his head.

"You ever think about adopting?" Jenson asked.

Barton stepped around the corpse, and Jenson followed.

"I've thought about it," Barton said.

"Because you'd be a good dad."

Barton waited for the punch line, but when it didn't come, he said, "Thanks."

Jenson looked down at the dead man. "You notice the angle? He was shot by a lefty."

Barton nodded. "That always helps, doesn't it?"

"He's not the same killer we're looking for," Jenson said.

Barton understood. There had been a rare killing spree along the affluent La Jolla coastline. Several homeless men had been murdered as they hunkered down for sleep in the dunes below the cliffs. The prototypical suspect would be a chemically unbalanced homeless person trying to secure his own territory. But this changed everything.

"No," Barton said. "The victim is different."

"And what's he still doing with his wallet?"

It was a good question. Why would a wealthy-looking gentleman still have a wallet full of money and credit cards if the killer was homeless? A random thought entered Barton's mind. He didn't like the sound of it, so he tried to wash it away by searching for evidence. A serpentine trail dragged out in the sand twelve inches wide moving away from the crime scene. As if someone raked the sand to cover up their footprints.

"I noticed that myself," Jenson said, following his stare. "Like the killer was covering up his tracks."

Barton folded his arms across his chest. The waves were lapping up to the corpse, but not compromising its integrity just yet. The tracks in the sand were about the same size as a large purse. That random thought began to develop some steam.

A voice called Barton's name from the darkness of the beach. A police officer waved him over.

Barton glanced at Jenson. "I'll be right back. Keep on searching the area, okay?"

"You got it, boss."

Barton ducked under the police tape and approached Officer Sam Welch. It was getting dark and Barton didn't recognize the officer until he was right next to him. Welch was tall and mildly overweight. He stood next to a much smaller young man who wore baggy shorts and a skin-tight tee-shirt.

"This here is Jimmy Hall," Welch said to Barton. "He has something to tell you."

The kid pulled a handful of long hair behind his ear and shuffled his feet. He was obviously out of his element.

"It's okay, son," Officer Welch assured him. "Just tell

this gentleman what you told me."

Jimmy Hall shrugged. "Can't you tell him?"

Welch smiled a paternal smile. "He'd like to hear your words." Then he placed a gentle hand on the young man's shoulder. "Look, you can't get in trouble by being honest. No matter what you say to Detective Barton, he will never judge you one way or another."

Barton waited for the kid to settle down. He knew Welch wouldn't waste his time if it wasn't relevant.

"I live up in those condos," the kid finally said, pointing up above the cliffs. "My folks are gone for the weekend, and I was walking past the sliding glass door when I saw something."

Barton stood there in the moonless night with his eyebrows raised.

"Well," the boy continued, "I watch a lot of those cop shows on TV—you know, CSI, that type of show."

"Yes," Barton said. "Very fine shows."

The kid dug a bare toe in the sand. "And it seems that whenever someone talks to the cops they automatically become a suspect."

Barton nodded. "Sure, I understand your concern. Let me ask you this—did you kill that guy over there?"

Jimmy jumped back with his hands up in absolute horror. "No, of course not. Dude, I would never do something like that."

"Well, that's good enough for me," Barton said. "I have no reason to doubt you. You are officially not a suspect."

"Really?" the kid asked, somewhat dubious.

"Look, Jimmy," Barton said, with his palms up. "I know you've been smoking weed, and I know you've tried to cover it up with some lemon-flavored breath mints. And I don't really give a crap. I'm looking for the person who murdered this gentleman over there. I know it wasn't you, so why don't you help me out and tell me what you know?"

The kid seemed to cower at the mention of his smoking habit, and Barton realized he was dealing with a somewhat paranoid witness. He decided to try another direction.

"You know," Barton added, "Officer Welch and I like to puff on the chronic now and again ourselves. We're all pretty much okay with the stuff. Right, Sam?"

Barton looked at Welch and found the cop winking back at him.

"You bet," Welch said. "It's used medically all the time. It reduces stress."

"See, that's what I always say," Jimmy said, coming on board for the ploy.

Barton smiled. "So, can we be friends and discuss what happened to this poor guy over there?"

"Sure," Jimmy replied. "When I went past my balcony, I noticed this woman following him."

Now Barton was interested. "Go on."

"And she was really close, almost like she was pushing him," the kid said.

Barton's mouth became dry. He didn't like where this was headed. "Along the beach, here?" he asked.

"Yeah." Jimmy pointed to the collection of rocks at the base of the cliffs. "She sort of led him there, then pointed something at his head. The next thing I know . . ."

Jimmy seemed unsure of the right words to choose.

"You're doing great, kid," Welch assured him.

"I heard sort of a pop. I think she shot the guy in the head with a gun, because the next thing I knew, the guy did a forward face plant right into those rocks."

"Did you recognize the woman?"

"No, I could barely tell it was a woman from where I was."

"Could you give me a description?"

"Well, not really. I mean she was kind of husky."

"Husky?" Barton asked.

"Like I said, they were a ways away, but she seemed to have a large gut, almost like she was pregnant."

Barton didn't know what to think of that, but he scribbled a couple of notes, then asked a few more questions before thanking the kid and letting him go.

As soon as the circle disbanded, Jenson approached Barton holding up a clear-plastic evidence baggie. With his free hand, Jenson shined a flashlight on the baggie to expose a plain, silver earring sitting at the bottom of the bag.

"A little gift from our killer," Jenson said with a satisfied smile. "He may be a pro, but he's a little careless."

Barton took a couple of steps away from the crowd surrounding the corpse, and his partner followed. "Listen, Nate, I need to tell you something."

Jenson cocked his head. "Go ahead, chief."

"You know how you're always teasing me about not having a girlfriend, right?"

"Right."

"Well, before we partnered up three years back, I had a steady girl. We even lived together for a couple of years."

Jenson smiled at the thought. "Okay. So what's the problem?"

"The problem is . . ." Barton rubbed the side of his face. The waves were creeping in and forcing them to step closer to the cliffs. "She was a professional killer. Hired by top executives from different countries all over the globe to rub out certain rebel dissidents threatening democracy."

Jenson's mouth opened slightly. "You knew about this while you were living with her?"

Barton nodded.

Jenson shook his head. "How?"

"I was trying to let love happen," Barton half-grinned.

Jenson had a questioning look on his face. "Why are you telling me . . ." He glanced down at the baggie in his hand. The lone earring. "Oh."

"We have a witness who believes he spotted a woman shooting Mr. Sinclair."

"Then I just have one question."

"Yes," Barton said, knowing his partner too well.

"She's left-handed."

"Wow," Jenson said, scratching the back of his head. "I can't believe you really had a girlfriend."

"Shut up," Barton said. "The only issue is, the witness said the woman was heavy, like she was pregnant. Sheila was rail thin. She almost made the Olympic swim team. And as far as being pregnant . . . well, that was never going to happen. She never wanted to have children. That was a big issue between us."

"Sure, she may have been an assassin, but not having your baby, that's a deal breaker, huh?"

Barton gave his partner a shove.

They stood there with their own thoughts, considering the next move when something happened that would change Barton's life forever.

The cell phone rang in the pocket of the dead man.

Barton looked at his partner. They both hesitated. They'd seen everything over the years, but not this.

"Better answer it," Jenson said, sealing up and tagging the evidence bag.

Barton stepped under the police tape, reached into the man's jacket, and opened the cell phone with his gloved fingers. The LED display announced the caller as "Private."

Barton touched the talk button and said, "Hello."

"What are you doing?" a woman's voice said.

"What do you mean?" Barton asked.

There was a frustrated breath, then, "I'm sitting here at Weatherby's for an hour thinking you're going to show. Now if you're not man enough to meet me . . . then . . ."

The line went dead. Barton recognized the voice. A loose thought ran through his mind. A bad thought. Weatherby's was just three blocks away. He handed Jenson the dead man's cell phone. "Tag this."

Barton ducked under the yellow police tape flapping in the wind and began walking away from the scene.

"Where are you going?" Jenson asked.

"To chase a lead," he called back.

"You need me?"

Barton shook him off. He dug his hands into his pockets and leaned into the stiff ocean breeze. As he trudged deep steps into the sand, he spied a young couple lying down on a large beach towel, groping each other like zombies trying to eat through their lover's mouths to get to their brains. Barton turned away and began a slow trot, lifting his knees in order to overcome the thick sand. Soon his trot became a sprint. After a few minutes, he realized he had gone too far, missing the staircase to the road. He stopped and leaned over, hands on his knees, gasping for air.

It took a minute for him to recover. He headed toward the staircase with a trickle of sweat meandering down his temple. The sand got thicker and his steps tougher until he began his ascent onto the staircase and eventually ended up on Coast Boulevard.

Barton found Prospect Street and made his way to Weatherby's. Thankfully, he wore a coat and tie, because once inside the ambiance hit him. Candlelit tables were spread out enough to allow a violin player to work his way through the dinner crowd. He squeezed past the group lined up in front of the hostess stand and poked his head into the dining room.

There she was. Sitting by herself in a booth.

Barton had to gather himself and remember the job. Always the job. He found himself approaching the table unprepared. He had a million questions, but not a single one came to mind as he eased into the seat across from her. They looked at each other, but neither one spoke. She hadn't aged much. The only noticeable difference was her obviously pregnant belly.

The silence grew awkward as he took a breadstick and snapped it in half.

"Am I going to need an attorney for this?" she asked.

Barton stabbed a square of cold butter with a knife and smeared it onto the end of his breadstick. He pointed the butter knife at her belly. "Congratulations."

"Don't."

"Don't what? I'm happy for you."

"You're looking at me the way a starving man stares at a stuffed turkey. We could never do this, and you know it."

"I know, I know."

"No you don't. You never did. So don't begin a stroll down memory lane with me like it was the yellow brick road, because there was no Oz for us."

"I didn't come here to reminisce."

"Then why are you here?"

He took a sip of her water. "I've got a stiff one down in La Jolla Cove."

"And?"

"And it's professional."

"And?"

"And it was done by a southpaw."

"Oh come on, Michael. Look at me. Do I look like I've been working tonight?"

He took a bite of the breadstick and shrugged.

She leaned back and folded her arms. "You knew I could never be a stay-at-home mom."

He chewed quickly. "I told you it's not about that."

"I mean think about it—how was I supposed to make a living while sharing my home with a homicide detective?"

"Do you know Elliot Sinclair?"

That stopped her. Her eyes roamed side to side as she ingested the news. She maintained her poker face, but he could tell she was trying too hard.

"It's not a tough question," Barton said.

Finally, she said, "Is that who's getting his photo taken over on the beach?"

"Spoken like a true pro. Always get more information than you give."

"Quit analyzing every little thing."

"I can't help it. It's my job."

She glanced over her shoulder toward the entrance of the restaurant. When she turned back, she sighed, "Are you going to arrest me?"

"Should I?"

"Because if you're not, I'd like you to leave. I'm meeting someone here."

That's the part that bothered Barton about his theory. Why would she be waiting for a man she'd just killed? Coming down from his suspicions, he looked at her with a fresh pair of eyes. She was truly a beautiful woman, even with the excess weight from the pregnancy.

"You look good," he said.

She frowned. "That's enough."

"See," he said, "that's why we didn't last. I was never good at giving compliments, and you were terrible at accepting them. It's like you try to scare off any chance of intimacy."

"Are you through, Dr. Freud?"

"See what I mean?"

"Here's what I see. I see a pathetic man who wants a family so bad he would actually try to convert an assassin into being his bride. That's what I see."

The tension mounted in his chest. She knew the exact button to push. He put down the breadstick and slid to the end of the booth. Before he stood, he thought about something. "Just exactly who are you waiting for?"

Her eyes gave nothing away. She simply pursed her lips and said, "Get out."

Barton wasn't going to learn anything this way. He would wait outside and see what happened. When he swung his legs from under the booth, he knocked over her purse. Several items spilled out. A checkbook, a pair of sunglasses, a set of keys, and an earring.

Barton stared at the earring. He heard the click of a .22 chamber being loaded.

"Sit back down," she said.

Her hands were under the table. Her expression was terminal. This wasn't the same woman he'd just complimented about her looks.

"Sit down," she repeated. This time she raised her eyebrows as if to say, "Don't tempt me."

He sat.

"Keep your hands on the table in front of you."

He did as she said. For a few moments, they said nothing. She kept her head still, but her eyes darted everywhere. It was the first time he'd seen her show indecision. It gave him hope.

"Why don't you tell me about it, Sheila?"

Her restless eyes appeared to settle on Barton by default. She took a deep breath. "He raped me."

"Who?"

"Elliot Sinclair."

"So you killed him?"

"It's not that simple."

"Just tell me why you were calling him on his cell after you did him?"

She seemed confused. "How—"

"Because I was there. I answered his cell phone when you called. That's how I found you."

This seemed to set her back. She shook her head and tried to piece it all together. "That was you on the phone?"

Barton nodded. "Leaving the earring was sloppy. It's not like you."

Her eyes went cold and dark, and Barton realized he'd gone too far. She was about to finish off the only person who could put her away.

"Don't do it, Sheila. The gunshot will only bring you more attention."

"It won't matter," she said. "The minute I'm out that door, I'll disappear into the landscape. They can have all the evidence in the world, but they won't have me."

He knew she was right. She was too involved with the underworld. She had the connections. She would never be found.

Sheila kept her attention on him as she reached down, swept up her loose items, and returned them to her purse. She sat upright, and her right arm seemed to extend under the table to zoom in on her target. Then, for a brief moment, a flash of compassion flickered across her eyes. "Sorry, Michael."

He braced for the shot. In the very moment he had shut his eyes, he heard a familiar voice.

"Mind if I join you kids?"

It was Jenson. His partner had a 9mm tucked discreetly by his side, and he motioned Sheila to make room for him in the booth.

Barton breathed.

Jenson sat next to the assassin and twisted to face her. He dug his automatic into her armpit.

"It's so nice to meet you, Sheila," Jenson said. "My partner told me he was chasing a lead, but I never imagined this."

Sheila never even looked at Jenson. She stared straight at Barton with the glare of a coldhearted killer.

"I'm taking one of you with me," she said.

Barton saw the determination on her face. He tried to diffuse the situation. "You're not thinking straight, Sheila," he said.

She shook her head. "No, I'm not. But I'm not going down without a fight."

"Take a good look around," Jenson said. "Notice anything?"

Sheila glanced briefly around the restaurant. Barton hadn't noticed, but the remaining customers had left their tables. Sheila was so focused on Barton that she didn't see it happen either.

"I had the place evacuated," Jenson said. "Now if you look out that picture window, besides the view of the ocean, you'll notice a nice group of friends I like to call the SWAT team."

Barton could see helmeted men tucked behind steel shields strapped to their arms. Their rifles were all trained on Sheila.

"You see," Jenson said. "There's no way out."

Over years of evolution, humans have developed the ability to warn their enemies of imminent danger. Their lips tighten. Their eyebrows merge. Sheila had adapted her own version of this autonomous skill. She smiled.

Barton had seen the look before, and he needed to

divert the tension before bullets started flying.

"He raped her," Barton said.

"Who?" Jenson asked.

"Elliot Sinclair."

"Our stiff?"

Barton nodded.

"How's a guy like Elliot get the jump on you?" Jenson asked Sheila.

"He slipped something strong in my drink while I was at Harvey's having a martini. The drug hit me hard. It took a while for my memory to return."

Jenson pointed to her belly. "Is that the result of—"

"Yes," she said. "It took me eight months, but I finally tracked him down tonight. I happened to spot him on the boardwalk on my way here, and I couldn't wait. I didn't have the patience. I was too emotional."

"But why would you call him after you shot him?" Barton asked.

"I know the answer to that," Jenson said. He removed a sheet of paper from his jacket with his left hand and unfolded it on the table. "I found this in his pants pocket. He printed this from your e-mail to him. Apparently you two met on a secure dating web site and only knew first names and cell phone numbers. Am I right?"

Sheila nodded.

"You made a blind date with the guy who raped you?" Barton said.

"Pisser, huh?" Jenson said.

"I didn't know he was the same guy until just now. I figured I'd do the guy, then have a date as an alibi thirty minutes later. I didn't know they'd be the same person. It was a good plan until Mr. Scruples here showed up."

"Trust me," Jenson said. "Your plan wasn't so hot to begin with."

"I was too emotional," Sheila said. Her face got tighter. "Like now. I'm capable of anything when I've got all these hormones raging in me."

"Now listen," Barton said. "This is not as bad as it

seems."

"Of course not," Jenson said. "I mean what are we doing here? He raped you. We get a DNA match with the child, and you've got yourself justifiable homicide."

"Who are you bullshitting?" Sheila sneered. "If I did him the night of the rape, maybe. But eight months later? No way. They're going to want me inside for at least twenty. And I'm not going inside. Never have. Never will."

Jenson dug his pistol into her side. "The only reason you're alive right now is because of that baby you're carrying. These guys outside could pick which nostril they want the bullet to enter. You get my drift?"

It seemed that she did. She acknowledged Jenson with a slight grin. It was a sadistic grin that made Barton's stomach twist.

Sheila quickly pulled the gun from under the table and jabbed it into the top of her belly. "If you don't let me out of here, he gets it."

Barton held up his hands. "Oh, man, let's not get stupid here. That kid's done nothing wrong. Leave him out of it."

Sheila looked at Jenson, then she held up her arm so the snipers outside could see what she was doing. There was a dead silence to the place. No silverware rattled. No music played in the background. Just a collective gasp from anyone who could view the assassin's next target.

Barton waved down the SWAT team. With great reluctance on their faces, one by one, they began to stand down.

Sheila gave Jenson a venomous glare. "Get out of the booth," she demanded.

Jenson looked at his partner. Barton nodded. Jenson backed out of the booth.

To a passerby, the scene must've looked bizarre. A pregnant woman backing away from the booth, all the while holding a .22 to her own belly. The entire time, Jenson stood still with his gun trained on her head. Barton knew that nothing good could come of this death dance. He held his hands up high and said, "Let me escort you out of here, Sheila."

The uncertainty lingered on her face as she swiveled her head to take in as much as she could. Barton caught Jenson's eye and made a circling motion with his finger: get a chopper in the air. Jenson nodded and stayed back while Barton followed her out.

She was at the door, backing out, holding the gun to her belly. The look of confusion on the snipers' faces said it all. They couldn't have known what to do. It wasn't a scenario they'd ever trained for.

Sheila used the confusion to move swiftly away from the restaurant. Barton stayed right with her. As long as she didn't object, Barton was going along for the ride. He had no plan. No solution. Just follow the assassin and react. Maybe even stay alive.

As she turned the corner down a side street, two police cars were parked nose to nose with their red and blue lights swirling silently, reflecting off of the row of small houses. The absence of pedestrians made them stand out even more.

Sheila was clearly startled by the events. She'd never even been close to being caught, and this was rattling her. She stumbled backward, glancing around for her next move.

"Please," Barton said, "let me take you in. I can help."

Sheila was in another world now. She barely held the gun to her stomach as she tried to run across the street toward the beach. Toward the crowd who were evacuated and watching the event like spectators at a reality show. Barton saw them for what they really were. Possible hostages.

He shuffled in front of her, trying to slow her pace. "No," he said. "That's not where you want to go. It's too open down there."

"Don't act like you're my accomplice, Mike," she snarled. "I'm on my own, like I've always been."

From the distance, the thumping of a helicopter came

surging toward them. She stood in the middle of Coast Boulevard, which was blocked off but for the SWAT team still lingering and the onlookers who were quickly being ushered away by police. Red and blue lights seemed to increase with every passing minute.

Sheila looked out at the ocean and, with a determined expression, trotted toward the stairs leading to the beach.

"What are you doing?" Barton asked.

"Stop following me," Sheila barked as she hurried down the sandy wooden stairs.

Barton ignored her and kept close as she kicked off her shoes at the base of the steps and headed toward the ocean.

"Sheila, what on earth are you doing?"

"I don't know."

"Well, can we talk about this?"

"Why, so you can get more reinforcements?"

Sheila's feet were kicking up sand into Barton's face as he turned to see the SWAT team take their sniper positions up on the cliffs. The thump of the helicopter's blades was louder now.

"We already have more law enforcement than we need," Barton said, slowing down as Sheila high-stepped into the oncoming waves.

"Sheila, stop!" Barton demanded.

For the first time since he'd known her, she listened to him. Sheila turned to see the wall of guns up on the cliffs and the helicopter now buzzing overhead. A spotlight came down and illuminated a wide circle around the two of them on the beach. Without ever looking up, Barton knew there would be at least two experienced snipers aboard.

"You can't outrun them," Barton said. His heart pumped extra hard, while he tried not to stare at the gun.

She swiveled her head back and forth between the ocean and the cliffs. Barton wasn't sure what she was thinking.

"Tell them to get rid of the helicopter," she yelled over the din of the chopper's powerful blades.

Barton felt the trained eyes of the snipers peering at them through their night-vision riflescopes. Nothing got the attention of the department as much as one of their own in danger.

The sand swirled around them, causing Barton to squint and spit out tiny fragments of sand. He waved off the helicopter and watched the snipers pull their heads away from their sights.

Barton waved furiously again, and the helicopter slowly tilted to the side and moved away from the beach.

Sheila must've realized the corner she was in, because she stopped fidgeting and faced Barton. Her expression caused him to skip a breath. "I have no family," she said.

"I know."

She looked down and patted her belly. It was as if she were all alone. Yet it still seemed creepy to see her point a gun at her belly with one hand and stroke it with the other.

"I can't do this," she said in a far away voice.

He wasn't sure what she meant, but was glad to see her stationary.

Barton's phone rang, and Sheila came out of her trance.

"Answer it," she commanded.

Barton pushed the talk button and pressed the phone to his ear. A moment later, he put the phone down and said, "They want to know what you want."

Sheila let out a psychotic laugh. "Well, let's see, I guess a week in St. Martin is out of the question."

Barton stared.

Then her expression went dark again. "Tell them to call for an ambulance," she said.

"Don't talk like that, Sheila."

"Tell them to send an ambulance right now." She had a permanent poker face, and Barton didn't want to guess any longer. An ambulance meant a chance for life.

Whose life, he didn't know.

"Now," she said.

Barton told Jenson her demand. He shut his phone.

"Five minutes," he said.

"Good." She shuffled in place. It was her nature to slither within the shadows of the streets, but now she stood there like a leopard caught out in a clearing. A killer, miles away from any cover.

"Just do what they want, Sheila. Life is worth living."

She shook her head. "You're such a dreamer. You're trying to save the world, but you haven't figured out that your world is just temporary. Nothing ever lasts."

"Listen to me. There's a better way, but you've taken on too much stress to be thinking clearly."

The helicopter could be heard lurking in the distance. The beach was barren now; the onlookers had been forced away from the scene, leaving the two of them alone.

"I have no past," she said. "I have no future. All I have is right now. Do you understand?"

"No."

"Of course you don't. You're Pollyanna with a badge."

"Sheila, you need—"

"I don't have your stamina for life," she said, looking down at her protruding abdomen. "It's funny. I could kill anyone on the planet without ever blinking an eye, but when it came time for me to have the abortion, I couldn't do it." She looked up at Barton with tears trickling down her cheeks. "Funny, huh?"

Barton nodded. He wanted to hug her and tell her he'd make it all right, but she couldn't make the feeling last. Her eyes became dark and dangerous.

Sheila glanced over Barton's shoulder and must've spotted the snipers positioned all along the cliffs above. Behind her, a vast barrier, like a giant wall. In front of her, a firing squad. The only thing which gave Barton hope was the fact that she kept stroking her large stomach with her free hand. Subconsciously or not, she felt something for that child.

Sheila looked down at the waves running in and out between her bare legs. "I could swim for it," she said, almost a question.

"No, you'd drown out there."

"They don't know how strong of a swimmer I am. I could go five or ten miles down the shoreline. They'd have a hard time tracking me at night."

Barton shook his head. "The Coast Guard would be on top of you before you could go a hundred yards."

Now, their eyes met, and she seemed smaller somehow, maybe even younger and more insecure.

"I don't want you to go," Barton said.

"I don't have much of a choice," she said with resignation in her voice. She clenched her lips together as if preparing for a vaccination. "You're a good man, Michael. A little naïve, but nonetheless . . ."

Barton sensed a softening in her tone. "Can we talk about this over coffee?"

She smiled a sad smile.

Behind him an ambulance siren approached. It seemed to snap the warmth from her tone.

"That's my cue," she said.

He held out his open hands. "Let me help you. I'll speak with the DA. I can—"

That's where it ended. She raised her gun deliberately and aimed it at Barton. Every finger was wrapped around the handle. Not one was on the trigger. If she wanted to kill him, she would have fired immediately, but she didn't. She was waiting for the snipers to put her down.

"Take care of him," she whispered.

"No!" Barton yelled.

The bullets came hard and furiously and seared through her head until there was nothing left. None of the shots hit below her neck. She collapsed onto the wet sand. A hideous sight.

Barton froze. He was trained to handle anything thrown at him, but now he stood there paralyzed. A stinging surge of vomit spiked up into his mouth, and he spit it out. Precious seconds passed as he stared at her bulging abdomen. The baby. Sheila was now a skintight prison to the child. He rolled Sheila on her back and dragged her away from the rushing waves until he was on dry sand. He pulled her dress up over her stomach, then pulled her panties off and left her naked from the chest down. He felt her belly for any movement.

None.

The ambulance screeched to a stop on the street above them. Barton saw Jenson pointing to him on the beach and yelling instructions into his cell phone at the same time. The thump of the helicopters blades seemed to get closer as the two EMTs came rushing out of the emergency vehicle with black bags and followed Jenson's instructions.

The EMTs high-stepped it over the thick sand and dropped their bags next to Sheila. When they saw what was left of her head, they seemed to hesitate. Out of instinct, they knelt next to her and felt for a pulse and searched for something to examine. One of them stuck a laryngoscope down a passageway where Sheila's mouth used to be. Barton recognized him. Nick McLane.

McLane groped furiously around her chin and neck area. "There's too much trauma," he said to the other EMT. "We've lost the trach."

"What does that mean?" Barton said.

McLane stopped and looked at Barton, who had both hands on Sheila's belly.

"It means we can't intubate her," McLane said. He must've noticed the blank stare on Barton's face, so he added, "We can't get her any oxygen."

"Which means?"

"Which means," McLane looked down at Sheila's belly, "she's not going to make it."

"Of course she's not," Barton said. "Now let's cut her open and get this kid out of there."

The two techs looked at each other. McLane said, "We can't."

"What do you mean, you can't."

"Look, Mike, we're EMTs, not obstetricians. We can't do C-sections."

"Look at her," Barton said. "You can't save her."

Sheila was missing half of her head. Her nose was an open passageway to the lower part of her brain. McLane reluctantly withdrew the laryngoscope from her severed mouth and nodded. He looked at his watch to denote the time of death.

The helicopter approached from over the cliffs. It hovered much higher this time, avoiding a sandstorm, while it beamed a large searchlight over the scene.

"All right then," Barton said. "Let's get this baby."

"I'm telling you," McLane said. "We have no training for that. The best we can do is get her to the hospital. Hope for the best."

"She has no family. There's nothing to lose."

His words had no effect.

Barton's hands trembled. He couldn't feel any movement inside of Sheila's taut belly.

"How long can this child survive in there?" Barton said.

McLane shrugged. "Maybe a couple of minutes."

Barton found himself panting. It had been longer than that since Sheila went down.

He heard the other EMT say, "I'm sorry."

Barton's head spun with unbearable thoughts. "Sorry? About what?"

"The baby's gone," the man said, avoiding eye contact.

From all sides, sirens approached. Flashing lights swirled around them as police vehicles stormed across the beach from the south. The local cops swarmed the scene while commanding voices barked a perimeter.

Barton stared at Sheila's belly. He was just inches away from saving an innocent life, and yet, he might as well be on the moon. The child didn't deserve to go this far and fall short. He fought back the urge to vomit again. McLane closed his black case and came to his feet.

"Give me a scalpel," Barton said.

McLane didn't move.

"Give me a damn scalpel now!" he demanded.

McLane unzipped his bag and handed Barton a slender package with the number 15 imprinted on the outside. Barton ripped open the paper packaging and grabbed the scalpel by the handle. The spotlight from the helicopter was his only true illumination. He had to move aside to avoid his own shadow from covering the sight. With a shaky hand he pressed the blade to Sheila's stomach.

He looked up at the EMT. "Like this?"

McLane made a half-shrug. "At this point, I don't think it matters."

Barton pressed the blade straight down the length of Sheila's stomach. He created a long, deep laceration, but he couldn't see anything but tissue and a straight line of blood.

"Harder," McLane said. "You've got muscles to get through."

A group of uniforms surrounded them, but Barton's focus was the scalpel twitching between his fingers. There was no time to worry about injuring the baby or fictitious lawsuits. He had to cut deep and fast.

He plunged the blade down until he felt it break through a barrier. He yanked hard and tore through tissue and muscle until Sheila's belly split open like an overripe watermelon. He pulled apart the two sides of her abdomen and fell back as a clear fluid spilled out onto his pant legs and muddied up the sand. That's when he finally saw the baby huddled up into a ball. Even in the dark confines of his womb, Barton could see the baby boy was blue. He wrapped his right hand behind the baby's head and slowly pulled the child from his death chamber. The infant was limp, slimy, and unresponsive. The umbilical cord kept him from getting too far from the womb.

Barton cradled the fragile lump of flesh, but had no idea what to do next. The two EMTs, however, finally had someone to revive. McLane slipped a forceps onto the umbilical cord, and the other EMT cut the cord with bandage scissors. McLane began pinching the child's toes. The other guy ruffled the boy's thin hair, trying to get a response. Barton had the sense they were guessing a bit.

McLane placed a tiny plastic mask that molded around the infant's nose and mouth and pumped the bag that fed into the bottom of the mask. He was introducing oxygen into the child's lungs while the other EMT continued to pinch and ruffle.

Barton felt helpless holding the wilted life in his arms. The poor kid was so close to making it. Barton could feel a tear drip over his left eyelid and trickle down his cheek. His hopes faded with every unresponsive pump of the resuscitator.

He looked up and realized that there were at least thirty law enforcement officers of varying rank surrounding them and staring at the lost child. The only sound was the constant thumping of the helicopter. Nothing else. A deep, morose mourning spread over the crowd as McLane pumped the bag with less and less enthusiasm. Barton's eyes were blurry with moisture.

Then it happened. A high-pitched scream that pierced through the night like the call of a wild animal. Barton wasn't sure if it was the final wail of a dying infant or the beginning of life right there in his arms. He wasn't sure, that is, until he heard a juicy sniffle next to him and saw McLane wipe his eyes with the back of his hand.

"You did it." McLane choked.

Barton pulled the child close and watched him grasp for newfound air with every new scream. He was no longer blue, and his limbs moved in concert with his cry. It was the dance of life. He'd never seen anything more beautiful. Barton felt a hand on his shoulder and turned to see his partner smiling down at him.

"He couldn't be in better hands," Jenson said.

They both stared at the beautiful boy with ten

beautiful fingers and ten tiny toes, and Barton said, "Welcome to the world, buddy. I'm going to make it a safer place just for you."

# About the Author of *Lethal Connection*

**Gary Ponzo** has been writing short stories for almost fifteen years and has been published in some highly popular literary magazines, including *Amazing Stories* and *Potpourri*. Two of his stories have been nominated for the very prestigious Pushcart Prize. He is also the author of the award-winning novel, *A Touch of Deceit*.

His Nick Bracco series includes *A Touch of Revenge* and *A Touch of Greed*. Gary is working on the next installment in the series, where FBI agent Nick Bracco uses his mafia cousin to track down terrorists.

Gary currently lives in Chandler, Arizona, with his wife Jennifer and two children, Jessica and Kyle.

# Bullet River

*by Dani Amore*

~~~

For life and death are one,
even as the river and the sea are one.
- Khalil Gibran -

~~~

# 1.

Just before I found the dead girl in the river, I had been thinking about how strange it was to get a sunburn just a few days after Christmas. Ordinarily, back home in Michigan, I'd be dressed in jeans, a T-shirt, and a thick sweater. And I would be fairly pale, with that washed-out, pensive expression people in the Midwest get when they know the worst of winter is yet to come.

But right now, I wasn't wearing a sweater. In fact, I wasn't even wearing pants.

Instead, I was floating on an inflatable lounge chair, a beer in my hand, my pale skin turning bright red. The best part was the beer was by no means my first. Which meant the pain of the sunburn had yet to actually register. I figured it would hit me tomorrow morning along with any aftereffects of a half-dozen Heinekens.

I'd been in Florida for a week now, ever since I'd helped a young woman escape from the clutches of one of my former clients: a dangerous and vindictive law firm in Detroit.

They had sent me after her, claiming she was a lawyer at the firm who had stolen highly sensitive information and was now blackmailing the partners. Turned out not to be the case. The woman was an honest lawyer who the partners had invited to take part in their money-laundering operations. She declined and went to the Feds, but the firm tried to kill her, so she ran.

Once I figured everything out, I took her away from a couple of bad guys and got her to Arizona. A buddy of mine who lived there was an expert at helping people disappear. The last time I saw her, she was happy.

The guys back in Detroit, though? They hated the Garbage Collector. That's my nickname, by the way. At first, I didn't really care for the name all that much, but after a while, it kind of grew on me.

So now I'm known in Detroit, Chicago, New York, and Los Angeles as the Garbage Collector. Which means I retrieve people and things that are usually tainted, illegal, or just downright dangerous.

I have a real name, but I keep that to myself, thank you very much.

So, not wanting to head back to Michigan and find out what those nasty lawyers might have planned for my homecoming, I got in touch with a friend here in Estero, Florida, who put me in touch with an old Italian couple, also from Michigan, who were heading to Italy for the winter. It hadn't been a part of their plan—most come to Florida in the winter and go somewhere else during the uncomfortable, blazing heat of summer. But according to my friend, apparently something had happened back in Italy that required their attention, and they wanted some security for their house.

That's where I came in.

The house was very nice. It consisted of three floors. The top was the master suite. The middle level was the living space, which consisted of a great room, kitchen, dining room, and two bedrooms with two bathrooms. There was also a two-story, screened-in lanai with an outdoor sitting area that overlooked the pool below. Just down from the pool were a dock and the Estero River.

The lower level was the pool, the garage, and a small apartment. I'd agreed to stay in the apartment and provide security for the main house. Apparently, someone(s) had broken in last year. They had vandalized a few rooms, stolen very little, and then helped themselves to the swimming pool for a few days. They had apparently also brought along their dog and let it swim in the pool. The homeowners figured that out when the pump and pool heater stopped working, and they traced the problem to about three pounds of dog hair stuck in the filter.

So this time, the couple refused to leave their place

unattended. What my friend had told them about me, I wasn't sure. Probably that I was a security professional with an impeccable background. Which was half true.

The long and short of it? I agreed to spend a few months in Florida, stay in the apartment for free, and receive a monthly stipend for my security services.

I figured no one back in Michigan would miss the Garbage Collector. It might also be enough time to let the lawyers cool down and reconsider arranging any payback for yours truly. Cooler heads would realize just how bad an idea that could turn out to be.

I was honest with the old Italian folks, though. Even though there was a private investigator's license in my wallet with my real name, I didn't show it to them. I also didn't tell them I was known as the Garbage Collector and that my specialty was collecting undesirables: people who skipped bail, blackmailers, runaways, thieves, and miscreants in general.

Not to sound egotistical, but the folks liked me.

Hey, first time for everything.

•

My Heineken was empty, so I paddled to the shallow end of the pool with my free hand, slid off the lounge chair, and used the steps to climb out of the pool.

The reflection in the apartment's sliding glass doors caught my eye. Not bad. You couldn't make out the slight gray at the edge of my temples, and the silhouette of my body was good enough—broad shoulders, narrow waist, dimmed scar on my shoulder, and the old bullet wound in my leg.

A beauty contest trophy would never be in my future, but I didn't have a problem with that. I had once rescued a former beauty queen who'd gotten hooked on crack and was being abused by her drug-dealing boyfriend. Her family hired me to bring her back, which I did. She went into rehab and is doing fine now. But in my opinion, that whole beauty-contest industry can really fuck people up.

The big towel with the University of Florida logo went around my waist, and I padded into the apartment. It was a simple set up: a single great room broken up into a small living room with a couch and television set, and a dining room with a blue dining table and four chairs. The kitchen was next to the dining area. It was small: a fridge, a stove, a dishwasher, and sink. A few cupboards. There was a hallway off the kitchen that led to a small bathroom with a shower, and further on, two bedrooms—one a bit bigger than the other. The smaller bedroom had two twin beds, and the bigger bedroom had a queen.

I was sleeping in the big bedroom.

The empty beer bottle went into an empty six-pack case. I pulled two more beers from the fridge, changed out my swim trunks for a pair of cargo shorts, and walked down to the small dock.

There was a boat hoist but no boat. Just a kayak locked to the dock's support posts. I worked the combination, sprang the lock, and freed the kayak along with its carbon-fiber paddle.

I lowered the kayak into the water, sat on the edge of the dock, and held the vessel steady with my feet. I lowered the beers into the little hatch behind the seat, then lowered my ass into the kayak.

I pushed away from the dock and paddled out into the middle of the Estero River.

The river had become quite a surprise for me. In Michigan I'd spent most of my time in powerboats roaring across vast stretches of lake, usually for a destination, never just to enjoy the water itself.

Now the tide was going out, so I was naturally pulled away from the dock toward a large, sweeping bend in the river.

I glanced over my shoulder; the large house was still visible over the top of the mangroves lining the bank. It looked especially impressive from the river.

Wind ruffled the surface of the water and bent the tall reeds back toward the river bank.

I popped off the cap of a beer and drank half of it in one long pull, set it between my legs, grabbed the paddle, and leaned forward.

The kayak shot ahead with smooth, balanced power. I paddled all the way down to where the river opened up onto the Gulf of Mexico. The trip took me twenty minutes. I celebrated by draining the rest of my first beer and opening the second.

I took a more leisurely paddle on the way back, upstream, aided by the fact that the tide had stopped going out and the water was in a relatively neutral state.

My second beer was only half-finished when I came around the bend in the river. The house I was watching still loomed high above the mangrove plants.

I steered the kayak into a little area of backwater surrounded by tall grass to finish the rest of my beer before I loaded the kayak back onto the dock.

There wasn't a stitch of breeze in this little protected spot.

I rested the paddle across my thighs, casually checked for alligators. (I'd been told there really weren't any around this area anymore, but I refused to take anyone's word for it.)

The beer came to my lips, and I saw a glow of white off to my right. I emptied the beer and put it back into place on the floor of the kayak.

I put the paddle back in the water and gently stroked the still water, sending the kayak toward the glow of white.

There was the possibility it was a turtle shell; I'd heard they show up from time to time and are valuable.

As I got closer, I realized it wasn't the shell of a turtle.

It was a woman.

Or at least, what was left of her.

I stopped the kayak from getting any closer, but a small wave I had created pushed up against the corpse, and she lolled slightly toward me.

A ravaged face turned toward me.

The sight froze me, sent a shaft of ice through my

insides.

Not because of the horrors of death. And not because of the ravages inflicted by death, time, and the river.

The face shocked me for a very simple reason.

It was a face I knew.

# 2.

I had no choice but to leave her there.

Like anyone associated on some level with crime, cops, lawyers, and all of the bullshit that goes with it, I knew from experience that irrational decisions could lead to some pretty horrible results.

The fact was I desperately wanted to free her from her soggy grave, even though I knew it was a terrible idea. But in my business, you have to be able to shut off emotions like you're blowing out a candle.

So that's what I did.

I didn't feel good about it. In fact, I felt like a piece of shit. But she was already dead. Her dignity . . . well, not much left of that either.

Instead, I paddled back to the dock, got out, tied the kayak to its mooring rack, carried my empty bottles inside the apartment, and put them in recycling.

Next, I left the apartment and did a perimeter walk of the property. It was my job now, after all. But I really did it because it gave me time to think. And because I also couldn't help but wonder if there were any other surprises nearby.

The stairs from the pool led up to the second-floor lanai. I checked all of the sliding doors and the little pass-through to the kitchen. Everything was locked up tight.

Back down the stairs, I used the screen door off one end of the pool area and stepped into the yard. I walked the property from the river all the way down the long, rectangular lot to the street. Then I returned on the other side of the property.

Nothing was amiss.

I let myself back in via the screen door on the other side of the pool, then sat in the white plastic chair outside the sliding door to the apartment.

The girl's face I had instantly recognized. No doubt about it.

I knew her.

In fact, I had known her quite well.

I pulled my cell phone out of my pocket and held it in my hand.

The screen was clear, just a hint of reflection from the water in the pool.

I took a deep breath.

Then called the cops.

# 3.

There wasn't a whole lot to Estero, Florida. It didn't have an actual "downtown." Or a Main Street. It was essentially a stretch of road along and just off of Highway 41.

Because it was unincorporated, the law enforcement agency responsible for Estero was the Lee County Sheriff's Office.

One of their cars pulled up the driveway.

"Afternoon," the cop said. "Nice place."

There was a look of not-so-subtle skepticism on his face. He knew instinctively that I didn't own the house or the property.

"Thanks," I said.

"You live here?" he asked.

"I'm staying in the apartment," I said, nodding my head toward the back of the house.

He nodded back.

"Did you call about a body?" he asked.

Before I could answer, paramedics in a Lee County vehicle roared down the driveway.

"Yeah, I called 911," I said.

The paramedics screeched to a halt.

"You're not going to need them," I said.

"Show me what you saw," the cop said.

"You're going to need a boat."

"Got one coming," he said.

"All right, this way," I said and turned back toward the house. I skirted the main building, cut through the grass, and walked around the pool to the dock.

I walked out onto the dock, went to the far right corner that looked out over the river.

The little backwater area was barely visible. I pointed toward it.

"See that little offshoot of the river over there? Looks

like it goes back into a lagoon or something?" I said.

The cop looked along the direction of my finger.

"Yeah," he said.

"That's where I saw a body, looked like a woman, about twenty minutes ago," I said. "I was kayaking."

On cue, a Lee County Sheriff's boat putted around the bend in the river. The cop thumbed the little mike on his shoulder.

"Adam, stop; go into that little backwater right there. That's where the body supposedly is." The cop shot a little sideways glance at me, letting me know he assumed there was a fairly good chance I would turn out to be full of shit.

Not a bad assumption, actually.

"You been drinkin' today, sir?" he said.

"Sure have, Officer," I said. "I had a few of my friends from Holland over."

He just looked at me.

"Heinekens," I explained. "Just a few, sitting by the pool."

"Any while you were out on the water?"

I wasn't sure what the rules were in Florida for that kind of thing. Lying to the cops is something I've certainly done my share of, but it's not first on my list.

Nonetheless, I said, "No, sir."

He nodded, clearly not believing me.

A blast of static erupted from somewhere on his uniform or belt; I couldn't tell where.

I did understand the message that followed, though.

The guys from the boat had confirmed what I'd found and added one little detail with just one word.

*Homicide.*

# 4.

I sat in the interrogation room, euphemistically labeled a "conference room." Two guys, one old and tan, the other young and tan, sat with me. We were having our own little "conference," law-enforcement style. We'd gone over my story several times. Why I was in Florida, who I was, and how I'd found the girl.

"Pretty big coincidence, don't you think?" the young one said. He had sunglasses, Maui Jim's, pushed back onto the top of his head. He had a peach-colored goatee that was so thin I almost felt sorry for him.

"What do you mean?" I said. Young & Tan shot a look to Old & Tan.

"Well, you move into that apartment, and bam, we got a floater," he said.

I just shrugged, perhaps a bit too dismissively because his face got flushed, and I could see the skin turn pink underneath his Noatee.

"Tell me again what brought you here," Old & Tan said.

"A job."

"And you do what for a living?" he said.

"I'm a security consultant."

"Yeah, right," Young & Tan said, scoffing it out of his mouth like a hairball.

"What were you hired to do?" the old one said.

"Security on the estate where I'm currently staying."

Young & Tan rolled his eyes. His hand went to his sunglasses like he wanted to drop them onto his nose, but then he remembered he was indoors, so he scratched his girl-stubble instead.

Old & Tan spoke again. Clearly, he had wanted the younger one to lead the interview, but that hadn't gone very well; so he finally just took over.

"Tell us again why you were on the river and how you

managed to find the body," he said.

By now, telling the story again felt like reciting a poem I'd had to memorize in elementary school. I repeated it the same exact way I'd told it the first seven times.

Young & Tan looked at the ceiling, clearly bored with me.

"Know a girl named Crystal Stafford?" Old & Tan said.

I thought for a moment. "No." If he was talking about the girl in the river, well, I knew her all right. I just didn't know her as Crystal Stafford.

O&T tapped a pen against a blank pad of paper. Clearly, my answers hadn't been worthy of a lot of note-taking. I took a little bit of pride in that.

"When is this security project expected to end?" he said.

Y&T laughed outright at that one. "I don't get how you can say shit like that with a straight face," he said to his partner.

"He's a good cop; that's why you don't understand it," I said.

Y&T almost stood up like he was going to throw a punch at me, but the older one waved him down.

"We'll be in touch," he said to me.

# 5.

I grew up in a world without religion. In fact, when I was younger and perfecting my skills at hurting people, I was always somewhat amused when they called out for God to help them. Begging for Jesus. Praising Allah, etc. As far as I could tell, those benign beings never helped out any of them.

Maybe they didn't want to mess with me.

So even though I've never set foot in a church my whole life—except that one time to kill a pedophilic priest, which probably doesn't count—I felt a little guilty doing so much lie-telling.

Because unfortunately, the correct answer to the detectives' question would have been, "I don't know Crystal Stafford, but I sure know who that girl in the river is."

But they hadn't asked me that, in those exact words. Nor did they tell me not to leave the area.

Which explained why I was on Delta Flight 1419 as it touched down at Detroit Metro at about seven o'clock. By eight, I was in a rental car headed for a strip club called the Bermuda Triangle on the infamous 8 Mile Road.

Okay, continuing on the religion theme: I have a confession to make.

My relationships with women have been exclusively transactional in nature. Why? Generally speaking, a few reasons, I suspect. A lifetime with virtually no permanent address. Instead of friends, a loose network of less-than-prominent lawyers, bail bondsmen, and other employers in the field of fugitive apprehension. And a need for some form of environmental isolation to help identify the approach of those harboring ill will toward yours truly.

So escorts and strippers. Which are usually one in

the same.

I thought of this as I left the rented white Chevy Malibu with the strip club's valet, an ambitious young man in a white shirt and tie. I then went inside, got a booth, and a bucket of beer.

I felt nothing of the somewhat relaxed state I had been in during my stay in Florida. I was back in Detroit. Where people knew me. And knew the things I'd done. Maybe even the things I'd done recently.

It was a dead feeling inside me. This is where I'd met "Crystal." It was all coming back to me, even as the waitress took away my first empty, and the first girl slid in beside me.

She looked like Gwyneth Paltrow with a weak chin.

"What time did you get here?" she asked me. Strippers always ask this so they can gauge how much you may have had to drink and how desperate you are for some company, and to get an idea if other girls had taken a shot at you.

"Ten minutes ago," I said, as I polished off my first beer. Nothing makes me want to drink like airplane travel. I hate it.

It would have been nice to dispense with trying to get some questions answered, but the club had very little privacy. The booths were right next to each other, and there was even an elevated walkway behind the booths. You never knew when someone might be listening.

So when she offered to take me back to the VIP rooms, I agreed.

She led the way to a section of the club guarded by a bouncer. He nodded to us as we passed him. The dancer guided us past at least a dozen small booths with black curtains pulled across their entrances. She went to a booth at the very back of the space, pulled the curtain aside. I sat on the leather bench as she closed the curtain.

I held onto my beer as she took off her top, kicked off her giant, clear, plastic stripper shoes, and sat on my lap.

"Let me ask you a question," I said.

"Sure," she said. She started grinding out of habit.

"Did you ever know a girl whose stage name was Kiki? Her real first name was Kristen."

The girl looked at me. "Sounds familiar. What did she look like?" As she said this, she turned around, bent over, and shook her ass in front of my face.

I looked past her butt cheeks.

"She had short brown hair, muscular legs, a little tattoo of a butterfly on her lower back."

She stood up and turned back to me, shook her head. "No, but you should ask Viv. She's been here forever and remembers everyone. She's kind of the House Mom around here, always taking care of the younger girls."

The song ended, and I stood up. I gave the girl a fifty—twice the cost of a lap dance.

She thanked me, and when we emerged from the VIP section, I had her point out Viv.

Viv looked to be of Arabian descent, with big black hair, a hawk nose, and barbed-wire tattoos coming out of her panties.

She turned and smiled at me as I approached. Beautiful teeth, and I could just make out crow's feet at the corners of her eyes, buried beneath an inch of pancake.

"How about a dance," I said to her.

She smiled like she hadn't been asked that in a long time.

Viv hooked her arm through mine, and we found another VIP room.

"First time here?" she said.

"No, I've been here a couple times, mostly to see a girl named Kiki. Know her?"

"Kiki! Sure I knew her," Viv said. "She left here a few weeks ago, not sure why. Never said goodbye to any of us. Sometimes that happens, but I wouldn't have expected it from her."

By now, Viv was rocking back and forth on me, and

she wasn't petite by any means.

"How can I find out where she went?" I said.

Viv narrowed her eyes at me. She stopped gyrating.

Old strippers, man. They can see a lie from a mile away.

I pulled a hundred-dollar bill out of my wallet.

Viv raised an eyebrow.

She snatched it out of my hand.

"Juju would know," she said. "He's over at the main bar, in the yellow baseball cap. He runs a lot of the younger girls. Don't tell him I mentioned his name, though. It's not a good idea to get on his bad side. Do you understand what I'm saying?"

I nodded.

"You've been warned." She got off my lap and left.

After a minute or two, I walked out and found the main bar.

Juju was an Albanian guy. I'd never met him, but I knew who he was. His love of Ralph Lauren clothes was obvious. He always wore Ralph Lauren khakis, Ralph Lauren shirts, and he was never without a Ralph Lauren baseball cap just to make sure you noticed the logo.

"Are you Juju? The manager?" I asked. Albanian mobsters were infamous for imitating their Sicilian counterparts, right down to the goofy nicknames. I had no idea what Juju's real name was. Probably Juhitsigov Markozuliac or something like it.

"Is there a problem?" he said.

"Yeah, I don't see Kiki around."

"Who?" He had a bored expression on his face. He had already pegged me as another desperate loser, a sucker who'd fallen for one of his employees.

"Kiki. She's a dancer," I said. "Really nice-looking girl, athletic body, short brown hair, muscular legs."

Juju laughed and spread his hands out wide. "That's half the girls who work here, man. Are you kidding me?"

"Oh, gosh darn it," I said.

But Juju was lying. I suddenly had the idea that it would be a lot of fun to take an actual polo club and bash Juju's teeth in.

He may have sensed it.

"What can I tell you?" he said. "Lots of pretty girls here for you. Take your pick." He turned his back on me.

"Maybe I will," I said as he walked away. I went back to my booth. The waitress had refilled my bucket. I drank two beers in four minutes and had another idea.

After a half hour watching the girls, I had picked out the oldest, nastiest, most desperate woman I could find. She was getting no free drinks, no dances, no attention at all.

She was perfect.

I drank and waited until she looked at me. When she did, I held her eye contact and gave a slight lift of the chin.

Within thirty seconds, she appeared at my booth like a dog who'd just graduated from obedience school.

"Would you like some company?" she said. Her voice sounded like a worn-out belt sander.

"Boy, would I," I said.

"My name's Pammy," she said.

"Great."

Compassion has never been my strong suit. But the sagging skin, the wrinkles, the faded tattoos, I knew she was prepped for serious exploitation.

I bought her two shots of tequila at ten bucks a pop and slipped her a hundred-dollar bill.

"Look, I'm not gonna lie," I said. "I don't want a dance; I only want information."

"What do you want to know?" she said. This girl had seen it all. Nothing surprised her.

"Kiki."

"What about her?"

"Who ran her?" I said. "And don't say Juju."

"Same guy who runs most of the young ones," she said. Her voice took on an especially bitter tone when she said the word "young."

"And that would be Juju's boss, right?" I said. "Who is he?"

Pammy glanced around the club. She knew where Juju was, and if he was watching.

"Okay, here's the deal," she said. "I'll tell you, but you have to take me in the back, get a dance, then come back and take a couple more girls back, so they don't know who told you."

"I'm not the kind of guy who talks," I said.

"They can make you talk," she assured me. "They can make anyone talk."

I made a mental note of the cash I had on me. More than enough.

"You got it," I said.

She tossed off a third shot that had magically appeared at our table.

"His name is Darko Fama," she said. "Everyone just calls him Darkie."

"That's nice," I said. I thought about a Dalai Lama joke but figured it'd been done a few million times.

"Where can I find him?" I said.

"He hangs out at a coffee place around 15 Mile and Hayes. Called Goodfellows. He's there all day, every day."

I nodded.

"Time for you to take me back," she said.

"No problem," I said.

I was a man of my word, after all.

# 6.

I knew I had a decision to make. Until now, I'd just asked around a bit, bought drinks for some dancers, maybe gotten a lap dance or two.

But going into Goodfellows was a whole new step.

There would be no going back.

I sat in my rental car outside the coffee shop. I'd spent the night at a Holiday Inn a few blocks away. The breakfast buffet had looked like a scene from Overeaters Gone Wild. I'd stuck with some toast and coffee.

As I waited for my Albanian friends to show some signs of life in Goodfellows, I thought about why I was doing all of this in the first place. And was there a way to avoid it? I could, after all, just skedaddle back to my hideaway in northern Michigan on Drummond Island. No one could get to me there.

But I'd taken the little Florida housesitting gig, and it had gone off the rails. No point in looking back.

The easy answer: I knew Crystal Stafford. I actually knew her as Kristen, even though her stage name was Kiki.

And I had known her quite well.

Since I had found her body, the Lee County Sheriff's detectives would be looking at me as their prime suspect. I had to figure out who was responsible fast and get back to Florida before they realized I was gone.

Which brought me back to Goodfellows and Darko Fama, or the politically incorrect nickname "Darkie" to his friends.

Things were about to get ugly, but I saw no better option.

Two guys pulled up in front of the coffee shop in a silver Cadillac.

One of them looked familiar to me.

After a few minutes, I got out of the car and went

inside.

•

The first thing I noticed was a tattoo on the forearm of a short, squat guy with a T-shirt that read "The only thing to fear . . . is a lack of beer."

Classy.

The tattoo, however, was nothing to scoff at. It was worn by a lot of Albanian gangsters and more than a few soldiers who had fought, if you want to call it that, for the Kosovo Liberation Army. As a group, they were legendary for the kind of atrocities that would give John Wayne Gacy nightmares. I'm sure their opposing counterparts were equally guilty of war crimes, but the only gangsters from that part of the world I'd run into were all from Kosovo.

There were two other guys in the shop besides Squatty. A thin guy in a track suit sitting at the coffee bar with an iPhone in his hand. He was just playing with his phone. I could tell that most of his attention was focused on me, try as he might to not make it look that way.

There was an old man standing behind the counter, next to a wall of stainless-steel, coffee-brewing equipment from the 1950s.

I walked up to the counter.

No one said hello. The old man didn't speak. I glanced around, saw a security camera in the back, and a door that was partially open.

Sloppy.

"I'll take an espresso," I said. The old man contemplated me for a moment, then slowly turned and started making my coffee.

I turned to the guy in the track suit, who had set down then picked up his phone twice. Clearly, I was creating a bit of anxiety for the young man.

"How you doin', Darkie?" I said to him. Much like Juju, I'd never met Darkie, but I knew who he was. He seemed to twitch a bit at the sound of his nickname but tried to act like he hadn't heard me.

Over the sound of the old man clanking around near the coffeemaker, I heard a strange sound behind me, which I identified instantly.

When a man wearing a ring slides his hand along a wooden baseball bat to get a better grip, the little scrape is unmistakable.

Trust me on this one. It's years of experience talking.

The stainless-steel coffeemaker in front of me was not a good mirror, but the reflection of something light-colored moving up and to my right told me exactly what was about to happen.

I spun and caught Squatty in full backswing. I lashed out with my steel-toed boot and caved in his knee. There is nothing quite like seeing the confusion on someone's face when they feel a key body part is suddenly not working correctly.

The swinging bat still came, but its force was vastly reduced. I blocked it easily, then wrenched the bat from his hands and swung a huge looping strike that landed squarely on top of his bald head. If it had been an axe, I would have cleaved his skull nicely in two. Squatty's neck bulged oddly to the side. He sank to his knees and then tipped over onto his face.

I swung from the same position at Darkie, who had flung his iPhone onto the counter and was trying to fumble a gun from his waistband.

The bat connected solidly on his left side, and I heard—and felt—a little crack. It could have been audible, or simply the vibration through the wooden bat.

Gosh, I really liked this bat. It was a beauty.

Darkie went down, and I carefully retrieved the gun from his waistband.

The old man hadn't moved.

Darkie struggled back to his feet. His face was pale, and he was hugging his midsection.

Self-love is so important to one's well-being.

I pointed at the old man with the baseball bat.

"See that, Darkie?" I said. "That's experience."

"Fuck you," Darkie said, wincing with each word.

The old man just stared at me.

"He didn't do anything stupid like you did," I continued. "He knew immediately what was happening. His thought process centered on surviving what I was about to do and then figuring out how to kill me, eventually. And as painfully as possible."

I glanced over at Darkie.

"I think I got your eleventh or twelfth rib," I said. "Those are called floating ribs, not really connected to the sternum. Also less likely, if broken, to puncture anything serious. So you should consider yourself lucky."

"Fuck off," Darkie said. His voice was somewhat high-pitched, something he'd probably spent a lot of his life trying to compensate for.

I looked at the gun. It was a Glock .40, all the rage these days. Walking backwards I went to the coffee shop's door and slid the lock, then flipped the OPEN sign to CLOSED.

"Where's my coffee?" I said to the old man.

He put my cup on the counter, but I ignored it. Using the barrel of the gun, I waved Darkie and the old man toward the partially open door in back.

"Move," I said.

The old man walked slowly without complaint. Darkie shuffled along, muttering curses under his breath.

The old man opened the door, and I made sure the safety was off the Glock. There was a chance, extremely slim, that someone else was in the office. But I doubted it. The last occupant had left the door slightly ajar.

My little Albanian coffee party went into the office, where there were two chairs facing an old steel desk.

"Have a seat," I said to them.

"You asshole, you are a dead piece of man-shit," Darkie said.

"Well put," I said.

I was at a crossroads. Darkie seemed like a punk, but sometimes the Albanians could be stubborn, even after a lot of torture. I know this from experience.

The old man was no pussy. It would be even harder to get the truth out of him. He probably despised Darkie, so threatening injury to the younger man was not a viable option.

So I could torture and kill both of them.

Or I could snoop.

I chose to snoop.

The office was a treasure trove of information. Bills on the desk, a calendar, and a computer. File folders.

I leaned the baseball bat up against a small, metal filing cabinet. With the Glock pointed squarely at Darkie, I flipped through the paperwork on the desk.

The bills were mostly utilitarian: water, energy, a couple of credit cards, a phone bill. There was a brochure from Kohl's. A catalog from Victoria's Secret.

"Buying yourself a nightie?" I said to Darkie.

"Shitty head," he said.

"I wish I had your vocabulary," I said.

At the bottom of the pile, I came across another phone bill. This one from Century Link. That was not a Michigan company.

I knew.

It was from Florida.

I looked closely at the name on the phone bill. It was a business. There was a Florida address with a post-office sticker partially covering it that said the letter had been forwarded.

I committed the name of the business and the Florida address both to memory then slid it back into the pile of mail. I spent a few more minutes going through the desk and some files, but I already had what I wanted. There was no need for Darkie and the old man to know that, though.

Before I could leave, however, I still had to do two things.

It took me three more minutes to find the hard drive linked to the security camera. I unhooked it.

"Let's go," I said.

The old man and Darkie walked out of the office. There was no desire on my part to kill the old man, so I swung a bit easier than when I had clobbered Squatty. Instead of trying for a home run, this was more like going for an opposite-field base hit. The old man dropped to the floor. I was quite pleased with my bat control.

Darkie made a break for the door, but I tripped him with the bat then dragged him back to the coffee bar.

I put the security camera's hard drive on the counter. The bat whistled through the air, and the hard drive exploded. Next to it, Darkie's iPhone still sat on the counter, undisturbed.

I swung again, this time a beautiful arc, and the phone shattered. Bits of plastic bounced off of Darkie's face. He looked very sad to see his phone demolished. Yet not a trace of emotion over the old man.

Kids these days.

I reached into the old man's pockets, found a set of car keys, nodded to Darkie, who reached into the pocket of his sweatpants.

I picked a point on the center of his left temple.

The bat was still in my hands.

This time, I went for extra bases.

# 7.

I landed back at Fort Myers Airport, got a rental car, and drove directly to the name on the phone bill.

*Dream Breezes, Inc.*
*74200 Cypress Cove Road. Estero*

Just a half mile from my house-sitting job.

I took 41 South, hooked over onto a road called Jamaica Bay Road, then followed that to Cypress Cove.

It was a run-down street full of small houses about to fall down with the occasional brand-new subdivision thrown in for comic relief.

One yard had two small horses in the yard.

The last house on the street was 74202. Next to it was a giant electric installation complete with towers and coils and metallic objects looking like something from a sci-fi movie.

I looked across the street.

There was no 74200 Cypress Cove.

Not surprised, but I sighed just the same.

When would these guys learn that these cheap parlor tricks never worked?

It just took me longer to track them down.

It did succeed in pissing me off, though.

•

Back at my apartment, I dug out the Yellow Pages. Dream Breezes had a little ad touting their work installing screens over pools and lanais. Even fake businesses have to run advertisements. It's enough to fool the tax people but not enough to dupe the Feds.

Dream Breezes' motto: No bugs, just the breeze. No address. But a phone number with the area code 239. Same as mine.

I called the number.

After twelve rings, it was finally answered. The guy didn't say "Dream Breezes," he just kind of grunted.

When I said I had a job for him, he told me they were booked.

His voice had a thick accent, yet it conveyed the tone of his unfriendliness quite clearly.

"I want to put a big screen over an entire property," I said. "Even the house. I'm an architect, and my client has an unlimited budget. This thing will be massive. I'm prepared to pay top dollar, sir."

He told me to hold on.

A different guy came on the line.

"What's the address?" he said.

# 8.

I was expecting something ridiculous, and I pretty much got it. Instead of, say, a working pickup truck with a side decal displaying the Dream Breezes logo, two thick-looking guys showed up in a white Lincoln Town Car.

"Thought you said you were building a house," the first guy said. He stood with his legs spread. He had on dress slacks and a black T-shirt. Inside his right forearm was a tattoo. The red, double-headed eagle.

"Building an addition," I said. "The world's biggest lanai. I'm hoping to get into Architectural Digest." I paused. "Again."

It sounded ridiculous, even to me.

"Seventy-five grand," the second guy said. He was dressed like the first, but he was younger and had black Vans on his feet.

I could tell by the way he stood that he had a gun in the back of his waistband.

"Wow, that's the fastest estimate I've ever gotten," I said. "You don't want to walk around? Take some measurements?"

"I already did," the second guy said and tapped his temple. And then he nodded, knowingly.

"Me too," the first guy said.

It took everything I had not to bust out laughing. These clowns needed to go to gangster finishing school.

"So, for seventy-five grand, you'll build a screen over this entire house?" I said. "Guaranteed to keep bugs out?"

"Guaranteed," the first guy said.

"Okay," I nodded. "Do you have any examples of your work? You know, a portfolio? Testimonials from previous customers?"

The two guys looked at each other.

"We don't work that way," the first guy said.

"How do you work?" I asked.

"You cut us the check for half, we'll be here tomorrow and start working," he said. "When we're done, you pay us the second half."

I shook my head, tried to look like I was tempted. "I need to know a little bit more about your company. You know, where you're headquartered, your address, who owns the business," I said. "Just so I can check with the Better Business Bureau to make sure you're, you know, on the up and up. I mean, I'm sure you guys are."

Their matching two-pound eyebrows furrowed in unison.

"The fuck's that supposed to mean?" the second guy said.

I acted a little scared. "Whoa, whoa, no offense meant. You guys seem like legitimate businessmen. I mean, that Town Car is bitchin'."

They looked at me, trying to decide if I was fucking with them.

"However, I've got another guy coming to give me an estimate." I glanced at my watch. "In fact, he should be here in about ten minutes. Do you want to leave me a card?"

The second guy looked at the first. I could tell what he was silently asking. He wanted permission to kick the shit out of me, or at least create enough pain and fear to result in a nice, big check.

The first guy looked up at the house. There was a little security camera over the rear of the house.

"You've got our number," he said.

They turned and got back into the Lincoln.

They backed down the driveway and when I heard their tires squeal on Broadway, I jumped into my rental, roared down the driveway and out, just in time to see them turning onto Highway 41 North.

•

I knew where they were going before they got there.

Fort Myers.

More accurately, North Fort Myers.

It only made sense. There were three strip clubs in the entire area. From Fort Myers south to Naples. The best was Angel Station, second best Candy Assets. The third one, Real Dolls, was out in the boondocks. I know, I checked it out. And it was unpleasant, to say the least. Most likely a front for a biker meth lab.

These guys pulled into the parking lot of Candy Assets.

It made sense the Albanians had control of at least one of the strip clubs in the area. Hell, they might have all three.

I parked on a side street and went inside.

The place was cheese incarnate.

They had tried to re-create some kind of candy-store decorations, but it mostly amounted to a bunch of photographs of women licking lollipops.

So creative.

I took a seat at the bar.

"I'll take a Heineken, please," I said to the bartender. She was a tall redhead with an apron that parted down the back to show off a silver thong between two bright-white ass cheeks.

"Seven dollars," she said.

I pushed a ten across the bar. "All set," I said.

"Thanks," she said without emotion and walked down to the end of the bar. Not gonna lie—I watched her the whole way.

I considered what my best plan would be, and then the solution presented itself.

Her name was Java. She was dark-skinned (again, the creativity!), probably Native American, and she wasn't young. Her boobs were small and obviously real, which meant for a stripper her age that she either had ethics or not enough cash for the procedure.

If it were for ethical reasons, my plan wouldn't work.

If, however, it had to do with a financial issue, I might have a temporary employee sitting next to me.

I pulled out a fifty and told her what I wanted her to do.

She said, "Easy money. I like it."

•

The two men were reflected in the mirror behind the bar. I took a long drink of beer, then turned with a look of irritation on my face.

"Awfully tough to see tits and ass with you two standing there," I said. "Actually, I *do* see asses. Two of them."

They were both big, thick thugs. Heavy arms and foreheads the size of toasters.

"A girl said you were harassing her," the one closest to me said.

"So fucking what?" I said. I loved playing an unruly customer. It was my favorite role. "Isn't that what they're here for, douche bag?"

"No, that's not why they're here," the second one said. "I think maybe you should step outside, sir."

"You know what, asshole?" I said. "If Fama tells me to leave, I'll leave. Until then, buy me a beer, or a lap dance, or just fuck right off."

The redhead glanced over from the end of the bar. I waved her over.

"These two meatballs are buying me another Heineken," I said.

They didn't say anything to her, so she gave me one, a slightly curious look on her face.

The thugs left, but one of them came back after a little more than half of my beer was gone.

He spoke.

"Mr. Fama would like a word with you, sir."

It may have just been me, but his "sir" sounded a bit sarcastic.

# 9.

He sat behind a desk, an iPad in his hands.

I recognized him instantly. He was a short man, wide, with a beer belly and man-titties. His face was the very definition of bulbous: big, thick lips and a blubbery nose. A heavy forehead that hung over his eyes like a bone visor.

"Do you have one of these?" he asked, tilting the iPad toward me.

"Nope," I said.

"It's the new one. Look at how nice this picture is," he said.

He turned the screen to me. It was a video of a young girl having sex with three men at the same time.

For a brief moment, I wondered if it was Kiki. But it wasn't.

"I can tell you don't like this, even though you are pretending to not care," he said, pointing at the video.

"How old is she?" I said.

"Old enough."

The other two guys laughed at the boss's joke.

I looked at Fama. I knew his first name was Bruno, and that I had last seen him about a year ago at a brothel in Detroit, from which I had pulled Kiki out at gunpoint. Bruno Fama hadn't been in charge then, but he'd been present. So had his little brother, Darko.

"So you remember me?" Fama said. "Because I remember you. You cost us some money. Maybe you want to pay me back now. We take credit cards. Everything but American Express. Their merchant's transaction tax is too much. Fuckin' robbery if you ask me."

"Don't think so, Bruno," I said.

He gave a half-shrug and an I-could-care-less smile.

"What is it they call you?" he said.

I just stared at him.

"The Garbage Collector, right?" He laughed. "Maybe that is why you carry such a bad smell with you, no?"

The other guys laughed some more. No one is ever as funny as the boss. Just ask these guys.

"So why did you dump her in the river right across from me?"

"What on this Earth are you talking about?" he said. He put the iPad down on the desk again. The porn video was still playing.

"You're just going to piss me off by lying," I said.

He chuckled.

"You know," he said. "After you stole one of our products back in Detroit, we put word out that we wanted to get to know you."

I nodded.

"No one wanted to tell us anything," he said. "But then a couple weeks ago, some friends of yours— lawyers, I believe—called me and said they'd heard a rumor you were in my neighborhood. They suggested I give you a gift, sort of like a . . . what do they call it . . . a Welcome Wagon?"

He picked up the iPad again and started tapping on the screen.

"We already knew how much you liked Kiki," he said. "In fact, your lawyer friends said they'd heard that you and Kiki had become very good friends after you abducted her."

I shook my head, but it was the truth. I'd made a mistake. Kiki's relatives had asked me to deliver her to them, sober. I'd taken her to my place on Drummond Island and helped her kick the drugs. It became more than that, briefly, until I reunited her with her family. That was the last time I'd seen her, until we met again. On the river.

Fama continued his story. "And since it was time for her to go, we were going to feed her to the crabs, but then someone had an idea. Maybe it was me. That we could turn her into . . . what do they call it? The gift that keeps on giving, right? And you *still* haven't said thank you! So rude."

This got a big laugh from the assholes.

I knew the only reason Fama was telling me this was because he planned to kill me.

I smiled at him.

Fama laughed. "I can see you cared about her. I don't give a shit and two halves about these bitches. These girls aren't people to me. They're product."

"I bet that's not what you tell them, though, is it?" I said.

"Tell them? I don't talk to them, you idiot." He held up a finger. "But I do fuck them. I believe I fucked this girl you talk about. Crystal. Kiki. I break them in, make sure they can suck dick like nobody's business, then I am done. It's like a test drive. Kiki told me I was the best fuck she'd ever had."

I'd had enough of Fama. But I knew this wasn't the place. Still, I wanted to make sure he would come after me as soon as possible. I couldn't wait to get my hands on him.

"So were you in the KLA too?" I said, gesturing at the red double-eagle on his forearm.

He didn't bother glancing down. He knew what I was referring to.

He also didn't answer.

"I almost said the 'army,' but it wasn't really an army, was it?" I asked. "Just a bunch of criminals running around, killing kids and raping young girls. Sort of like a training ground for Albanian scum."

I let out a big sigh.

"Guess some things never change," I said.

To his credit, he kept his face still. His dark eyes were flat.

"Goodbye, Mr. Garbage Collector," he said. But his voice had lost any trace of joviality.

"How are Darkie's ribs, by the way?" I said. "That guy is a pussy. Just like every Fama I've ever met. You guys probably *want* to go to prison so you can take it up the ass every night."

Fama got to his feet, and the two thugs moved toward me.

I didn't bother waiting for a response.

"Thanks for the beer, guys," I said to the thugs.

They didn't try to stop me.

# 10.

One thing I learned during my housesitting stint: a river makes a lot of noise. Day or night, twenty-four hours a day, seven days a week, either the river itself is creating sound or something on the river is making noise. Maybe it's an alligator. Or a snake. Or a fish.

In this part of the Estero River, odds are the sound is man-made.

A fisherman returning from a long day out on the Gulf. A late-night kayaker. Or a pontoon boat full of drunken retirees.

But it was simply the sound of an occasional bird call and the splash of a fish jumping that accompanied the arrival of my friends from Albania.

They had waited until after the club closed. By my estimation, it was around three in the morning. There was a slight cloud cover, just enough to mask any light from the stars.

I stood among the palmettos and scrub oak, next to the post that held the motion detector for the driveway. There were two posts, and the installer hadn't bothered to try to camouflage them.

I figured my late-night visitors had spotted them on their first trip to see me.

And I wasn't wrong.

They parked the same car about ten feet from the detectors, shut the engine off, and got out.

They must have agreed on the best approach because they split off, one going to the right, the other going to the left.

Toward me.

The motion detector was on a short, metal pole that had been buried directly in front of an oak tree. In order to get around the motion detector, he would have to step behind the tree. The ground behind the tree sloped down toward a gulley that had been dug to drain rainfall toward the river.

When the thug stepped behind the tree, his head dipped down. I came out of the scrub oak without making a sound and executed one of the finest sucker punches of my career.

My fist crashed into his jaw, and I felt bone give way—in his face, not my hand.

He toppled forward, and I caught him before he landed in a stand of small palmettos. I lowered him gently to the ground.

I patted him down, then freed the 9mm from his shoulder holster.

From the other side of the driveway, I heard someone whisper.

"Pudge." He sounded annoyed.

"What the fuck, you takin' a piss?" he said.

I circled back behind the big car, then into the woods behind the second man.

I took great care not to brush up against the larger palmettos on this side of the drive. When their fronds rubbed together, it sounded like a violin lesson gone terribly wrong.

The second guy had come out of the woods and now stood in the middle of the driveway on the other side of the motion detectors. Subtlety and stealth were clearly not lessons taught in the KLA.

"Quit fucking around," he whispered, this time with a bit more volume.

I stepped up behind him and put the muzzle of Pudge's gun behind his left ear.

"He's not taking a piss," I said. "But he probably did shit his pants."

•

I pulled the Albanians' Lincoln, with Pudge safely ensconced in the trunk, into the parking lot of the Estero Bay Preserve. It was a huge tract of land, thousands upon thousands of acres, a lot of it swamp, that had been "saved" from developers. It had several walking trails, including one that went for eighteen miles.

I popped the trunk, pulled the second thug out, checked to make sure the duct tape was still across his mouth, then marched him into the preserve.

We walked for at least two miles until we got to a stand of dead trees, all standing in about two feet of water.

I stripped the duct tape from his mouth.

"Fuck you!" he said, and he pressed his lips together. Before he could spit, I whipped the barrel of the gun into his teeth.

He fell on his ass.

I put the muzzle of the gun against the top of his head.

"So what was the plan?" I said to him.

He hesitated, so I pressed the muzzle of the gun into the vertebrae of his neck.

"The boat," he said. "He was going to take you out on the boat." He then described to me in great detail what Fama had planned for me.

None of it was a surprise. Fama had mentioned something similar about his original plan for Kiki.

"So what did she do? Why'd he kill her?"

He shook his head. "She did the one thing he never lets his dancers do."

I waited.

"She tried to leave," he said.

That's what I'd figured. I tried not to think about Kiki's failed escape. Maybe it was guilt or maybe disappointment that she hadn't tried to contact me. I would have helped her.

She had to have known that.

"Call him," I said.

"Pudge has the phone," he said.

I pulled it from my pocket. "You mean this one?"

Fama was on the call history, so I held down the call button.

When I heard him answer, I put the phone to the thug's ear, and he said what I told him to say.

After I disconnected the call, I introduced the barrel of the 9mm to my hostage's temple. It was a fairly vicious blow, but I was pretty confident I hadn't fractured his skull. I take pride in my violence, to the point where I'm arrogant enough to consider myself a craftsman of sorts.

I took apart the cell phone and threw the pieces out into the brackish water.

I didn't know if alligators made it out this far and if they would be able to turn Sleeping Albanian Beauty into dinner, but one could always hope.

# 11.

The white Lincoln Town Car's headlights caught Fama's Range Rover as it pulled into the marina.

Fama got out first, followed by yet another one of his thugs.

"Pudge, you asshole, turn off your lights," Fama said.

I left them on but got out of the car with the 9mm in my hand.

"Oh, hello there," I said.

They were both caught off guard. Fama's bodyguard made the first move.

I shot him in the knee.

Fama didn't move.

Keeping him in my line of sight, I went to the bodyguard, dug the gun out of his shoulder holster, and kicked him in the ribs.

"Help him up," I said. Fama bent down to help the man, and I cracked him on the back of the head with the pistol.

He went down like the sack of shit he was.

"Roll him over," I said to the guy who was now sitting up but holding his knee. When he leaned over to grab Fama, I cracked him on the back of the head too.

I was four for four in rendering my victims unconscious. Those were All-Star type numbers.

I slipped the gun into my waistband, then dragged Fama by the heels down the dock to his boat, described to me in great detail by my Albanian friend now sleeping in the Estero Preserve.

The boat was a cabin cruiser, several years old, that looked like someone had tried to convert it into a crab-fishing boat but had given up.

I dumped Fama without ceremony on the deck at the back of the boat, then did the same with his companion. I dug through the bodyguard's pockets, found the key to the boat, fired up the engines, untied it from the dock, and eased out of the mooring into the Estero River.

The little marina where Fama kept his boat was much closer to the Gulf than the dock of my house-sitting job. From which I'd launched my kayak trip that had started this whole mess.

The bends of the river were familiar to me by now, and even in the early morning darkness, I soon found my way out into Estero Bay.

I put the engine at a slow idle and went to the back of the boat, next to a large plastic tray bolted to the gunwale.

Beneath it was a small storage compartment. I opened it, and found the large, razor-sharp meat cleaver Fama's associate had assured me would be there.

Next, I went to the pile of crab traps, grabbed three, and set them next to the cutting board.

I dragged Fama and propped him against the side of the boat, then lifted his right arm and laid his hand across the board.

"This is for Kristen," I said.

The cleaver cut through his wrist with a whisper and a thud. His Rolex slid right off the stump and landed on the deck.

The pain roused Fama from his sleep, and he let out a garbled scream. He half stood, which was perfect for me. I grabbed his hair, slammed him face-first into the cutting board, and lined the blade's edge along Fama's neck.

"This one's for me," I said.

I chopped down, and Fama's head popped from his neck, then rolled off the cutting board onto the boat's deck.

With a knee, I pinned Fama's headless torso against the side of the boat, grabbed his other arm and chopped off his left hand. I grabbed it, dropped it into the first crab trap, and tossed it over the side. I went to the console, eased the throttle forward, and went another hundred yards into the bay.

Again, I shifted the engine to neutral, went back, grabbed the next hand and its matching crab-trap container, and tossed it over the side.

Back at the console and still navigating from memory, I eased the boat forward, past Coon Key to the mouth of San Carlos Pass, near the Estero Boulevard Bridge.

Fama's head went into a crab trap, and this too went over the side.

I was glad Fama's associate back in the Preserve had told me how Fama had planned to get rid of my body. I hoped Fama wasn't mad at me for stealing his idea.

I guided the boat under the bridge and followed it to where the pass widened out into the Gulf of Mexico. I pointed the nose of the boat due west, toward Texas, and eased the throttle forward until the boat was moving at a good clip directly out in the Gulf.

And then a major disappointment: I went to the back of the boat and discovered that Fama's companion wasn't unconscious. He was dead. I shrugged off the fact that my night's perfect batting average was spoiled.

I gave him a seat in the captain's chair and lashed him in securely with rope. With the same rope, I then tied him to the boat's steering wheel.

Next, I found a towel, wiped down the cleaver and tossed it out into the Gulf, then used the towel to wipe down anything else I had touched.

A spare gas can was at the stern of the boat. It was half-full. I splashed gasoline over everything above and below decks.

Next, I doused the towel with gasoline and poured a trail of gas right up to the bow of the boat.

When I was sure the boat was heading perfectly straight, I used a lighter I'd gotten from the boat's dashboard and lit the towel on fire.

There was a whump as I dove from the bow. I drove myself straight down and then out, back toward land. I swam underwater for as long as I could. When I finally surfaced, a wall of black smoke covered the water, and I caught sight of what was left of Fama's boat still motoring out into the Gulf.

Moments later, an explosion rocked the air and debris shot up into the sky.

I dove again and swam until my lungs were on fire.

This time when I surfaced, there was only the faint smell of something burning.

It took me nearly twenty minutes to make it to land for two reasons. One, I was not a very good swimmer. And two, I had to swim at an angle to make sure the current wouldn't reunite me with Fama.

I dragged myself onto the beach, took a minute to catch my breath, and then got to my feet.

The sun was just coming up.

A day at the beach.

I'd always wanted one of those.

## THE END

# About the Author of *Bullet River*

**Dani Amore** is a crime novelist living in Los Angeles, California. She is the winner of the 2011 Independent Book Award for Crime Fiction, and her novels have become best-sellers in the United States and abroad.

You can learn more about her at daniamore.com

Visit Dani Amore on Amazon.com

## Books by Dani Amore:

THE KILLING LEAGUE

DEAD WOOD (A John Rockne Mystery)

DEATH BY SARCASM (A Mary Cooper Mystery)

TO FIND A MOUNTAIN

SCALE OF JUSTICE

THE GARBAGE COLLECTOR

FOUR

HANGING CURVE

# *The Lighthouse*

*by Rick Murcer*

# Chapter-1

I never thought it would end like that. Who would? Especially in small, tourist communities like Silver Lake, Michigan. But like my dad always says, thinking can get you in a whole lot of trouble. He was right.

What Maggie Burrows and I did on most Saturday nights by going to the local make-out spot was innocent in the way of small-town traditions. It was our version of Lovers Lane or Park-A-Rama, whatever you want to call it. My parents even talked about their time in the old lighthouse. It was always innuendo and a sly wink between them that wasn't so sly, but the message was crystal clear: they had a moment or two at the top of the Little Sable Point Lighthouse that was forever theirs. That's how it should be, right? Lovers should have those nostalgic reminders of how they'd gotten from then to now. I wanted that, and I wanted it with Maggie.

Maggie.

She was beautiful with amazing dark eyes and a regal mane of long, black hair. Maggie was petite, but oh so competitive. Looking at her, one would never guess that she hid a fiery spirit for winning, and I suppose for living too, that I'd never seen in any other woman. All that in spite of her smallish stature . . . and the scar.

At age ten, Maggie had fallen through her front door after tripping over her beloved cat, Ingrid, and had twenty stitches sewn less than majestically across her right eyebrow. I knew it bothered her from time to time, but it was funny how I never noticed it unless she touched it or made some reference to the fact that she had to settle for me because of the faded railroad track on her brow.

"Chase Andrews, you're the luckiest man on the planet," she'd say. But that twinkle, that special turn of her head, would always lead to a grin and an accompanying kiss that was beyond description. Part of me *did* wonder what she saw in a tall, lanky kid with glasses who came up a little short in the social graces, but I didn't question it. I was almost afraid to.

As it turned out, those times would be one of the few "moments" that I'd be able to keep.

We had, Maggie and I, been breaking into the Little Sable Point Lighthouse that stood guard over our section of Lake Michigan for two years, ever since we started dating in our senior year of high school. She'd gone to Shelby High; I'd attended Hart. Our schools were the kind of natural rivals that books are written about. It was close to total traitorhood to date and to fall helplessly in love with someone from the other school, but we didn't care.

We'd met at the top of our famous sand dunes after I'd fallen from my ATV and she stopped to help . . . and laugh. Five minutes later, she was all I could think about. I must have had some effect on her too because she went out with me, though it took a few minutes to stammer out the "question." I practically flew home.

Even after we had gone on to college in separate parts of the state and pursued different ends of the academic spectrum, we found time for each other. She was studying chemistry at Michigan State, and I chose Muskegon Community College to further my knowledge regarding the family business: cherry and peach farming. I know, not sexy, but farming is honest. Anyway, we'd find time for a few trips up the cold, metal, spiral steps. The view was spectacular. I swear there were nights when Lake Michigan's breezes cleared away every wisp of cloud and haze, revealing the dancing stars in amazing contrast to the dark sky. And it was just for us. We even thought we could see Chicago, some one hundred twenty-five miles across the lake, a time or two. That's how it was last night.

Late May is when business really gears up for our community, and we didn't think we'd have a chance to do a Saturday rendezvous. I picked her up after her summer-job shift at the Sands restaurant on Thursday around midnight, drove through the village past Termite Bridge, and eventually parked at one of the vacant cabins along Natural Beauty Road. The moon was an evening away from being full, and the smell of cottonwood and late lilacs was unusually persuasive in the warm night's breeze, laying ground work for a romantic rendezvous. I was up for that.

We had walked the last half-mile along the beach, holding hands, bumping hips, and making plans that young lovers make. Kids, dogs, cars, vacations, winning the lotto so we could do whatever we wanted. We even talked about grandkids. I think that hurts the most, making plans, I mean. Now it just seems like words in a magazine or some forgotten book. You know, like it was someone else's life. But it wasn't. That part is sinking in, at least.

Anyway, when we had reached the door to the lighthouse, I took out the lock-picking tool I'd made in shop class and started for the lock, then I stopped and swore. I couldn't believe what the bright moonlight revealed. There were now two locks, one high and one lower, and they weren't padlocks. Bright, shiny, bolt locks were embedded in the black iron door, more imposing than Fort Knox. I swore again.

Maggie had giggled.

"What's so funny?"

"Your dumpy expression, for one. But wait. You're gonna like this, Chase."

She'd reached into the front pocket of her tight jeans and produced a key.

"My mom is volunteering to work the lighthouse and collect entrance fees for the rest of the month. She gave me the key before I left for work and told me not to lose it."

I was shocked. Not so much by the key, but that she'd given it to Maggie. Maggie's mom had always volunteered for stuff like that, but to give up a key so we could make out on the top of the lighthouse? Maybe I was growing on her.

Jill Burrows and I had gotten along okay, but it had been just Maggie and her mother for fifteen years, and her mother had no real trust in men—with good reason. Cheating spouses could do that to anyone.

"So maybe your mom thinks this is serious?" I asked.

"Oh, I think she gets that. Especially since I told her we've never had . . . you know . . . done it."

"Whoa. You told her we haven't fooled around yet?"

"Yeah," she smiled. "I tell her everything."

"Damn. She's going to think I don't like women."

". . . or that you're a gentleman, and I mean more to you than a few rolls in the sack. Not that rolls in the sack aren't important," she had said, smiling.

Maggie had me there, on both counts. Small-town manners were ingrained by great parents, and I'd wait for God to come back before I made love to her, if she wanted me to. It didn't mean it wasn't difficult or that we hadn't come real close a couple of times. It meant she was that important to me. I wanted to protect her from regrets and pain forever. I failed there too.

I closed the door behind us, and she started her patented race to the top of the tower, some one hundred and thirty-nine steps. I was feeling good, so I tried to catch her. About halfway up, I reached up to pinch her rear. As fingers gripped cheek, she jumped, then lost her balance. Only God knows how she fell backward instead of giving her shins the thump of a lifetime. I caught her, and then slammed into the dark brick wall as her fingernails dug into my forearm and raked down to my wrist. It had hurt, but I held tight.

As the staircase filled with the sound of adrenaline-enhanced breathing, she'd begun to laugh. You know the kind. Musical and as alive as any human expression. Being a little more terrified than Maggie, it took me a few moments to see what was so funny. But it wasn't really humor triggering her laughter, then eventually mine. It was relief and a sense of gratefulness that we'd be all right. That we'd make it another day . . . at least one of us would.

# Chapter-2

After one more deep breath, and a lingering kiss that brought me back to the moment, to her, we'd scrambled up the last sixty steps or so and burst through the door facing back away from the beach and lake. A moment later, we were sitting against the wall facing Lake Michigan. The waves waltzed to the shore in that mysterious rhythm that calmed every sense of distress and concern preying on one's mind. Visitors to the lake *thought* wave therapy worked, but beach people *knew* it.

Maggie snuggled close, and I'd wrapped both arms around her, nuzzling her hair and thinking how her scent was the best aroma ever . . . even better than freshly-baked cherry pies.

The large, glass octagon that housed the seventy-inch Fresnel lens loomed behind us. It was usually operational, but not every night, and it was much more for show than function. Tonight it wasn't lit because of one last cleaning session to be completed by the weekend. Funny how that worked. Maybe if it had been lit, things would have been different. Of course, if I'd kept my temper and not gotten so pissed off, things would've been different too.

After pointing out two cargo ships, lights blinking, easing through the water, Maggie had become silent. I hated that because it meant that she wanted to tell me something that I wasn't going to like. I was right, again.

"So, Chase. I don't know how to tell you this other than how I always tell you things that involve us."

"Shoot," I said, trying to sound confident and reassuring. Of course, I felt neither.

"I'm. Well, I have this professor at State, and he thinks I have a real future in chemical engineering. He graduated from MIT and got his doctorate there too."

I already hated where this was going, and a feeling of

dread and irritation brewed much faster than it should have.

"Okay. So what does that mean?"

Maggie sat up straight and drew her face close to mine. "It means he did some legwork, and I can transfer to MIT, beginning the fall semester, with a full, all-expenses-paid scholarship that practically ensures a six-figure job when I finish."

I stood up and leaned over the iron-rod railing, angrier at her than any other time I chose to remember. I could tell from her voice, her excitement, that she'd already made up her mind. Worse, she knew that I knew it. I continued focusing on nothing and everything as the silence between us expanded into an almost intolerable level. What an awful feeling that can be.

Squeezing my hands together, I panned to the right and saw someone walk down the beach, then disappear into the tree line. Late-night beach walks were not unusual for people around here, and I didn't care if anyone saw me because I was wallowing in every self-pitying emotion under the moon. I should have paid more attention.

I heard her stand, but she stayed behind me. I couldn't see her, but I knew her head was bowed, and her hands were folded in front of her. I also knew discussing this was out of the question, at least for her.

"Chase. It's a great opportunity for me, for us."

"Whatever happened to discussing everything? You'll be a thousand miles away, and it'll be months in between seeing each other," I said, seething.

"It won't be that bad. You can even come out to see me and we . . ."

"*We* won't do shit," I whispered.

I felt her hand reach for mine, and I pushed it away and then headed for the stairway, leaving her at the top of that Godforsaken lighthouse.

I hit the bottom step, pushed open the door, and circled the lighthouse to the beach and started north, hands in the pockets of my plaid shorts, feeling betrayed and as hurt as anyone could. And why shouldn't I? We had been talking about life plans twenty minutes ago, and now that was all on hold. At age twenty-one, I felt everything I had wanted was being jerked from me or, at the very least, delayed a few years. And of course, the thought that someone would sweep her off her feet, some rich dude who wore argyle sweater vests and socks to match, was the worst thing. It wasn't like it had never happened before, and it scared the hell out of me.

Ten minutes later, I pivoted in the cool sand, raised my arms to the sky, then started back to the lighthouse, my anger devolving to a shade of shame. Then I smiled. Maggie Burrows knew me better than myself and realized I needed to think about this before we could talk like we always talked. It wasn't going to change anything, because she was right. I'm young, but I recognize truth when it talks to me, mostly.

After walking around the small bend that led to Little Sable, my *I'm an ass and I'm sorry* speech running through my head, I stopped and shook out the sand from my sandals. Just as I'd put them back on, I heard it.

The scream that pierced the starry night was as horrifying as anything I'd ever heard, mostly because I recognized that voice. The only thing worse was the sickening thump echoing in my head a split second later. It shattered my world.

# Chapter-3

I wish I could tell you what ran through my mind as I sprinted toward the lighthouse. I could try to describe it, but unless you've been there, it would be impossible. All I can say is that it was the total culmination of every fear, anxiety, and terror I'd ever felt wrapped into one merciless package. Because I knew. I knew.

Splashing through the small pool that guarded the left side of the lighthouse, and then hurdling the old log embedded in the sand, I'd gotten within thirty feet of the large granite rocks piled in front of the structure, and then I saw her. I will forever try to blank out the image of Maggie lying across three of the gray stones, her head and left leg posed at impossible angles, but that'd be like raising the Titanic.

My whole body shook as I inched closer. The silvery moon seemed brighter than ever, giving me more nightmare material. There was blood running down the rock near her head, and it trickled down to the white sand, conjuring up some hellish, red-sand collage. Even from twenty feet, I could see her dark eyes were open.

I know people do dumb things in situations like that, but I think it was hope against reality that made me do it. My denial was alive and well.

I called her name.

"Maggie? Maggie?"

She didn't respond, just continued to stare. I don't know what I'd expected. Like I said, crazy thinking.

I was suddenly struck with the thought of how she'd reached the rocks. She must have fallen. She wouldn't have jumped. Had she gotten too close to the edge and lost her balance?

I'd glanced at the railing at the top of the lighthouse, still not understanding how this could have happened. It didn't make sense that she was where she was. Then, inexplicably, I blamed myself. Maybe it was my asshole attitude that led to this. The feeling was like getting blamed for doing something to your kid brother or sister, and you hadn't done anything at all, but felt guilty just the same. I know, more crazy ideas, but like I said, unless you've been there . . .

Shaking off that thought, I took a couple steps closer, then rushed the last few strides, tears running down my face.

As I kneeled against another group of rocks, I reached out and touched her cheek. She was already cold. I jerked my hand back, then immediately felt more guilt. I stood again and looked at her legs and the way her torso was turned, and the tears started again. I wanted to help, but didn't know what to do. My mind had never been so jumbled. But I had to do something, right? Then I recalled what I'd learned in lifeguard training: don't move the injured, call for help.

I remember pulling out my cell and dialing 9-1-1; but I also recall sirens already blaring and not far away. Someone must have heard Maggie's scream and called the police. I waited for my call to go through anyway. The operator answered and the conversation went something like this:

"9-1-1 operator. How may I help you?"

"My girlfriend is hurt down at Little Sable Lighthouse, send help, an ambulance."

"Who's calling, and what's your girlfriend's name?

"I'm Chase Andrews and Maggie Burrows is . . . just send an ambulance," I screamed.

The woman on the line told me to calm down. I started to scream again and then heard another sound— the iron door at the front of the tower had slammed shut.

Help was already here. Then again, I didn't remember hearing a police car pull up, and the siren still bellowed a few blocks away.

All that ran through my mind was that there was someone here to help me, us.

As I began to run, I said to the love of my life, "I'm getting help, Maggie."

Motoring around the south side of the lighthouse, wiping at my face, I held out hope that whoever was there could fix what was going on, and tomorrow it would all be okay. I recall feeling even a little relief, but that's not how it went down.

I'd reached the side of the lighthouse and saw a figure crest the sidewalk trail, just as I tripped over something metal. It jabbed my calf as I tumbled head first into the cool sand, but that didn't stop me from yelling.

"Help us! Please! Help. I need help."

I was at least a hundred fifty feet away and couldn't make out any detail of the figure as they disappeared over the hill, but I do, and will always, remember the slight hesitation the person had made, as if contemplating a great truth, or lie, before moving out of the picture.

Scrambling to my feet, I started to run again and went down immediately, getting a face full of sand this time . . . and sharp pain coursing through my ankle. I looked down and saw a tire iron wedged between my sandal strap and my foot. I did the classic double-take because I felt something sticky on the handle as I pried it from my sandal.

At that moment, the Oceans County Police Unit had arrived, lights flashing and sirens dying the way they do when their trip is over.

Standing, I was already yelling for them. As the two officers, one male, one female, stormed over the hill, their flashlights lighting up the beach like a new morning's dawn, I got another glimpse of the tire iron in my hand. Two things were certain: it had come from my car, and the sticky substance on the handle . . . well, it was blood.

# Chapter-4

"Please. I need your help," I yelled. "My girlfriend is hurt, over on the rocks."

The first officer had rumbled down the slope, a woman. She shined her light in my face, then stopped, slowly moving the light to the hand holding the tire iron, then flashed it back to my face.

"Drop the iron, son; then we can help you."

I didn't actually see her pull her gun, but I heard it as it ripped from her holster. A moment later, the second cop did the same. I didn't really think much about it because all I wanted was help and maybe release from the reality that I hoped to escape. That "strength in numbers" quote I'd heard my entire life was no longer just a phrase, but carried real substance for me. Maybe these two could make Maggie better, make all this go away.

Foolish man.

"I want you to put the tire iron on the ground and then lay face down, okay?" the lady officer said again, this time with more insistence.

"What? I don't understand how that helps Maggie. Please. Help her. She must have fallen from the lighthouse. I . . ."

"Now, young man." This time her partner was speaking, and he sounded pissed. Real pissed. Then I was hit with another light at an angle more to my right, blinding me for a moment. But out of the corner of my eye, I saw the tire iron, and the sand sticking to the blood, and finally realized what was happening. They thought I'd hurt Maggie. Thinking back, I guess I would have assumed the same.

"Wait. I didn't do anything to her. I tripped over this and . . ."

The next second, I was face down in the sand with a

huge weight on my back and shoulders. My ankle turned underneath the force as I went down, causing persistent flashes of pain to tango across my eyes. I yelped. But the two cops couldn't have cared less. Apparently, I was the object of their biggest moment in law enforcement and needed to be treated accordingly.

Struggling against the man on my back was useless. He wrenched my right hand around to my hip, and I felt the cuffs snap tightly, then on the other hand.

"Just lay there, boy, or my voice will be the last thing you ever hear," he barked.

"Better listen to him. He ain't a patient man," she warned.

He got off from me, and I didn't move. Partially because I believed him, partially because the gravity of the last five minutes had caught up with me, and I suddenly felt as tired as I'd ever felt in my life. I was more than ready to have someone else take control. I listened to the waves and rested my head on the sand, waiting for the tears to stop.

"You watch him, and I'll go check out the rocks," the male officer said.

She agreed.

The next thing I remember hearing was the male cop swearing, then he retched up his last meal. A moment later, I heard footsteps kicking up sand as he rushed back to me and his partner.

"Damn it. Call the State Police. Now. He's killed her. Good God. Hurry. I ain't ever seen nothing like that."

Hearing him talk was like someone throwing ice cold water on me in the middle of the night. They really *did* think I'd killed Maggie. Killed Maggie. That thought was far beyond terrifying.

"Wait. I didn't kill her. I found . . ."

"I told you to shut the hell up, you little bastard."

He jerked me up from the ground, and I felt something hit the back of my head, a sharp pain, and then my eyes couldn't focus.

"If you talk again, I'll make sure you get a nice, long

stay in some hospital . . . if we get you there on time, that is," he'd growled.

As the fog cleared, I sensed that he wasn't kidding. In fact, I totally believed him.

I was then hustled over the path and tossed into the backseat of the brown-and-white county cruiser, just as an ambulance and two state cop units pulled into the parking lot.

Then I saw something odd as I stared out the window, something that didn't really register until later. Maggie's yellow VW Beetle moved past the entrance of the park and disappeared around the bend, heading toward town.

# Chapter-5

So there I was. Sitting in the back of the Sands restaurant, where Maggie worked, surrounded by four cops, a State Police Detective, and the Sands owner, Jeff Clark.

The cops stared at me, like Satan and I were on a first-name basis. Detective Jan Green, a tall woman with short hair and a handsome face, was sipping coffee and going over the notes she'd made after grilling me two different times. Same questions, different wording. Good technique, I guess, for someone who had been lying to her. But I hadn't. Jeff, who was there because he'd always been tight with local law enforcement and made his place available as a pre-jail holdover, was the only one who hadn't condemned me, at least with his eyes. He was a man of faith and, for the most part, lived it.

They hadn't let him speak to me, but he'd given me a reassuring wink during the time he wasn't trying to shake the shock and sadness from his round face. I guess I understood that too. When you worked for Jeff, you were family, and Maggie had been one of his favorites. She'd been very much like a daughter to him. But he also knew how much in love we were, and I wanted to believe that he knew I hadn't killed her . . . but doubt and the heart were always uneasy bedfellows.

Detective Green came back to the booth where I was cornered, cuffs still clamped to my wrists, and sat down across from me for the third time, her face even harder than before. I got the impression that she had no difficulty being a bitch of the highest caliber. That thought made me even more nervous.

"I don't get something, Chase. You said you got upset when Maggie told you her plans, then you stood up and just kind of stared over the railing. Then you stormed down the steps, right?" I didn't like the tone in her voice.

"Yes. That's right. I told you that twice."

"And that's when she tried to talk to you and scratched your arm, right?"

I sighed. "No, detective. She scratched me when she fell back as we were going up the staircase."

I was suddenly struck with that replay in my mind's eye and felt the wind leave my sails. Her laugh, the way we were breathing, the smell of her hair were all vivid and alive. If I were designing torture techniques, forcing people to remember things would go to the top of the list.

"Okay, just wanted to make sure I got that right. So that must have been when you went back to your car to get the tire iron. I mean, you couldn't have that little hussy ruining your life . . ."

"What? I never went back to the car to get anything. I went down the beach, like I said. And what part of 'I wouldn't ever hurt her' don't you get? And don't call her a hussy."

She was starting to get under my skin—I guess that's what they do—but she was not even in the ballpark when it came to Maggie and me.

"Oh, I get it. And I've heard it a hundred times, but you know, what am I supposed to think? You were the last one to see Maggie alive; you were pissed; and your tire iron had blood and two strands of long black hair on it. As soon as we get the prelims back from the lab, I bet those hairs will be hers. So, can you see the problem I have?" She was glaring at me. I briefly wondered if her eyes were going to turn red. It was like she hated and pitied me at the same time.

"I don't care about your probl—" A vision of someone hitting Maggie with a tire iron exploded into full-blown imagery, and I couldn't finish what I was saying. Like I said before, if you haven't been there, you don't know what it's like. That image of Maggie being hit, along with the detective's matter-of-fact words, created a phrase that hadn't run across my thoughts, until now. Murder. My Maggie had been *murdered*.

"What's wrong, son? Are you ready to tell the real story here?" Green asked. Her voice was as soothing as the lake's waves.

"I . . . I . . . It just occurred to me that Maggie was murdered," I answered, but the voice didn't sound like mine. Maybe I was in full-blown shock after my trip down denial lane.

Leaning over the wooden table in the booth, her eyes grew soft. She sort of reminded me of my mom after I'd screwed up somewhere, and she wanted to tell me that it was okay.

"You want to tell me what really happened? I understand. People get mad; they lose it, then regret what they did. Do you regret what you did, hitting her, then sending her over the railing like that? It's all right. You can tell me, then it'll be over," she said, so understanding, so smooth. And it was all a lie. Damn. She was good. For a second, I thought I was going to say I did it. Then I got angry, again.

"I-DID-NOT-KILL-MAGGIE! Got it? I would die before that would ever happen. Just because we're young doesn't mean I don't understand the concept of sacrifice. We are . . . were . . . that much in love. She was the only thing I could count on as being totally real," I said, enraged.

"Okay. Take it easy."

She began leafing through her notes and looked up at me, her eyes were hard again. I guess she'd decided the good-cop approach hadn't worked.

"You said you heard the door slam and then tripped over the tire iron when you ran after whomever it was to get help. Is that—"

The front door burst open and my uncle, Jack Andrews, an attorney, stormed into the main dining floor, looked around, spotted me, and hurried toward us. He was a smallish man with round, wire-rimmed glasses, short, neat hair, and a gift for double-talk like no one I'd ever met.

On his heels strode my dad, my mom, and my two

best friends, Aaron Rich and Chuck Fowler. If that's what the cavalry looked like to a wagon train surrounded by hostiles, then the folks in the wagon must have gone crazy with relief. I know I did.

"I'm Chase's attorney, Jack Andrews. Are you charging him with anything?" my uncle asked, talking directly to Detective Green as he stepped between two of the county officers.

The detective looked at her hands, glanced at me, and sighed. "We're just trying to verify his story. If he's innocent, then he's got nothing to—"

"You didn't answer my question, Detective. Is he being charged?"

By then, my dad had worked his way through the cops and stood with his hand on my shoulder. He bent to my ear. "You okay?"

I nodded, then felt the tears well up.

How in God's name was I *ever* going to be okay?

He didn't look me in the face, but I could tell by his touch that he understood what I was thinking.

Letting out a breath, Detective Green slid out of the booth and motioned for Uncle Jack to follow. He shook his head, eyes blazing.

"Say what you got to say. But if you're not charging him, we're out of here. You've already broken about five different laws, as far as I can tell. And you and I both know that anything he's said to you, if you do charge him, won't be admissible because his attorney wasn't present."

"Look. We just want to find out what happened."

"So do we. But you, of all people, know there's a right way and a wrong way," answered my uncle.

"I can hold him for another twenty-four to forty-eight hours, you know, before I have to charge him or let him go."

"You can, but then we'd just get him released because you must only have circumstantial evidence or he'd already be booked. Besides that, he didn't do it, and I can tell by your face that you're not sure either."

She put her hands on her hips, looked toward the ceiling, and started to speak. But the door flew open again, and Maggie's mother rushed in. She turned toward me, and I could see she'd been more than crying. Her rage . . . well, I've never seen anyone wear a look like that. She cocked her head, flashed the scariest grin, screamed something at me, and then raised the pistol in my direction.

# Chapter-6

I sat frozen in place, wondering what it was going to be like to be shot. But that didn't happen. I'd never seen Aaron, my best friend from the time we were five, move that fast. He was always the brains in the group, but also the last one picked for any sandlot game we'd play. I won't say he was frail, but it was close. He barely hit a hundred forty pounds on his six-foot frame.

Before the cops, or anyone else, could react, Aaron tackled Mrs. Burrows, who was no heavyweight herself. I think her and Maggie could have been twins if they'd been born the same year.

They both hit the gray-tiled floor with collective grunts as the gun skittered under one of the booths at the front of the building. Maggie's mother struggled against Aaron, trying to get up and reach the gun. I heard him yell as one of her blows struck him in the face. But my friend held fast.

By then, two of the county officers had joined the fray, and Jill Burrows had little chance of getting off the floor and completing the task of shooting me. It didn't, however, stop her from threatening to finish her chore.

"You killed my little girl! I warned her. I told her all men were the same. You killed her. I'm going to make you pay, Chase Andrews. You hear me? I'll finish this."

Her words and sobs reverberated throughout the Sands as the two officers hustled her out of the glass doors and into one of the cruisers. One of the other cops retrieved the gun, looked it over, and took it outside. I supposed to give it to one of the other cops . . . and keep it far away from Maggie's mother.

Green had pulled her weapon during the scuffle. She now put it back in her shoulder holster and motioned for me to get up. "I don't think that woman likes you, but don't worry. She'll get some time to cool off."

She did that sighing thing again, and I almost felt sorry for her. I think she wasn't totally sure what to do.

"Your attorney is right. I don't have enough to hold you. Your story has been consistent, and you do have a mark on your leg that could back up what you've said about tripping over the tire iron. The CSU will see if they can put the science to your claims, and I'll get a report tomorrow."

By then, my family and friends were surrounding me, and I felt better. But I was sure I'd never be the same. Green spoke again, her face as determined as I'd seen it. "You better make sure you don't leave the area until I get what I need, one way or the other. I'm not convinced you didn't do this, and I'll have some more questions."

Pulling out her pad, she flipped pages, then stopped and let out a breath. "I have just one more, then you can go, for now."

I nodded.

"You said you couldn't make out anything about the person that you said had come out of the lighthouse and gone up over the hill."

"That's right."

"Which direction did this person go? The moon gave you plenty light enough to see that, at least."

I ran it over in my mind, including the slight hesitation the person had made. I felt my eyes grow larger.

"Right! They went right, to the south."

She finally smiled. But not the *let's do lunch* smile. More like a crocodile. "You sound sure. Okay. Go home, and I'll be in touch with your attorney. And Chase, I mean it. Don't leave the area, not even for dinner. Like I said, you're still my first choice for this, and if I thought I could make it stick, you'd be going with me."

"Yes, ma'am." Then my mom looped her arm through mine and ushered me toward our four-by-four truck.

Just before I climbed into the back, I stared at the setting moon, and it occurred to me, right then and there, that there had to be a second choice: the one who had really killed Maggie. Maybe I'd seen her killer, and not just her *murderer*, but the destroyer of my dreams.

# Chapter-7

"What happened, Chase? We all need to hear it from your lips. I don't ever remember you lying to your Mom or me, so talk to us."

It was almost five a.m., and the people I cared about the most, minus one, were gathered around our antique oak table. My mom, still pretty in the way older women are, was holding my hand. I think it's her eyes. The hazel in them seems to brighten with age. My dad, looking older than I could remember, set his gaze on me too. Not just because of what was happening, but because he'd loved Maggie from the start. I think his vision of grandkids and Maggie and I taking over the farm had been embedded far deeper into his subconscious than he, or I, had realized. My kid sister, Lizzy, all of fourteen, sat with tears on the brim of her lower lids, but never quite letting them come. She was a little jock and, in lots of ways, tougher than me.

Aaron, supporting an ice pack under his eye where Jill Burrows had thumped him, sat beside Chuck. Brawny, smartass Chuck sat speechless: truly a rarity for him.

It seemed we were all on the verge of one of those life-changing epiphanies, and each of them was connected to what had happened to Maggie . . . and me.

I went over the events again. I halted, momentarily, when they cried, when they swore, when I cried, when my brain refused to process what my eyes had seen. They say time heals. Maybe. But the image of her twisted body had left a tattoo on my heart that a million years would never remove.

After I finished, a pregnant silence filled the room, then Chuck broke it, his strong jaw determined to hide his emotion. I was thankful for that.

"Why didn't the cops check the area for footprints

and stuff?" he asked.

"I think they might have later, but they were pretty sure they had their man, so why bother? But I do think Detective Green had asked me that last question because she wasn't sure what really happened."

"Let's get this right: you got pissed, left the lighthouse, came back later, heard Maggie scream, and then after . . . after seeing her, you heard the door, fell over your tire iron, and then saw someone hitting the path as you yelled for help, right?" asked Aaron.

"Yeah, that's it, in a nutshell."

More silence. Then I realized why: the story did sound bad, even contrived. Like something from that old fugitive movie from the '90s.

"It does sound off, I guess. But it's true."

"I believe you, but it's not us you have to convince," said Aaron.

"So how'd the tire iron get out of your car? Didn't you lock it?" asked Lizzy.

Out of the mouth of babes.

"I don't always, especially around here. I had the keys in my pocket, but I really don't remember if I did or didn't, but probably not."

Aaron stood up and paced around the room, frowning and rubbing the back of his neck.

"You know what that means, right?" asked Aaron.

"It means someone was watching and following you two. Maybe even trying to make it look like you did it," said my dad.

I was quickly coming around to their train of thought. Maybe the shock was starting to wear off, or maybe it was becoming clearer to me that I was in deep trouble. Either way, with the help of mom's coffee, the light was getting brighter.

"Why in the hell would anyone do that? I mean, Maggie didn't have an enemy in the world, and I don't go around pissing people off. Except for Chuck and Aaron, once in a while. We weren't exactly target material for some mafia hit or drug gang after a deal went south."

"That might be true as far as you know, and since I spend half of my waking life around you, I can vouch for that," said Aaron, slowly. "I didn't see Maggie as much as you."

The tone in his voice made me uncomfortable, then it made me see red.

"What are you driving at? That maybe Maggie had something going on that no one knew about?" I yelled. Standing, the chair hitting the hardwood floor, I started around the table, fully intending to knock Aaron on his pious ass. I guess this was one of those times when *he* pissed *me* off. Chuck grabbed me, and my dad got between us.

"Don't you be saying stuff like that. She was as pure as they get. We hadn't even . . . you don't know shit!"

"Easy, Chase. I didn't say what you heard. I'm only trying to walk down every path here and make sure you don't go away for a long while. My life wouldn't be too cool if I had to hang around with just Chuck all of the time."

I was breathing hard, still wanting a piece of him, then Chuck snorted. My dad grinned as Aaron pushed his glasses up farther on his nose, his patented twinkle forcing me to shake my head and smile. That look got me every time, and he knew it.

I sat back down and put my hands on each side of my head. I noticed the aroma of baked cherry strudel coming from the kitchen and wondered when mom had done that. Man. My head had really been up my butt.

"I know. Its just—this is Maggie we're talking about."

"We all loved her too, man, so listen to what old Brainiac is saying," said Chuck.

"Okay. I'll try."

"Listen. Is there anything else you can remember? Anything weird, even a feeling?"

"Dude, you're watching too many crime shows on TV," said Chuck.

I searched my mind for something, and then it slapped me: Maggie's car.

I sat up straight. "After the cop threw me into the back of his car, he stood outside, talking to his partner for a minute, then just as they got in, I thought I saw Maggie's car drive past, heading back to town."

"Thought?" asked Mom, coming in from the kitchen with cherry strudel for everyone.

"No. It *was* her car. It wasn't just the moon that made her Bug stand out, but it went underneath those bright street lamps just outside the State's parking lot."

"Where was her car when you picked her up after work?" asked Aaron, a strain of excitement dancing in his voice.

"It was in the employee parking area behind the Sands restaurant, where it always is when she was working."

My dad reached for his cell and dialed a number. "I'm calling my brother Jack."

"Why call our attorney now?"

"Because her car wasn't there when we came to get you."

# Chapter-8

After an hour on the phone, we were able to arrange a get-together with Detective Green, my Uncle Jack, and us near the beach . . . and the lighthouse. My mom decided to stay home with Lizzy. We were all exhausted, but there was a special kind of tired in her eyes that I'd only seen once before. It was just after she'd received the call that her sister had been killed in a horrible car accident near Grand Rapids. The crash had been so intense that it took them three hours to get all of the body parts out of my aunt's car. This look was a little different, though. It was almost like she knew something none of the rest of us did. Anyway, I think that kind of news affects us all in different ways, but it was like she was reliving that experience all over again, and as much as she'd cared for Maggie, it was me she was really worried about. I think she thought it would be awhile before they got my body parts out of this wreck. But I knew it would work out because I hadn't done anything, and this is America, right?

My dad piled my friends and me into the SUV, and fifteen minutes later, we stood at the State Park's entrance, waiting. It was around seven a.m., but the sun had already risen, and the day was heating up. I could hear the waves and even got a whiff of the lake's fishy, but fresh, breeze. It struck me how much I loved this beach life, and wondered how anyone could ever leave it. It was addicting. More than that, it was home.

A few minutes later, Detective Green pulled up. She had someone with her, a man. They stayed in the car, talking and drinking coffee until Uncle Jack showed.

Jack got out of his Mercedes and motioned for us to follow him.

"Have they attempted to talk to you?" asked Jack.

I shook my head. "They haven't got out of the car."

"They're just trying to figure a way to pin this on Chase, that's all," lamented Chuck.

He wasn't the sharpest knife in the drawer, but his loyalty was unbelievably comforting.

Both doors of the blue state trooper unit opened, and the detective and the man got out.

He was over six foot, blond, kind of stocky, and had these blue eyes that just sort of saw right through you. Without even talking to him, I immediately felt uneasy, yet comfortable at the same time. Some people just have this presence, this . . . hell, I don't know, this charisma. It was like he knew my thoughts before I said anything. I glanced at dad, then Aaron and Chuck. Strangely, they all had the same kind of look on their faces.

*Who is this guy?*

I didn't have to wait long to find out. He stretched out a large hand and smiled.

"I'm Manny Williams. I'm a detective with the Lansing Police Department."

His grip was strong, and there was a sense of honesty about the man. He was easy to like.

He shook everyone else's hand, and even Uncle Jack, at least for a second, returned his smile.

"Manny and I go way back," said Detective Green, "and I invited him in on this one. He's the best detective I've ever met, and he does that profiling thing you see on TV . . . and he does it better than most."

"None of your shyster-ass tricks. We're here because we have more information, and we just want to find out what happened to . . . Maggie, got it?" said my uncle.

Detective Williams nodded and then turned to me, locking onto my eyes.

"I'm sorry for your loss. I know what it's like to lose someone you love. I'm only here to get to the truth. That's what you want, right?"

I felt the tears well up. That simple statement caused Maggie's face to flash across my mind and led, once again, to the scene at the rocks at the base of Little Sable Point Lighthouse. Her being gone didn't seem real, still. Would it ever?

"It is what we want," said my dad, knowing it'd be a minute before I could speak.

"Tell me when you saw Maggie's car, again," said Detective Green.

"Like I said, it was just before the cops got in the car, and I was sitting in the back," I answered.

"Show me where you were and then where you saw her vehicle," she said.

I walked over to the parking lot and then, some twenty feet later, stopped, turning toward the road.

"This was it," I said. "The car came over that ridge and went toward town."

"You're sure?" asked Detective Williams.

"Yes."

"Okay. And you were sitting in the back seat, behind the driver or on the passenger side?" he asked.

"The passenger side."

He ran his hand through his hair and frowned, but didn't say anything. More of that uneasiness whispered to me.

"Well, we found Maggie's car. It was parked a block from yours in another driveway that led up to a house near the dunes. The CSU folks are going over it now, and they'll let us know what they find. But I got to tell you, there was some blood smeared on the driver's seat, like the killer wiped their hand on it. Whoever did this was probably in her car."

"Is that like, well, don't killers sometimes come back to the scene?" asked Aaron.

Williams smiled. "That's what people think about killers, that they come back to the scene of their crime, but in reality, it doesn't happen unless the perp has a different agenda. Some serial killers and arsonists would fit into that minority, but 'no' is usually the right answer."

Detective Green crossed her arms and glanced at Uncle Jack, then me.

"That also means whoever did this went back to get

her car. The keys were still in the ignition. That says to me the killer had access to them. Do you have any idea how that could have happened, Chase?"

"Don't answer that, Chase. They're fishing," said my uncle.

My dad scowled at Uncle Jack and then motioned for me to answer. "We've nothing to hide."

"Well, she must have left her purse in the car. Or maybe she brought it with her. I honestly don't remember," I said.

"I agree with you that she must have left her purse in the car. I don't think whoever killed Maggie would have bothered to take her purse from her and then do what they did. Besides, we didn't find her purse anywhere near the lighthouse," said Detective Green.

It was my turn to frown. "What do you mean?"

She gazed out to the lake, the horizon becoming ever so brighter, then turned back to me.

"Chase. We found it down the beach, near where you said you had been walking."

# Chapter-9

"What the hell does that mean? You still think I did this?" I bellowed . Fatigue and stress don't play well together, and I was living proof.

Detective Williams stepped closer to me. "Chase. What we do in this cop world is try to eliminate possibilities and, in this case, suspects. I want you to think like Detective Green and me for a moment, then tell me what you would consider , understand?"

That voice of his was so disarming. The man had done this a time or two.

I tried to do what he asked, and for a moment, just a second, I understood what was going through their minds, I think. I hadn't really supplied them with options, and people lied all of the time for less serious reasons, far less.

"I, well, I guess that—"

My uncle took three steps, grabbed my arm, and pulled me back to where dad and the others were standing. Interesting how I had been kind of cut from the herd and hadn't even realized it. They were *really* good.

"Don't answer those kinds of questions, at least the way they're leading you. They want you to confess, even though you didn't do it. From now on, no more questions answered unless I say it's okay. Okay?"

I looked at my dad, then Chuck, then Aaron. I'm pretty sure we were all on the same page. I didn't do this, and I wanted to answer all of their questions.

My grandpa on my mom's side had been a different kind of man. Strong, fearless, full of that life energy we'd all like to have. He'd fought in Germany in 1944, and during one of those special talks that only granddads and grandsons have, he'd said, *Don't be afraid of nothing, walk boldly into the pit. You ain't going to live forever anyway, so living like a chicken shit is a waste.*

He was right. It was time to go boldly. I *didn't* have anything to hide.

Detective Williams had said to put myself in his shoes and tell him what I'd think. That was still a good idea to me.

"Uncle Jack. I'm going to talk to them about whatever they want. Maggie's gone, and someone has to pay. The sooner we stop with the games, the faster that will happen."

"You don't know how *this* game is played. Innocence isn't always the best way to avoid . . ."

"Stop. For God's sake and ours, stop," said my dad, that familiar, and sometimes dreadful authority reverberating through his voice. When dad got like that, it was time to listen.

"I believe in the truth, no matter what that is. So at least for now, Jack, you're fired. We'll do this the right way."

Jack stared at me and then dad. He threw up his hands. "You're both damn fools. Don't come running when this all blows up in your faces. Oh, and you'll get my bill, real soon," he called over his shoulder as he stomped toward his car.

"Yeah, I figured that," said my dad, quietly.

Got to love my dad.

Without another word, I motioned to the two cops.

"Listen. For the tenth time, I know what this looks like. I don't know how her purse got there. I don't know who would have followed us, then me. I just know what I've told you, and it's the truth."

The two cops exchanged glances.

"You sound like an honest man, but we have to follow the evidence, and right now, that's not looking so good," said Detective Green.

I started to answer and then realized that Detective Williams wasn't looking at me, but over my shoulder instead. I felt one of those *oh-no* chills. You know, like when you're sure there's some type of monster behind you, ready to tear your head off. I was close.

"What's on your mind, son?" asked Detective Williams.

I turned to see who he was speaking to. Aaron was moving sand with his right foot and watching the process. I could tell he was in one of his famous thinking spells. But the feel of intensity draped around him was out of character. He usually kept his calm, come hell or high water. Not this time.

"If you two are right, whoever was driving Maggie's car was probably the killer, right?" asked Aaron, that strange look not leaving his face.

"Let's just say that I'd like to have a little one-on-one session with that person," answered Detective Green. Williams said nothing; he just waited.

Aaron pursed his lips and spoke softly. "I saw who was driving her car last night."

# Chapter-10

I was stunned. My mouth wouldn't work, and I couldn't move. Detective Williams had no such ailment.

"What do you mean, Aaron?" he asked.

"Just what I said. It was around twelve thirty, and I'd just finished up at the Barbeque Ranch and was getting into my car, when I saw the yellow Bug heading south. I waved but—"

"Who was it? And why in the hell didn't you say something sooner?" I growled. "It could have saved us all of this crap. Damn, Aaron."

I felt like a million tons of manure had been lifted from my shoulders. Then, for no reason I could think of, I felt dread reach over and kiss me on the cheek. Aaron's answer was going to change each of us forever. I just knew it.

Aaron hesitated, looked down at his foot again, then shook his head slowly. Out of the corner of my eye, I watched Chuck back away from him like he thought whatever came out of his mouth would have the same effect as a grenade. Odd. My dad looked nervous too, but held his ground.

Aaron looked up and steadied himself.

"I didn't think it would be this hard, you know."

"Stop," said Detective Williams. He had one of those *about-time* looks on his face and, like I said before, when this man spoke, you listened. There was something else there, almost like he wanted to protect Aaron. That if he let him say what he saw, Aaron would blame himself forever.

"What the hell do you mean, stop? I have to know who did this."

"Just hang on, Chase. It's more complex than giving us a name, okay?"

"All right. All right."

He put his hand on my shoulder and smiled, then the two detectives moved away, speaking in low tones.

In those maddening moments, I felt everything and then nothing at all. It was like my emotion box was empty, and it'd be awhile before it was filled again. Maybe it never would.

I turned toward Lake Michigan and felt the morning breeze freshen on my face. I saw a red transport ship heading north, maybe a half mile off the coast, and focused on part of its journey, knowing the next time I saw one of them like this, my world wouldn't be the same.

"Chase?"

I jumped and spun toward the sound of Detective Williams's voice.

"Yes."

"Let's go sit by the lighthouse for a few minutes. Detective Green is going to go wait by Aaron and the others."

"Anything to get this over with."

Then it struck me like an eight-foot wave. *Aaron.* Aaron had killed Maggie. It made total sense.

I turned to confront him, and Detective Williams grabbed me. The man was powerful and stopped me in my tracks.

"Wait. Don't say anything. We have to do this the right way," he said, seeming to read my mind.

"But . . . okay. You're the boss."

A minute later, we were sitting on the sand about thirty feet from where Maggie had died. I couldn't stop the flashbacks. That scream, her stare, the walk up the lighthouse steps—a walk I'd never make again, ever.

"Chase. I'm worried about Aaron."

"Why? I mean he killed her, right? He must have followed us. You know, I always wondered about him. He'd say how much he loved her as a friend, but he was jealous. I could tell."

I caught my breath and wondered why I had just unloaded all of that on the detective. It felt good, though.

He ran his hand through his hair and smiled. "I think you're right. But let me tell you why I'm worried about him. People who do this kind of thing, kill someone close to them, can become so distraught that they block it out and have no memory of it."

"You mean like amnesia?"

"Exactly. It's called dissociative amnesia. Something a person has done, or seen, causes so much psychological stress that the person simply forgets what happened. The mind is powerful and frail at the same time. If we confront him with what's going on, he may dive deeper into denial and never come out again, got it?"

"Yes," I said, not really understanding how that could happen, but sure the man wasn't lying. "What do we do?"

"Well, it'll help if we go over your story so we have all of the details together. I've had a couple of these cases, and it works to show the facts. You with me?"

I said I was.

"I know this is going to be tough, but let's start from the beginning. Right after you picked Maggie up from work."

"Really?"

"Really," he said.

"All right," I sighed.

I went through it again. He stopped me once in a while, got a clarification, and told me to continue. Each time he did, I felt more anxiety for Aaron. There was hate too, but I'd known him longer than Maggie, and I suppose I loved him as much. But I just couldn't get how he could do that to her and me.

"I think I have what I need, Chase. So let's go talk with Aaron. It'll be good to have you there. It might help him stay grounded."

I got up and turned to look at the lighthouse and was surrounded with more flashbacks than I could shake a stick at. Gruesome flashbacks.

Detective Williams stood beside me. "I do have another question."

"Shoot."

You said Maggie fell backward after she fell on the steps, right?

"Yes."

"So she would have reached behind her to grab your arm, causing the fingernail scratches to start at the bottom of your forearm and work up. Is that right too?"

"Yeah. I caught her, and we just stood there for a few minutes."

He let out a sigh and I felt my head start to spin. What the hell was happening here?

"The scratch marks, according to the police photos and as I see them now, indicate just the opposite, Chase. Evidence shows that the scratches started at the top of your arm and ended by your wrist. That happens when people are facing each other and maybe struggling."

"Well. Maybe I was wrong. It happened so fast."

"That could be. I have another question. Remember, we have to get this right."

I felt myself growing impatient. "What?"

"You said you were sitting in the back of the police car on the passenger side, and the in-car video confirms that. We're about the same height, so, before you got here, I got in the back of the car, cuffed myself, and tried to see out the window where you saw Maggie's car drive by, and for the life of me, I couldn't. In fact, it was almost impossible to see out the driver's side rear window at all."

I rubbed my face, my mind wandering back to Maggie. The curve of her face. The shape of her body. The smell of her hair. I never loved or missed her more than I did at that second.

"Maybe I saw it out the other window, but I saw it," I answered, my voice faltering.

"That's possible," he said quietly.

Detective Williams took a step closer and drove those eyes to the very core of my soul.

"I want you to close your eyes, Chase, and

concentrate on the man you saw at the top of the trail leading away from the lighthouse."

"I told you a hundred times, I couldn't see him."

"Trust me here. I think you can, but something's blocking it. I need you to try. Aaron needs you to try. Maggie and her mother need you to try."

The man should have been one of those motivational coaches. I didn't want to let anyone down, especially Maggie, and do less than I could. Furthermore, Detective Williams knew that about me.

I shut my eyes and concentrated. I relived running around the lighthouse and felt the pain as the tire iron jammed into my sandal and struck my calf, causing me to go down. Then I dug deep. The pale light of the moon grew brighter, and I watched the figure hesitate and then look my way. It occurred to me that Detective Williams wanted me to concentrate on the man I'd seen. I don't know how he knew that, but he was right. It was a man, wearing a familiar ball cap.

In my mind's eye, the moon seemed to get a little brighter, then I saw his face. Good God in heaven, I saw his face.

# Chapter-11

I stared at Detective Williams, then slowly turned to the group of men waiting with Detective Green. The sun felt a little warmer on my back as it rose higher, but that's not why I was sweating. I've read about those out-of-body feelings people have. They say it happens in situations when someone just can't escape any other way. You could count me to be in that group.

I'd read a few things in college I didn't like. I suppose anyone who'd traveled that route felt the same way sometimes. But there was this book written by Henry David Thoreau, *Walden Pond.* In it, he'd written about his life near that small lake. I'd researched him after reading the book and found something he'd written that turned my head. That quote came rushing back to me and, for some unknown reason, stabbed my heart.

*Rather than love, than money, than fame, give me truth.*

Truth. I didn't need this truth, but I began up the slope anyway, knowing life would never be the same.

Manny Williams didn't speak but instead followed as I shuffled through the sand, finally reaching the destination my legs seemed to acknowledge without being told.

Silence is golden, like the saying goes, and if it had been up to me, this silence would have lasted until the end of time or whenever God came back, whichever was first. But I didn't have the luxury of choices like that. Immortality wasn't on my resume.

"It's time," said Detective Williams, softly, in that voice that could force a dead man to speak.

I panned the circle of people that included three of the most important men in my life. The disappointment and pure dread at identifying the killer of my Maggie was going to tear us apart for an eternity.

I glanced at Detective Green and then over to Detective Williams. His slight nod somehow gave me courage. I wanted to run away and hide, but in the end, Maggie's killer had to pay. Oh God in Heaven, this was going hurt.

I let out the last remnants of a breath that I'd held jealously. Pain began to pound at my temples, and my lips trembled. "Detective Williams and I have been talking," I said softly. The throbbing in my head was louder, drowning out my voice. Memories and unwelcome pictures began to flash at me, piercing my heart and threatening my breath. I gasped for air. I had to say the words, somehow. Then I did. Even I couldn't believe it. "It was me. I saw my own face on the man going over the hill," I blurted.

I had to say it. Truth was truth, as my dad would say, but this was more than that. It was Hell.

Aaron moved closer to me, his face full of questions. I turned my eyes away. I never wanted to see him look at me that way again. He reached out, grabbed my arm with a boney grip, and whispered. "Why?"

Detective Green stood next to my dad, who looked like he'd just been stabbed through the heart. Maybe he had.

"I think I'd like to know that too, Chase," Green said.

I slumped slowly to the sand, and once there, I remembered everything. Not just the face of the man who stood in that silver moon's light, but—please, God, forgive me—everything that had happened. How I'd killed her.

The movie in my mind started again; this time, there were no scenes deleted.

Maggie had climbed to the top of the lighthouse, me in close pursuit, both of us laughing in that out-of-breath way that was funny and hurt at the same time. We held hands, stared at the lake, listened to the waves. I'd bent to kiss her, but she'd moved away and said she had something to tell me. That it would be better to hear it up here, in a place where we'd had great memories. I recalled how my heart started to beat, like when you think you're in deep trouble. Maggie didn't keep me waiting. She really was going to go to MIT, that part was true. But she was going to move there, for good, to be with the new love of her life—the professor who had gotten her into the school and who was twenty years older than her. I'd thought she was joking, but she hadn't been. I'd never felt that kind of betrayal. And betrayal was the right word. We had just talked about having kids, for God's sake.

I saw red. I swung the iron I'd brought to pry off the locks. It struck her with a glancing blow as she ducked and grabbed my arm. I pushed her and she almost went over the railing. I swung again and felt the left side of her skull give. She hurtled over the edge.

I hadn't meant to kill her. I'd just lost it. I rushed down the steps, took one look at her lying on the rocks, and felt like I had died inside.

I then ran all the way back to our cars. I hadn't really picked her up at work; she had met me at the vacant cabin. That's when I squeezed into the front seat of her car and drove back to the lighthouse. I really can't explain that, other than to say that's where her scent was still the strongest. I know it was sick, but until you walk in my shoes . . .

Ten minutes later, I was back at the beach, calling 9-1-1. You know the rest.

That movie had only taken seconds to show in my brain, but the reruns would last until the day I died.

"Chase?" said Detective Williams.

The hot tears welled up, then disappeared. More crying wasn't going to bring her back either. I'd made sure that nothing would.

"I . . . I was angry. I guess I just lost my cool. I've never . . ."

Detective Williams put his hand on my shoulder not saying anything, but it spoke more than you'd think a touch could. In a way, I think he was telling me he understood, at least in part. But there was that other side of his touch. The one that said *you're coming with us.*

I stood. Life is full of curves, and as I heard the waves prance to the shore, I decided I was only going to one place.

I twisted away from Detective Williams and sprinted toward the beach. He yelled for me to stop, but oddly, only once. I guess he had his reasons. I heard echoes of someone running behind me, but I didn't look back. I was never going to look back again.

I reached the lake's edge and dove into the icy waters of Lake Michigan. I'd swim as far as I could then let nature take its course. It'd be better that way, at least for me. I swam hard. It wouldn't take long to tire and just sink to the bottom . . . if I didn't die from hypothermia first.

A few minutes later, I heard another swimmer and looked a few feet behind me.

Aaron.

"Get your skinny ass back to the beach," I yelled. "This ain't about you."

His glasses were gone, and his teeth were chattering. His appearance reminded me of a cartoon version of a drowned rat, but his look of determination was something special.

"Hey-y we're in this t-together. I'll help-p you through this-s. But like y-o-u always tel-l-l me: truth is truth. So i-f-f you go, I-I go. So do a man-n a solid and let-t me live-live long enough to get lu-lucky."

I was still treading water when a wave hit me in the face, but not with anywhere the impact of my friend's actions. In spite of what I'd done to Maggie, here he was. No condemnation, just a determination to stick with me. I felt my heart change, at least a little.

I went to him, nodded, and then we swam back toward Little Sable Point Lighthouse.

## About the Author of *The Lighthouse*

**Rick Murcer** is a *New York Times* and *USA Today* best-selling author.

He lives in Michigan and graduated from Michigan State University. He has two grown children, three beautiful grandkids, and a blind black Lab named Max, who serves as his "writing" dog.

He loves to answer your e-mails, so talk to him.
Website: www.rickmurcer.com
E-mail: rickmurcer@gmail.com

## Manny Williams Books

*Caribbean Moon*

*Deceitful Moon*

*Emerald Moon*

*Caribbean Rain*

## Sophie Lee Short Stories

*Capital Murder*

# The Honeymooners
## Jekyll Island – Book 1

*by Traci Hohenstein*

# Prologue—*six months earlier*

The champagne chilled on ice, and plump strawberries coated with rich dark chocolate sat atop a sterling silver tray.

Straightening his tie, the man knocked hard on the door of Room 314, calling out, "Room Service!"

"Just a second," came a voice from behind the door.

The man fingered the glass vial in his pocket. He took a quick glance down the hallway before the hotel guest opened the door.

"Good evening. I've got some champagne for the happy couple, compliments of hotel management," he said, rolling the cart into the room.

"You can just put it over there." The groom pointed next to the bed. He was partially dressed in his tuxedo, with his tie and jacket off, shirt untucked and unbuttoned.

The man pulled out the champagne and started to open the bottle.

"Just leave it, dude. I can do that," the groom said.

"It's all part of the five-star service."

"Okay. Whatever." The groom walked toward the bathroom.

The man waited until the groom was out of sight and then slipped the vial out of his pocket. He poured the clear, odorless liquid into the two champagne flutes, then filled them with the chilled bubbly. For the finishing touch, he removed the strawberries and artfully arranged them on a china plate. He heard giggles coming from the bathroom.

"Have a nice evening!" he called out, closing the door behind him. "Thanks for the tip, asshole," he mumbled to himself while hanging the DO NOT DISTURB sign on the front of the doorknob. Instead of the elevator, he took the stairwell two steps at a time, humming the

"Jeopardy" theme song.

***

Tuesday morning, Maria Gonzalez, head housekeeper of the Tropicana Hotel and Casino in Atlantic City, rapped on the door a few times before sliding her key card in the slot. She ripped off the DO NOT DISTURB sign before opening the door. The guests were supposed to have checked out, and sometimes they did so without notifying the front desk. Since all guests had a credit card on file, it was not unusual to just leave when they were ready. Still, Maria sang out, "Housekeeping!" as she peeked inside the room.

Satisfied the room was empty, Maria engaged the doorstopper and stepped back to grab a load of towels off her cart. She was short-staffed this morning with half her staff coming down with a stomach virus. Thankfully, she only had nine rooms to clean this morning. Maria proceeded to the bathroom when she almost tripped over something. She looked down and saw a nude male body on the floor. The body had a sick, green tinge to it, and the smell of vomit assaulted her nose. Maria screamed and bolted out of the room, feeling like she was going to be sick. "Help me!" she yelled as she ran down the hotel corridor. "Somebody is dead! Help me!"

# Chapter One

Jake and Tessie McBride arrived at the quaint, yet luxurious, bed-and-breakfast on Jekyll Island just after midnight. Jake pulled into the gravel driveway and parked in front of the sign announcing "Welcome to The Hibiscus House." He reached over and grabbed Tessie's hand.

"Are you ready, Mrs. McBride, to start our honeymoon?"

Tessie smiled brightly at her husband. "Why, yes, Mr. McBride." She leaned over and gave him a lingering kiss on the lips.

"Mmmm . . . you taste so good," he said as he ran his hand down to her breast. He gave it a hard squeeze as he nibbled on her left ear.

"Are we going in?" Tessie asked.

"I could take you right here," Jake whispered in her ear.

Tessie responded by running her hand across the large bulge in the front of his pants. "How could I turn this away?" She unzipped his pants, lifted her skirt, and moved over to his side of the car, lowering herself down onto his lap. She started slowly, and then moved her hips faster and faster, relishing the sound of Jake moaning in her ear.

They'd been so into each other, Tessie hadn't noticed a car pull up next to them, until a door slammed. Jake had her nipple in his mouth as she looked over at the sleek, silver Lexus. A tall, handsome man was walking around to the passenger-side door. Their eyes locked for a moment, before surprise, then amusement, passed over his face. Moving even faster now with Jake's face firmly planted in her chest, Tessie smiled sweetly at the guy and gave him a small wave. He smiled back as he opened the door for someone. Tessie watched as the handsome man and his partner, a petite, blond woman, walked to the entrance of the bed-and-breakfast. The woman never noticed Tessie and Jake.

Tessie felt Jake tense up as he exploded into her. A few seconds later, he kissed her on the forehead. "Now are you ready to check in, Mrs. McBride?"

She checked her reflection in the rearview mirror. Digging out some lip gloss from her purse, she swiped it across her supple lips. "Let's go."

# Chapter Two

The smell of fresh chocolate chip cookies mixed with the salty ocean breeze was intoxicating.

"Welcome to Hibiscus! You must be the McBrides, our honeymooners! What a lovely and appropriate last name! I'm Elsa, the owner." The slightly overweight woman with a bubbly personality met them in the foyer. She held out her chubby hand. "It's so nice to meet you!"

Tessie smiled and shook her hand. "It's nice to finally meet you." Tessie remembered Elsa's very detailed and complete e-mails regarding their reservation at the luxurious, ocean-front bed-and-breakfast.

"You must be tired after that long drive," Elsa said.

"A little," Jake acknowledged, rubbing Tessie's back.

"Well, your room is ready to go. All I need is a signature on our reservation card, and then you'll be all set."

Jake stepped forward to take care of the paperwork while Tessie looked around. The foyer was decorated nicely with a West Indies theme. Dark wood furniture mixed with cream and soft-blue fabrics and accents. A large, intricate-cut glass bowl held white sand and various-sized, exotic, baby-pink seashells. Next to the bowl was a handwritten breakfast menu.

### *Blueberry Muffins*

### *Scrambled Eggs*

### *Maple Brown Sugar Bacon*

### *Parmesan Cheese Grits*

### *Mango-Orange Juice*

### *Colombian Coffee*

"Fresh breakfast is served in the dining room area every morning at eight. You're welcome to have it delivered to your room as well," Elsa said, winking at Jake.

"Do you need help with your bags?" A young teenage boy appeared from behind the reservation desk.

"This is my son, Mickey," Elsa said.

While Jake and Mickey went to grab their bags, Tessie turned her attention to a small stack of newspapers sitting next to the breakfast menu placard.

### *"Honeymoon Killer Strikes Again!"*

Her eyes skimmed the first few sentences of the article.

*"Tiffani and Blake Cunningham, a young couple from Charlotte, North Carolina, were found murdered in their rented beach house in Myrtle Beach. They'd been on their honeymoon when the suspected serial killer struck. A maintenance man found their bodies on Sunday morning . . ."*

"Ready, babe?" Jake asked, startling her. "Everything okay?"

"I was just reading something." Tessie pulled herself away from the newspaper, an unsettling feeling in her stomach. She gave Jake a quick smile and tossed her long, dark hair over her shoulder.

Elsa and her son led them up the stairs. "We have you in the Endless Love room," she said, opening the door to their suite. Tessie walked in first. The walls were painted a soft blue, the king-sized bed faced the French doors, which led out to a balcony overlooking the infinity pool and the Atlantic Ocean. A large en suite bath held a luxurious shower with seven separate nozzles and a roomy, claw-foot tub. A small desk and chair were tucked away in the corner of the room.

"Dinner is served nightly at seven thirty. There's a directory on the desk with restaurant and deli recommendations for lunch. All are within a short distance from the Hibiscus. Turn down service is offered nightly around ten. We bring up warm, chocolate chip cookies and milk. There's also a list of activities, like scuba diving and horseback riding, available at a discount rate to our guests." Elsa smiled at the couple. "Sorry, I'm rambling. Any questions and I'll be out of your way."

"Honey?" Jake wrapped his arms around Tessie.

"Oh, everything looks good. Thank you, Elsa."

"Okay then. Gina will bring you guys a little snack, and we'll leave you honeymooners alone. Good night."

"See ya in the morning," Jake said, tipping the teenage boy before closing the door.

"You okay, Tess?" he asked.

Tessie opened the French doors and breathed in the scent of the ocean. "The newspaper downstairs. It had an article about the Honeymoon Killer." She waited for his reaction.

Jake wrapped his arms around his wife and kissed the top of her head. "Baby, you don't worry about that. We're here to relax, remember?"

Tessie turned around to face Jake. "Seriously, honey. I don't want to spend our . . ."

Jake put his finger on her lips. "Shhh . . . no worries." He removed his finger and slid his tongue in her mouth tasting her sweetness. A knocking at the door interrupted their kiss.

"I'll get it. You stay here and *relax*," he instructed her.

Tessie leaned over the balcony and spotted a couple in the pool. It was well after midnight, and the couple had the whole pool area to themselves. She marveled at this perfect place to spend a honeymoon. Jake was right; she needed to let loose.

The Hibiscus Inn was a luxury B&B that Tessie had found while reading an article in *Southern Living* magazine. She was instantly attracted to the quaint, three-story Victorian inn situated on the ocean. It boasted eight suites with six of them dedicated to honeymooners. The inn catered to upscale clientele and offered luxurious amenities. It sounded like heaven, and Tessie had booked it right away—not even batting an eye at the four-hundred-a-night price tag.

The sound of a woman's giggle floated up to her. The woman's back was facing Tessie, and Tessie got a good look at the man with her. It was the same guy from the parking lot. The soft lights from the pool highlighted their tanned bodies. The man held his partner against the back of the pool, her hips rising up and down to meet his. Tessie couldn't keep her eyes off him. Even from a distance, she could make out that he was very handsome. Not good-looking in the movie star way, like Jake was. No, this guy had a mop of curly hair, tall and lanky. More like a surfer-boy look. Another giggle followed by a soft moan from the woman. Then Tessie realized the man was looking up at her. Embarrassed she was caught spying, Tessie stepped back into the safe shadow of the night. That didn't stop the guy from giving her a smile and wave. Not unlike the one she gave him earlier in the parking lot. But something in his smile made her stomach muscles tense up. While keeping his eyes trained on Tessie's balcony, he grabbed the woman's hair and gave it a hard tug as she moaned louder. Tessie heard the door close, and she took one last look at the couple before stepping back inside.

Jake picked a cracker from the sterling-silver tray and topped it with a piece of white, creamy cheese. He held the cracker up to Tessie's mouth, then slid it in. He watched her chew with satisfaction.

"Eat up." He motioned to the tray loaded with crackers, cheese, and fruit. "You'll need your strength for later."

Tessie washed her cracker down with a glass of champagne that Jake handed her.

"Big day of doing nothing," she responded.

Jake playfully swatted her on the bottom. "That's what *you* think."

# Chapter Three

The pool deck was empty when Tessie laid her beach towel on the lounge chair. She adjusted the straps on her pink bikini bottoms and sat down to rub suntan oil on her legs. Jake had stayed behind in the room to make a few business calls that couldn't wait. Or so he told her. This was supposed to be a relaxing honeymoon, not a time to work—she had reminded him of his exact words to her the night before. Jake was already on the phone before she could argue her point. Tessie had grabbed her bag and stormed out.

"Need help with that?" a deep voice said behind her.

She turned to find the guy from last night right in front of her.

He looked a little older than she'd originally thought. She had him pegged around twenty-ish last night. Now up close and in the daylight, she thought he looked closer to thirty. He still had the surfer-boy look, with a mess of curly hair, pretty blue eyes, and a deep tan.

"Sure." Tessie handed him the bottle of oil. He massaged her upper back with the oil in quick, efficient strokes, his hands nice and strong. Tessie felt a twinge down below. When he finished, she thanked him and laid back on the lounge. "I'm Tessie McBride."

"Clay Myers."

"You're on your honeymoon as well?" she asked him.

Clay laughed. "It's obvious we both are, huh?"

Tessie remembered Clay watching her have sex in the parking lot. And she reciprocated by spying on him in the pool with his wife. She felt herself blushing. "Yeah, I guess so."

Clay cleared his throat and looked around the pool deck. "So where is the lucky fellow?"

Tessie smiled. "Upstairs. Business calls. And the lucky lady?"

"Spa day. Ramona likes massages and having her nails done. Or whatever it is that you girls do," he answered.

Tessie peered at her own toenails. "I could use a pedi myself."

"Nonsense. You look beautiful."

Tessie felt herself blushing again at the compliment. What was this guy doing to her? She was usually immune to such bullshit from guys. She decided to change the subject.

"Where do you guys live?" she asked.

"Atlanta. How about you?"

"DC."

"What made you decide to come here for your honeymoon?" he asked.

"I saw an ad in a magazine," she said. This was in part the truth. "You?"

"This is a mini-moon for us. I couldn't get a lot of time off for a proper honeymoon so we came here for a few days. Next year, we'll go to Europe for a month."

"What do you do?" Tessie asked, truly intrigued by him.

"I'm a cardiologist."

"Nice, noble profession."

"Yeah, I guess. It runs in the family. My father and grandfather are both cardiologists."

Tessie thought about it for a minute. The name Clay Myers was ringing a bell. "Wait, your dad isn't Dr. Clayton Myers is he?"

Clay smiled. "The one and only."

Dr. Clayton Myers was the renowned cardiologist, famous for his heart-healthy diet plan and cookbook. His books were on the best-seller list and Dr. Myers was a popular guest on the talk-show circuit. Now that Tessie saw Clay up close, she recognized the resemblance between father and son.

"And what does the lovely Tessie do back in DC?"

Tessie gave him a smile that could melt the sun out of the sky. She reached in her beach bag and pulled out a ponytail holder. In one swift move, she gathered her long, brunette hair and piled it on top of her head. "I'm a freelance writer." She stretched out on the lounge chair and closed her eyes. "Not as exciting as saving lives, I guess." She could feel Clay's eyes on her. Men wanted to sleep with her, and women wanted to be like her. Tessie had known that she held a special power over men all her life and learned at an early age to use it to her advantage.

"Trust me; cardiology is not all that exciting. What kind of writing?"

"A little of this and a little of that," Tessie answered coyly. "Mostly financial and business pieces." She peeked over at Clay, who was intently staring at her. With what? Intrigue? Lust?

"Pretty and smart to boot . . ." Clay started to say.

"Hey, babe." Jake's voice behind her made Tessie sit up in her chair.

"Hey, babe." Tessie leaned over for a kiss. "Clay, this is my husband, Jake McBride."

Tessie watched as the two men shook hands.

"Keeping my wife company?" Jake asked.

"We're keeping each other company," Clay answered. "My wife Ramona is at the spa. How long are you guys at Jekyll?"

"Until next Saturday," Jake answered for them.

"Ya'll should go diving with us tomorrow morning. They do a dive certification here at the pool," Clay said.

"No need. We got our certifications last year," Tessie said. "Jake and I are both self-professed adrenaline junkies. Sky diving, cave diving, mountain climbing . . . you name it, we've probably done it."

"Nothing spectacular about this dive trip, but I guarantee it'll be fun. We have to go about twenty miles out, seventy feet of water for some good visibility, but it's worth it. Afterward, we can head to a spot where we could do some spear fishing. Gag grouper, snapper, cobia, and flounder by the dozens," Clay said.

"We're game," Jake said, looking at Tessie for

confirmation. She nodded.

After thirty minutes of chatting, Ramona showed up. Tessie really didn't get a good look at her the first time she saw her, but up close she was pretty. Strawberry-blond hair and shoulder-length, blue eyes, about five-four and petite. Tessie envied her glowing, tanned skin and freshly painted nails. She spent far too many hours inside writing. This week she vowed to work on her tan and go back to DC with some color on her skin.

"OPI Cajun Shrimp?" she asked Ramona, peering at her toenails, referring to the name of the nail polish.

Ramona gave her husband a quick peck on the cheek. "It's my favorite color for the beach."

"I've invited the McBride's to go scuba diving with us tomorrow," Clay said.

"Great. It'll be nice to have another couple join us," Ramona agreed.

"Anyone up for lunch? They have a great deli next door that serves salads and sandwiches," Clay asked. "We can eat by the pool."

Jake looked over at Tessie who nodded. "I'll walk over with you."

While Jake and Clay left to go pick up some lunch and drinks for them, Ramona reached in her bag for her copy of the *USA Today* newspaper.

"Did you hear about this Honeymoon Killer on the loose?" she asked Tessie in her sugary-sweet Southern accent.

Tessie shrugged. "I heard something about it on the news."

"It's creepy. He just struck this past weekend in Myrtle Beach. Killed two young kids from Duke. They'd just graduated college. The police think he dressed up like a repairman to get access to their beach house. They were hung." Ramona shuddered. "Just terrible, isn't it?"

Tessie slid her sunglasses up to the top of her head. She watched as an older couple walked up from the beach access ramp. "Very terrible," she agreed.

"Wonder why he kills honeymooners?" Ramona

asked.

"Dunno. I guess honeymooners are an easy target."

"What makes you say that?"

"They're easily distracted. Horny," Tessie answered.

Ramona laughed. "That's one possibility." She looked at the older couple who were settling in by the pool, sitting a few feet away from them. "It could be that guy over there," Ramona said as a matter of fact, pointing to the older guy.

Tessie peered at the couple. He was bald and wearing loud, Hawaiian-print trunks, socks, and a pair of Crocs. The wife was in a matching bright-orange bikini, crochet sarong, and flip-flops. She guessed they were in their mid-fifties. "He hardly strikes me as a ruthless killer."

"Well, no one suspected Ted Bundy either. Isn't it always the ones you expect the least?" Ramona asked. Not waiting for an answer, she continued, "The news reporter is always interviewing the neighbor or friend of the serial killer who says 'He was a nice guy. Helped old ladies across the street. I'd never guess that he was kidnapping girls and hiding their bodies in the basement.'"

"True," Tessie laughed, agreeing. "Chances are slim, though, the Honeymoon Killer is here on Jekyll Island. Even slimmer that he would strike at this particular B&B."

"What are you ladies talking about?" Clay asked as he put down a tray of grilled fish and salads.

"The serial killer on the loose," Ramona answered.

Clay laughed. "My wife is obsessed with that story. She's a bit of an amateur sleuth."

"Just because I solved a petty burglary in our neighborhood when the police didn't have a clue, my husband thinks I'm a regular Agatha Christie."

"Well, honey, you have to admit you've become a little infatuated with that case," Clay said.

"The guy has killed three couples already! We could be the fourth!" Ramona claimed. "All the deaths were along the eastern seaboard, Atlantic City, Hamptons, and Myrtle Beach. What's to say the Georgia coast isn't next?"

"She has a point," Jake winked at Tessie before handing her a salad.

"If the killer were to strike here," Clay said to his wife, reaching over and patting her on the leg, "I'd protect you."

"Thanks, honey," Ramona said, rolling her eyes.

"Forget serial killers. Let's talk about this dive trip," Jake said.

# Chapter Four

The water was calm on the way out to Gray's Reef. Tessie was surprised to see the older couple from the pool was joining them. They were recently married (first marriage for the bride, third for the groom). He was a traveling salesman—pharmaceutical—and she was a dance instructor. Tim and Marlo Mathis.

The captain expertly made his way to the spot where the three couples would spend four hours diving, snorkeling, and swimming in and around Gray's Reef. While Billy, their dive master and guide, went to get all their equipment ready, the couples sat on the deck discussing—what else but Ramona's favorite topic—the Honeymoon Killers.

"I heard the first victims were poisoned. Until the second couple was found, the police thought the first was a suicide pact," Ramona said. "Could you imagine dying on what's supposed to be the best night of your life?"

"What happened to the second couple?" Marlo asked. She was just as intrigued as Ramona.

"They were electrocuted!" Ramona exclaimed. "They were the couple from the Hamptons. The maid found them in the hot tub the next morning when she showed up to clean. They had been fried while skinny dipping in the Jacuzzi. Who knows what murderous method the honeymoon killer will come up with next time? He seems to like to change it up."

"How awful! When did this happen?" Marlo asked.

"About a month ago," Tessie answered.

"Tim, you were in the Hamptons last month. Do you remember that happening?" Marlo asked.

Tessie and Ramona exchanged glances. Ramona gave her an I-told-you-so look.

"I heard something about it," Tim said, shrugging his

shoulders.

"What were you doing in the Hamptons?" Ramona asked Tim, in an accusing tone.

"Ramona!" Clay scolded his wife. "You'll have to excuse her. She's a little obsessed with this honeymoon-killer case."

Tim waved off the husband. "It's okay. I was there for a company function."

"Did you know the area where the couple was found?" Ramona asked him.

Tessie saw Clay gave his wife a warning look.

Tim laughed it off. "Yeah. The Hamptons is a small place." He stood up and gave his wife a pat on the leg. "Now, if you'll excuse me. I think I'll go give Billy a hand with those tanks."

Marlo gave a small, nervous laugh, desperate to change the awkward conversation. "So, have you guys tried horseback riding yet? Tim and I went yesterday morning, and it was so much fun."

Tessie tuned Marlo out, taking in her surroundings. Clay and Jake seemed to be doing the same thing: looking at Marlo, but not really listening to her babble on about riding horses. Only Ramona seemed to be studying Marlo with great interest, hanging on to every word she said.

Marlo had platinum-blond hair (obviously dyed), fake (obvious) tits, booth spray-tan ala orange-creamsicle color, and long, claw-like, red nails. Tessie was sure she would get a recap of this conversation plus a complete analysis from Ramona later—about why or why not Ramona suspected Tim of being the serial killer preying on honeymooners. Even though they'd known each other about twenty-four hours, Ramona had recruited Tessie to be her partner in crime in all things serial killer. Clay was right about his wife. Ramona was obsessed.

". . . and so I would recommend riding Thunder if you want a gentle horse. Don't let the name fool you," Marlo continued.

"I'm going to see if they need any help." Jake was the

next guy to up and leave the conversation.

"I'll go with you," Clay offered.

And then there were just the three girls.

"The horseback riding sounds like fun," Tessie said, jumping back into the conversation. "I think we'll try that tomorrow."

"You should!" Marlo said with a little too much enthusiasm.

"Tim sells pharmaceutical drugs, huh?" Ramona asked.

Tessie groaned inwardly. Ramona's questions were starting to sound more like an interrogation.

"He does. Tim's worked for the same company his entire career. Top salesman, five years in a row," Marlo said proudly.

"How'd you two meet?" Tessie asked, beating Ramona to the punch.

"A convention in Raleigh. My dance studio was hired to perform at the convention. Tim and I met at the cocktail reception afterward. It was love at first sight, as they say." Marlo fingered the hem of her sarong, playing with an unraveling piece of yarn. "Tim doesn't have the best track record when it comes to relationships. But I think he's changed. He's much calmer since we've been together. So his friends and colleagues tell me." She shrugged, her boobs bobbing up and down.

Ramona took this as an invitation to delve into the psyche of the Mathis's relationship. "What do you mean he's calmer? Did he have an anger problem?"

Marlo looked a little unsure, like she'd said too much. "Well, no not really. He's just a little uptight sometimes. He's got a stressful job, on the road a lot, and then he's got to deal with two ex-wives and three teenage children." Marlo laughed nervously. "Wouldn't you be a little strung out?"

Tessie came to her rescue. She had enough of Ramona's digging. "We all react differently to life's little situations. Now, we're going to relax and do some diving, see things from a different perspective." She stood up to stretch just as the men came back with Billy and the dive equipment.

"Who's ready to dive?" Billy asked.

# Chapter Five

Tessie loved being under the ocean, swimming alongside the colorful tropical fish, where it was quiet and magical. In another life, Tessie was sure she would've been a mermaid. Swimming by Jake's side, she took his hand as they glided through the cerulean blue waters, exploring the coral reefs and admiring all the marine life. Tessie kept an eye on Clay and Ramona, noting they were about fifty feet away from them.

Clay was excitedly pointing to a large tortoise that lazily swam by them—not a care in the world. Jake pulled them away from the group, and they swam to the other side of the reef. Tessie spotted a lone barracuda peeking out of a coral rock formation waiting for prey. The barracuda flashed his pointy, sharp teeth at her before disappearing back into the safety of the dark. A group of silver angelfish seemed to be following her and Jake around the reef. Jake got excited when he found a large cobia swimming around the bottom of the reef, seemingly playing hide and seek with him. Jake stuck out his forefinger and thumb like he was cocking a gun and then rubbed his stomach. Tessie smiled to herself. There was nothing more Jake loved than fishing. After their dive this morning, the captain was going to take them to another spot so the men could go spear fishing while the girls sunbathed on the deck.

Just as Jake started to follow the cobia, Tessie spotted Clay and Ramona again. She started to wave them over when she noticed Ramona was in trouble. Through the thick diver's mask, she could see that Ramona's eyes were wide with panic. Then Tessie noticed Clay was giving the distress signal that divers use when in trouble. Clay was fighting to keep Ramona from swimming up to the surface. Tessie knew that if Ramona panicked and surfaced too quickly, she would be in danger of getting decompression sickness.

Tessie sprang into action and got Jake's attention. They made their way over to the distressed couple and started to perform the buddy breathing system, slowly making their way to the top. When they finally broke the surface, Ramona flung her mask across the deck and gasped for breath. Tessie followed her up the ladder.

"What the hell happened down there?" Ramona peeled off her wet suit. Her face was beet red.

Jake and Clay climbed aboard the boat as Billy and the Mathis couple followed close behind.

"We saw you guys go up. What happened?" Tim asked.

"I'll tell you what happened!" Ramona stormed over to the side of the boat, screaming at Tim while he hesitated by the ladder. "You messed with our tanks!"

Clay grabbed his wife by the arm. "Ramona! Calm down. You don't know that."

Tessie watched as Tim laughed at Ramona's outburst, which caused Ramona to go hysterical.

"That's the most absurd thing I've ever heard," Tim said, while climbing the ladder. "Why would I even do that?"

"Because you were trying to kill us!" Ramona exclaimed.

Marlo came up the ladder behind Tim, looking confused and terrified at the same time. "What's going on here?"

"Your husband is the Honeymoon Killer! He messed with our tanks and tried to kill us. That's what's going on here!" Ramona pushed Clay away and tried to stand up, but he put his arm around her and held her down in her seat.

"Your wife is crazy and delusional," Tim said while he stripped off his equipment.

Billy stepped in to diffuse the situation. "I was with Mr. Mathis the whole time we were getting the equipment ready. If the tanks were tampered with, I would know it."

Tessie watched as Billy and Jake carefully examined the tanks and the rest of the scuba equipment.

"Well, it's very suspect that Tim's the one who handed us the tanks before the dive. He had to know they were low on air," Ramona said.

"I had no idea. All the tanks were full," Tim countered as he walked over to Billy and watched them inspect the tanks.

Tessie gave Tim credit for being so calm during Ramona's tirade.

"I'm not sure why the tanks malfunctioned, but I assure you that I'll get to the bottom of this." Billy picked up the equipment and headed back to the cabin.

Jake put his arm around Tessie and whispered in her ear. "Great job down there, babe."

Tessie wondered what would've happened if she hadn't noticed the couple was in trouble when she did. Ramona was so wrapped up on thinking Tim tried to kill them that she didn't even bother to thank Tessie and Jake for saving their lives. Tessie continued to watch Ramona fume about the tanks and Tim's possible involvement, slowly beginning to wonder if taking this trip to Jekyll Island was a mistake.

# Chapter Six

"How's your headache?" Jake asked as he rubbed his wife's back.

"Better." Tessie rolled over and opened her eyes. She'd dealt with mind-blowing migraines since she was fourteen. This one was probably brought on by the dive incident, coupled with dealing with Ramona's antics.

"Feel up to dinner?" Jake asked.

"I don't think I can face another round of drama. I just want some time with you," Tessie said as she reached up and kissed Jake.

"That can be arranged. Why don't I go downstairs and have Elsa make us a to-go plate?"

Tessie looked at the clock. "Damn. It's already seven o'clock. How long did I sleep?"

"About six hours."

They'd nixed the fishing part of the dive trip when Ramona went haywire, and they came straight back to the B&B. Tessie went right up to the room, the blinding headache already raging full force, and took some painkillers.

"I'm going to take a shower while you grab dinner."

"'K, sweetie. I'll be right back."

After a long, hot shower, Tessie felt better. She decided to forgo the clothing and slid into the cool, satiny sheets a la nude and waited for Jake. Grabbing the remote, she turned on the TV. Tessie flipped through the channels until a news show caught her attention. A buxom, brunette reporter was discussing the Honeymoon Killer. Tessie turned the volume up.

". . . the young couple who was found dead in their luxury honeymoon suite. Police have now confirmed they are looking for two, not one, serial killers. The FBI in charge of the case is not releasing information on how they've come to the conclusion there are two suspects involved, but it has been speculated the killers were spotted on surveillance cameras."

Tessie heard the door open and muted the TV.

"Jerk chicken with fig and walnut pilaf, steamed garlic broccolini, and ginger pear rum cake with vanilla bean ice cream," Jake announced as he sat down a large tray of food. Gina, one of the B&B employees, followed behind him with a bottle of wine.

"Enjoy dinner. I hope you feel better, Mrs. McBride," Gina said before closing the door behind her.

"Elsa sends her best," Jake smiled as he arranged a plate for Tessie. She sat up, letting the sheet fall from her body.

"Wow." Jake looked at Tessie's naked body appreciatively. "Dinner may have to wait."

# Chapter Seven

*Another beautiful day on the Georgia coast,* Tessie thought as she looked out over the balcony, waves lapping up on the beach. Jake came up from behind and wrapped his arms around her waist.

"Are you sure you don't mind?" he asked again.

"Of course. Go, have a good time!"

Clay had invited Jake to play golf at the famed Pine Island course. Afterward, the foursome would meet for dinner at the B&B and then hit up a local jazz club.

"I just don't want to leave you again with Ramona. Seeing how that all ended yesterday," Jake said.

"It's okay. We're going shopping. We'll be nowhere near Tim or Marlo, so I think she'll be pretty tame."

"You're the best." Jake gave his wife a kiss before heading out the door. "I'll see you around six."

Tessie chose a sleeveless, tangerine-colored sundress and a big, floppy sunhat. While she was putting on gold earrings and matching bangles, someone knocked on the door.

"Hiya. Ready to go?" Ramona asked as she opened the door, poking her head in.

Tessie didn't realize that the door could be opened from the outside without a key. She was used to self-locking doors at hotels and would have to remember to lock the door next time.

"Yep," Tessie answered, grabbing her own bag on the way out the door.

On their way down the staircase, they overheard someone arguing. Ramona put her finger to her lips, and they stopped midway down the stairs. Tessie didn't feel comfortable eavesdropping on someone's conversation, but Ramona held her firmly by the arm.

". . . not going to worry our guests about this, Elsa. This is supposed to be a special time in their lives. We're not going to make a fuss about it."

"Don't patronize me, Frank. I just think we need to give them a heads up to be careful. The last thing we need is a murder on our hands," Elsa responded in a hushed tone.

"The sheriff didn't think it was a big deal. He just said for *us* to take some extra precautions, like locking the doors at night and keeping a watchful eye. This is something *we* need to do. The guests don't need to be bothered with it."

"Well, if the sheriff didn't think it was a big deal, then why did he drive all the way . . ."

Tessie recognized the voices of the couple who owned the B&B. She removed Ramona's arm from hers and cleared her throat. Ramona shot her a dirty look as Tessie continued down the stairs.

Elsa and Frank were standing at the reservation desk, looking busy shuffling papers around.

"Good morning, ladies. I hear that you are off to go shopping," Elsa said, smiling brightly.

"We have to punish our husbands somehow for playing golf on our honeymoon!" Tessie said.

"Right you are!" Elsa answered. "Would you like me to have someone drive you? You can never be too careful."

Tessie caught the frustrated look Frank gave Elsa.

"No need. I'm driving our car," Ramona answered for them. "Thanks for the offer, though."

Ramona waited until they were safe inside the Lexus until she spoke to Tessie. "I wonder what that was all about."

"I don't know. So, where to first?" Tessie asked, eager to change the conversation.

Ramona adjusted the mirror, swiped on some brightly colored, coral lip gloss, and turned over the engine. "We're going to hit up the shops on Pier Road. There's a place that sells exquisite sterling-silver jewelry."

"I'm always up for new jewelry." Tessie looked out at the beautiful scenery: tall oak trees draped with moss, glimpses of the ocean, and old cottages lining the road. As soon as they turned onto Pier Road, Tessie saw familiar faces coming out of a general store. "Hey, isn't that the Mathis couple?" she asked Ramona, instantly regretting the words.

Ramona slowed, almost coming to a stop in front of the store. Tessie slouched in her seat. They watched as Tim, wearing a Carolina Panthers ball cap on his bald head, carried a paper bag out to the car. Marlo followed behind him, her boobs popping out of the tight V-neck sundress she was wearing. They appeared to be arguing about something, Marlo's high-pitched voice carrying over to Ramona's rental car.

"What are you doing?" Tessie asked Ramona, as she turned the car around.

"Let's follow them," Ramona suggested.

Tessie sighed. "I don't want to spend my free day following Tim and Marlo around."

Ramona pulled the car into a parking lot across from the store. She kept an eye on the Mathis's car, which was pulling out of the lot. Marlo was driving and still appeared to be annoyed with Tim.

"Just for a few minutes. I just want to see what they're up to. Then we'll go shopping. Please?" Ramona begged.

Tessie knew this wasn't going to end well. She could feel a faint pulse behind her left eye, signaling a possible migraine coming on. "Fine," she relented.

They followed the Mathis vehicle for a couple of miles, when it turned onto Riverview Road and into the parking lot of the Jekyll Island Airport.

Ramona and Tessie watched as Tim got out of the passenger side door with a small carry-on bag and headed inside the airport. Marlo gave a wave to her husband out of the window before pulling out of the lot.

"Weird. Where's Tim going?" Ramona asked.

"Don't know, don't care. Let's go shopping now," Tessie said.

Ramona blew out a sigh. "It's their honeymoon. Why

would he leave her alone?"

"I'm sure you'll find out tonight at dinner."

# Chapter Eight

The long mahogany table seated twelve people and was elegantly decorated with cream silk placemats, sterling-silver napkin rings, bone white china, and crystal cut glasses and wine goblets. Jake and Tessie were the last couple to the table. Thankfully, Ramona and Clay were seated at the other end with two other couples. Marlo was absent from the table as was her husband Tim.

"Tonight, we have a treat in store for you guys. Our guest chef is from Beachwood Bistro. Chef Thomas cooked up a wonderful meal for you. For starters, we have fried green tomatoes and bacon-wrapped scallops. The main course is a grilled ten-ounce sirloin steak with sautéed mushrooms and onions, shrimp and grits, and steamed broccolini and glazed carrots. Dessert tonight will be your choice of key lime pie or Georgia bourbon peach cobbler. I hope you enjoy," Elsa said before her dining staff started bringing out the platters of appetizers and filling water and wine glasses. Tessie found herself starting to relax with her first sip of wine. She had told Jake about her day with Ramona. Once she got the Mathis couple out of Ramona's mind, they actually had a nice day of shopping and lunch on Pier Road.

"The tomatoes are delicious," Jake said scooping up another bite of southern delicacy.

"All the food has been great." Tessie chose the scallops, relishing the crunchy bacon paired with the chewy scallops.

As Elsa was refilling the wine glasses, Tessie overheard Ramona ask her about the Mathis couple.

"Oh dear, I'm afraid that Mr. Mathis is ill. They took dinner in their room tonight."

Tessie and Ramona exchanged glances. They both

knew that wasn't true. Even though they didn't actually see Tim get on a plane, Marlo had driven off and left him at the airport. Why lie and say he was ill?

"How about a walk on the beach after dinner?" Jake whispered in Tessie's ear.

"Sounds wonderful," she replied.

*** 

The waves were lapping gently along the shoreline and a slight ocean breeze kept lifting up the hem of Tessie's skirt, showing off her shapely legs.

"Tess," Jake wrapped his arm around her shoulder, "is everything okay?" He played with the long braid down her back.

Jake had been attracted to Tessie since day one. She, with her long, dark hair, wide emerald-green eyes, and perfectly proportioned body; he, with his tall, movie-star good looks—together, they made a handsome couple. People on the street would often stop and stare at them, trying to recognize if they were somebody special.

"All this talk about the Honeymoon Killers is starting to get to me. I didn't think it would affect me as much as it does," she answered. "I keep having bad flashbacks."

"We could always cut our trip short, hop on a plane to south Florida, maybe Miami? Spend the rest of our honeymoon down there," Jake suggested.

"Possibly. But I don't think running away from everything is going to help."

"Your headaches are getting worse. I can tell."

"I just need to keep my distance from Ramona," Tessie laughed.

Jake gently yanked her braid, pulling her head back before going in for a kiss. He then grabbed her hand and led her up to a sand dune that afforded some privacy. Tessie pulled up her dress, revealing a black, lacy thong.

"Frank was telling me about a boat we could rent from the marina. Elsa will make us a nice appetizer tray, and we'll take a sunset cruise around the Atlantic," Jake said as he ran his hand up her thigh, then slipping his finger between the lacy thong and Tessie's warm skin. "We could invite the other couples. Then we can do what we do best."

"You're forgetting something." Tessie said before sighing deeply as Jake inserted his finger deep inside her. "They know who we are."

"And you're forgetting something. Ramona is already convinced that Tim is the Honeymoon Killer." Jake nibbled on her ear. "This could help with your headaches."

"What do you have in mind? You know Tim is gone. We saw Marlo drop him off at the airport."

"When Clay and I got back from the golf course, we sat at the bar. Marlo was on the other side on the chaise lounge by the pool. I overheard her talking to Tim on her cell phone. Wherever he went, he's scheduled to be back tomorrow. Marlo is picking him up in the morning," Jake said, struggling to pull down his pants. "She was pretty upset that he left her on their honeymoon to take care of some business. At least, that's what I got out of the conversation."

"And you're just now sharing this with me?"

"I've been devising a plan since I heard her conversation. I wanted to think it through before I told you."

Tessie sighed. "It would be nice to shut up Ramona. I would personally relish that job. How do you suppose we do all of this?"

Jake told her his plan. When Tessie agreed, he said, "Great. I'll book the boat in the morning. You work your charm and invite everyone." Jake put his shorts down on the sand and sat on top of them before pulling Tessie onto his lap. He loved the feel of her lowering herself onto him, clenching her thighs tight as she rode him. "Now, no more talk about this. Let's have some fun."

# Chapter Nine

"We've got a problem," Jake said as he handed Tessie a cup of coffee. She sat up in bed, rubbing her eyes before putting on her eye glasses.

"What?" Tessie took a tentative sip of the strong, black coffee.

Jake reached for the TV remote and searched for a news station. He settled on CNN, which was covering a live broadcast. On the border of the screen, flashing in red, were the words "Honeymoon Serial Killers Claim Next Victims."

"The owner of the private beach house in Panama City Beach is confirming that a couple he'd rented the house to was found dead last night. The couple's names and the cause of death have not been released yet, but the owner has told us they were on their honeymoon. Speculation is that it is the work of the Honeymoon Killers. Myrtle Beach is the last known place the serial killers targeted, and investigators are saying that more than one person is involved. We'll be reporting more on this gruesome murder once details become available. Back to you, Bob."

Jake muted the TV. "What do you think about that?"

Tessie drained the rest of her coffee. "Copycat killer? Or coincidence?"

"I'm going for the copycat theory. The question is, who and why?"

"I thought we were going to leave work behind this morning and concentrate on us."

Jake slid between the covers with Tessie. "Good point. You know how much I love you?"

"Show me."

***

At breakfast, Tim sat at the table looking a little tired.

Marlo was still keeping up with the story that he'd been sick. Tessie thought it was believable, seeing the black circles and bags under Tim's eyes. It looked like he hadn't slept the last twenty-four hours. Thankfully, Ramona and Clay hadn't shown up for breakfast.

"Feeling better?" Tessie asked Tim.

He nodded. "Just a stomach bug."

Tessie wondered how he was able to slip by yesterday morning without any of the staff or other guests noticing he was gone.

Jake fixed his and Tessie's plate from the breakfast buffet. Fruit and coffee for her. A spinach egg-white omelet for him.

"If you are feeling up to it, Jake and I would like to invite you guys to a sunset cruise tonight. It's our last night at the inn; we'd like to take a catamaran out. We'll have some champagne and tapas."

"Thank you for the offer, but I'm not sure if Tim is up for it," Marlo answered for them.

Tim waved her off. "I'll be fine. What time did you have in mind?"

"We'll set sail at seven o'clock sharp," Jake said. He then gave directions to Tim to the marina. "We'll see you then."

"That went good. Now to get Ramona and Clay on board. Literally," Tessie whispered in Jake's ear before laughing at her own joke.

"That shouldn't be a problem. Let's hit the pool for a bit before we get ready for tonight."

# Chapter Ten

Jake and Tessie had taken the catamaran out for a test ride before bringing it back to the marina. While Tessie drove back to the B&B to pick up the champagne and appetizers, Jake got the boat ready to sail. Nervous excitement floated through his belly as he thought through every scenario that could happen tonight. He liked to be prepared for anything and everything.

While waiting for Tessie to come back, he went through the cabin, double-checking everything. Tonight would be a perfect night for a cruise, with cloudless skies, light breeze, and a full moon. If everything went as planned, Tessie would be rid of her headaches for a while, and he would be able to sleep well for a few nights. They could take off for south Florida and enjoy the rest of their honeymoon.

The catamaran was a thirty-six-footer that slept six people comfortably with three cabins, small kitchen, and a main saloon. Jake had a similar model back home and was comfortable with sailing the boat. Just as he was checking the compartments under the sink, he heard Tessie come aboard. She was carrying two large bags of food. He went to help her.

"The others should be on their way," she said, putting the bags down on the small dining table.

"Smells good," Jake said, kissing his wife on the lips.

"Elsa is a dream. She made us crab cakes, stuffed mushrooms, bruschetta with tomatoes and garlic, cocktail shrimp, and mini key-lime custards." Tessie began to unload the food. "She also threw in a couple bottles of wine, one red, one white, and some coffee with a bottle of Kahlua."

"So our guests will be full and happy," Jake said.

"They won't know what hit them." Tessie smiled.

# Chapter Eleven

Ramona stepped out of the bath and wrapped a warm towel around her. "I still don't understand why they invited Tim and Marlo. Tessie knows that I despise that man."

Clay pulled off his swimming trunks and stepped into the steamy shower. "Ramona, let's not fight about this. I told you at lunch that we don't have to go. It's our honeymoon too. We can stay here and have dinner in bed. They'll understand."

"No, I want to go. A sunset cruise sounds romantic. I just don't want to have to look behind my back every five seconds, wondering when Tim is going to put a knife in it."

Clay laughed as he soaped up. "Tim isn't the Honeymoon Killer any more than I am."

"That murder happened in Florida last night! He hopped on a plane yesterday, but he claimed he was here sick in bed. What a perfect cover."

Clay laughed again. "Whatever you say, darling."

Ramona left the bathroom to go in search of the jewelry she'd bought at the cute shop on Pier Road. She looked in the bag and pulled out a few pieces of sterling silver. Bracelets, earrings, and a starburst-shaped ring. Ramona sighed as she realized that she had the wrong bag. Tessie must have grabbed hers when they got out of the car. Ramona was going to wear a white, gauzy sundress, and she had specifically bought a silver and turquoise necklace to go with it. She walked back into the bathroom and yelled at Clay. "I'll be right back," Ramona said, explaining to Clay about the mixed-up shopping bags.

Ramona tightened the belt on her robe as she made her way down the carpeted hallway. Tessie's room was just a few doors down from her room. She hoped that she hadn't left yet.

She thought about what Clay said earlier about Tim. She knew Clay wasn't convinced that Tim had anything to do with the recent murders and didn't take her allegations seriously. But he'd done the same thing when she was worried about the neighborhood burglar. Ramona had great instincts, which helped in catching that teenager stealing a TV from her neighbor's house. No one believed Ramona when she tried to tell all her neighbors and the local police that a certain teenager was responsible. She took satisfaction when the boy was caught. Now Tim may not have had anything to do with honeymoon killings, but he was guilty of something bad. She just knew it. Maybe if she did find out what was going on, Clay would finally quit teasing her.

She knocked on Tessie's door. No answer. Jiggling the handle, she realized the door was unlocked.

"Tessie?" she called out.

Again, no answer.

Ramona proceeded to walk inside the McBride suite. The king-sized bed was neatly made, and the room was clean and tidy. Ramona looked around for the shopping bag. All their clothes were neatly folded in the dresser bureau or hanging up in the closet. Ramona thought back to her own suite, which was strewn with clothing, makeup, and jewelry. Tessie and Jake were apparently OCD neat freaks.

She felt a little guilty for being in their room, snooping around. The bathroom was just as neat as the rest of the suite. All makeup and toiletries were stashed in a cabinet under the sink. Not a drop of water in the double sinks or tub. Two damp towels hung from the towel bar.

"I must have overlooked it the first time," Ramona said aloud as she walked back into the bedroom. Methodically, she pulled each drawer open and went through their clothing. Her hand hit on something hard under one of Tessie's nightgowns. She pulled out a denim-covered scrapbook.

Curiosity getting the better of her, Ramona sat down on the bed and opened the book. She stifled a scream when a picture of a nude body floated out of the book.

# Chapter Twelve

Once she got her breath under control, Ramona flipped through the book slowly, taking in all the news articles and photographs on each page.

*Mysterious Death of Honeymoon Couple in Atlantic City*

*Couple Found Electrocuted in Hamptons Beach House*

*Atlantic City Honeymoon Deaths – Suicide or Murder?*

*Myrtle Beach Honeymooners Found Dead*

*Hampton Honeymoon Deaths May Be Connected To Others*

Ramona was confused. She knew Tessie was a freelance journalist, but she thought she worked with the financial and political sector. Maybe the Honeymoon Killer was an obsession of Tessie's as well. If so, Tessie had no right chastising her for being preoccupied with the case as well.

How in the world did Tessie get photos of the crime scene, though? She felt sick to her stomach as she perused the photos of nude young couples in various positions.

She recognized the Atlantic City honeymooners from the news photos. Except the newspaper ran pictures of the couples when they were alive.

This picture showed a nude male body sprawled out on the floor. A young woman lying in a tub with her eyes closed, just like she was sleeping.

Another picture of a couple in a hot tub. Their grotesque bodies under water, the woman's hair fanned out covering most of her face.

The last photo was of a young couple still dressed in their wedding finery, hanging from a rafter, looking bizarre with their shoes off. Their faces were beet red.

There was something Ramona was missing. Her traumatized mind couldn't think straight. She was thinking more about why Tessie would have these disturbing photos more than she was really looking at the details of the photos.

Then it hit her.

She thought back to the news stories she'd heard. And for a second time, she stifled a scream.

These photos were taken right after each couple had died. *Before* their bodies were allegedly found. Tessie was there when the murders took place? Not after? That only meant one thing. Tessie and Jake were the Honeymoon Killers.

Ramona picked up the phone to call the authorities. She knew Tessie and Jake were probably waiting for them at the marina. Tim and Marlo would be there as well. She thought of Clay back in the room getting ready. Ramona started to dial for help. While she waited to be connected, she thought of her husband who thought she was crazy for thinking Tim had something to do with the murders. She thought about his endless teasing of her being a neurotic nosy-body. She thought about all the physical and verbal abuse he'd put her through that nobody knew about. She thought about all the times she wanted to call 9-1-1 on her own abusive husband.

"911. What's your emergency?" the operator asked.

Ramona started to formulate a plan of her own. "Sorry, there is no emergency." She hung up the phone.

# Chapter Thirteen

"Welcome aboard!" Tessie greeted as Ramona and Clay stepped on the glittering white catamaran.

Ramona gave Tessie a quick hug, stepping back and seeing her friend in a new light.

They followed their hosts down below to the main saloon where Tim and Marlo were already waiting. Platters of appetizers were laid out on the dining room table along with two bottles of wine and a bottle of Christophe Champagne.

"Nice spread," Ramona said as she plucked a stuffed mushroom from a plate.

Tessie handed her a glass of wine. Ramona swirled the Chardonnay around before taking a tentative sip. Tessie winked at Ramona. "I think Tim will be on his best behavior tonight."

"Everyone set to go?" Jake asked. "We'll be heading out in five minutes. Sunset is supposed to be beautiful tonight, so grab your drinks and let's head up to the deck."

"I can take your purse," Tessie offered Ramona as they prepared to go above board.

Ramona gripped it tight. "That's okay. I've got my camera on me. I want to take some pictures."

"Great idea. I'm afraid I forgot to pack my camera." Tessie smiled at her.

"I'll e-mail you some photos from this evening," Ramona said.

They sat on the deck, watching the coastline fade as Jake took them farther away from shore. The bright, orange sun was starting to make its descent into the horizon. Clay wrapped his arm around Ramona and whispered in her ear. "I don't know what you are up to, but I know it's no good." He squeezed her shoulder so hard, Ramona winced.

# Chapter Fourteen

Ramona excused herself, volunteering to go downstairs and grab the bottle of wine to refill everyone's glasses. Patting the side of her purse, she was reassured when she felt the small pill bottle.

*Thank goodness for my anxiety attacks,* she thought.

Positioning herself facing the interior steps, she quickly opened the pill bottle. She had crushed the sedatives before leaving her room this afternoon, saving her some time. She just wasn't sure how much to pour into the bottle. The men would require more of the medicine to effectively knock them out, she thought. So she ended up dumping all the medicine in the wine bottle. She corked it, swirled the wine, while keeping an eye out for anyone who may come down to check on her. Satisfied the powder had melted into the red liquid effectively, she put the empty pill bottle back in her purse.

Pouring a small amount in a plastic cup, Ramona took a taste test. The sedative didn't affect the taste at all. She smacked her lips and headed back.

"Refill anyone?" she asked, joining the others on the deck.

She topped off everyone's glass, including her own.

***

Jake anchored the catamaran about a mile offshore from the Jekyll Island coastline. Luckily, the water was pretty calm with only a light chop. The last thing he wanted was someone getting seasick and throwing a wrench in the plans.

How lucky was he that he not only found his soul mate in Tessie, but that they shared the same ideals, the same cravings for adrenaline-pumping activities, and the same need to kill. When he met Tessie, he was not only impressed with her beauty but with her brains. She was highly intelligent and continued to impress him on a daily basis.

Killing the three honeymoon couples was her most brilliant plan yet. The authorities were scrambling to connect the dots, but they never would. The FBI would have a hard time profiling the honeymoon killers. He relished that thought.

No one would have ever expected that this beautiful, popular couple had committed three perfect murders together over the course of six months. The copy-cat Panama City Beach murder had his blood boiling, though. But that was something he would think about later. Tonight, they had an opportunity to get things back on track.

Jake looked back over at his wife, beaming with pride. Tessie's long, dark hair cascaded in waves down her back. Her green eyes were alive with excitement as they always were before a big kill. She was talking to Clay about some new cholesterol drug when suddenly she swayed and then fell off her chair, hitting the deck with a thud.

"Tessie!" Jake yelled as he jumped up from the captain's chair and rushed over to her. Just as he was kneeling down, Clay tumbled over on top of him. Jake pushed him off.

"What the hell?" Jake asked.

"I don't feel so good," Marlo said as she laid her head down on Tim's lap.

Jake felt a faint pulse on Tessie's neck. He looked up in time to see Tim close his eyes, while his head lobbed crazily back and forth like he was a puppet on a string.

He looked over at Ramona who sat perfectly still watching her husband lay on the cool deck. She seemed to be the only one not affected by the weird things happening around them.

Food poison? Bad wine? A virus? All these thoughts ran through Jake's mind. He started feeling a little woozy himself. Was that real or just a reaction to what was going on around him? He tried to fight off the dizziness.

"What's happening?" His words came out slurred as he tried to focus on Ramona. He was starting to see double.

She shrugged. "I feel fine. Really relaxed."

All of a sudden, he was very tired. He grasped Tessie's hand and fought the urge to lie down.

"What did you do?" he tried to ask Ramona, but it came out more like "Wadda dooo?"

His last thought before passing out was that he hadn't planned as well as he should have. He'd underestimated his opponent.

# Chapter Fifteen

Ramona had to get busy. Jake was the biggest of the men, and she didn't think he'd had much to drink. Now was the time to see what she was made of.

She ran downstairs to the kitchen and grabbed the butcher knife she'd seen earlier that evening, along with a pair of latex gloves she'd stashed in her purse.

"Focus on the big picture," she kept telling herself. Hauling Tim and Clay off the boat was going to be a challenge. Ramona weighed one hundred nineteen pounds and was five-four. Jake was at least six-one and probably weighed over two hundred pounds.

She raced back upstairs and was relieved to see everyone was still knocked out. She took a deep breath, gripped the butcher knife in her gloved hand, and stood over Jake's body. Taking her right foot, she firmly placed it on his stomach and prepared to push him on his back. As soon as her foot hit his stomach, Jake grabbed her foot and pulled.

Ramona tumbled sideways, the butcher knife slicing her left forearm as she fell on the deck. She felt a crack in her right foot where Jake still had a firm grip.

Pain shot up simultaneously through her right foot and up her left arm. Blood was oozing out of the wound, and she fought to stay conscious and not throw up. She jerked her ankle free as Jake tried to sit up. Fighting through the pain, Ramona hopped up at the same time Jake pushed up on his knees. She scooted behind him and held the knife high up, ready to plunge into his back. As he tried to stand, she drove the knife into his back, connecting with his spinal cord, severing it.

She pulled the knife out as he groaned and fell back on the deck. Ramona sunk to her knees, sucking in deep breaths while trying not to pass out. She needed to tend to the deep wound in her forearm before she passed out from blood loss.

This was going to be hard enough with two functioning hands, but with an injury to her left arm, this was almost impossible. What the hell was she thinking? How was she going to pull off murdering five people all by herself?

# Chapter Sixteen

Tackling Tim's body next, she was thankful he was lighter than Jake. She grabbed Marlo by the hair and lifted her off of Tim's lap. She pulled Tim by his legs, dragging him to the stairs. Ramona got him as far down the stairs as she could before stepping over his body to push him feet first into the ocean. Her heart was hammering wildly as she gave one final push on his shoulder, then Tim's body hit the water, and he immediately sank. Marlo's body followed behind him. Ramona watched to make sure they went completely under the water, hoping they'd drown quickly.

The makeshift bandage was already soaked with blood when she sat down to rest for a minute. She looked at her watch. An hour had already passed by quickly. The sun had set, and the others could be waking up at any minute. She didn't know if she had the strength to continue.

Now, Tessie and Clay were the last ones left. She wanted to save Clay for last. All the torment he'd put her through the last few years was getting ready to come back to him threefold.

She was beyond tired as she dragged Tessie by her arms and got her as close as she could to the back steps. This was going to be hard. Tessie had become her friend in the last few days. Ramona had few friends back home due to Clay's jealous behavior. But she reminded herself that Tessie and Jake had done bad things to those innocent couples. Ramona was just righting a wrong. Clay had abused her over the years. And Tim was a creepy guy who she was sure had done something wrong. Marlo was the only innocent in this matter, as far as Ramona was concerned. Unfortunately, Ramona couldn't let her live. Marlo would tell everyone the truth.

With some regret, Ramona heaved Tessie over the

edge of the last step. Just as Tessie hit the water, she thought she saw Tessie open her eyes. Ramona held her breath, watching Tessie sink slowly down into the dark, inky water. By now, it was pitch dark, and even with the full moon shining down, it was hard to see anything more than five feet beyond the boat. Thinking her eyes were playing tricks on her, she quickly forgot about Tessie and went about taking care of the last person on the boat besides herself.

Ramona stood next to Clay. She surprised herself by crying. "You charmed me and made me fall in love with you. I thought you were my knight in shining armor. Then you turned on me. Showed me a side of you that I didn't see coming. The first time you laid a hand on me, you made me think it was my fault. You made me alienate all my friends and family. You took away everything that I loved. You made me feel dirty and shameful." Ramona plunged the knife deep in his chest. "I hate you." She collapsed on the deck next to him and passed out.

# Chapter Seventeen

Ramona awoke in a panic. Clay was still lying next to her, his white dress shirt soaked in blood. She checked her watch. It was nine thirty. She got up, stripped off the bloody gloves before tossing them overboard. She proceeded downstairs to call for help. It took her a few minutes to figure out the boat's phone system and to get the Coast Guard on the line. Exhausted, she curled up in ball on the couch and cried herself to sleep again.

An hour later, she felt someone tapping her on the arm.

"Ma'am? Are you okay?" A man stood before her in a dark-blue uniform.

She slowly sat up and nodded.

"Are you the one who called?"

Another nod.

"What happened here?" he asked as another man joined him, also in uniform and flashing a light around the darkened room.

"They're all dead," she whispered.

"Who are the two men on the deck?" he asked.

"My husband, Clay Myers. And the other is Jake McBride." Ramona started shaking violently. "She killed my husband."

"Who killed your husband?"

"Tessie McBride. The Honeymoon Killer."

# Epilogue – *a year later*

Tessie sat calmly in her Mercedes, watching as the bride came out of the hotel entrance wearing a champagne-colored wedding dress with her strawberry-blond hair cascading down her slim shoulders. The bride was accompanied by her sister, who was carrying a small makeup case and a bouquet of flowers.

As the limo whisked the bride and her sister away, Tessie cranked up the engine and prepared to follow them. She didn't need to stay on their tail. Tessie knew where the wedding would take place. Reaching over to the passenger seat, she grabbed a copy of the latest *People* magazine and read the article again.

*Lone Survivor of the Jekyll Island Murders Marries Again*

*Ramona Myers, the only survivor of the Jekyll Island Massacre, is getting married.*

*Ramona and her then-husband, Dr. Clay Myers, were attacked a year ago while on their honeymoon at Jekyll Island, Georgia. Clay was killed by Tessie McBride, who authorities had dubbed the Honeymoon Killer. Tessie and her husband, Jake, had been targeting honeymooners and killing them for over six months when they'd lured Clay and Ramona on a sunset cruise and planned to murder them along with another couple, Tim and Marlo Mathis.*

*Against all odds, Ramona survived. After a distress call to the Coast Guard was sent out, authorities found an injured Ramona on the rented catamaran. She told authorities that Tessie and Jake had used sedatives to spike the other couple's drinks and then proceeded to murder their guests, one by one. Ramona said she had awakened from the sedative to find Tessie and Jake arguing while dumping the body of Marlo Mathis overboard. Ramona crawled away while the couple was distracted and was able to get hold of a kitchen knife for self-defense. She recounted to authorities that she'd crept back to the deck where the McBride's were preoccupied with killing Ramona's husband. Ramona had approached Jake from behind and stabbed him in the back. Tessie and Ramona then fought for the knife, and Ramona received a cut to the forearm. Tessie slipped on a puddle of blood, lost her balance, and hit her head before falling overboard. Ramona called for help before passing out.*

*The body of Marlo Mathis was found by authorities a week later on the shores of Jekyll Island. The bodies of Tessie McBride and Tim Mathis were never found.*

*Fast forward a year later, Ramona has found love again and is marrying technology tycoon, Lucas Perrona. Their wedding is taking place in the beautiful wine country of Napa Valley. Ramona moved out to California a couple months after the incident to work with her sister, Julia Capstone, who owns the famed Capstone Advertising Agency. Ramona met Lucas Perrona during a photo shoot that her sister's agency was overseeing. After a whirlwind courtship, Lucas and Ramona will be married this month at the Blue Duck Winery. This story is a great example of one woman who found love again after enduring a great tragedy.*

Tessie snorted as closed the magazine and tossed it in the backseat.

"Tragedy, my ass." Tessie remembered the night of the sunset cruise very clearly, and what Ramona told the authorities was a complete farce. The only truth in what Ramona had said was that she'd killed Jake, the one and only true love of Tessie's life.

Tessie picked up the hunting knife and twirled it around by the handle. Now Ramona was going to pay in spades.

# About the Author of *The Honeymooners*

**Traci Hohenstein** is the best-selling author of the Rachel Scott series, *Burn Out* and *Asylum Harbor*.

She lives in Northwest Florida with her husband and three children. In her spare time, Traci likes to paddleboard and play with her kids at the beach. She is working on her next Rachel Scott novel.

You can visit her at:
Website: www.tracihohenstein.com

Or send an e-mail to:
E-mail: tracihohenstein@gmail.com

**The Rachel Scott Series (suspense)**
Burn Out
Asylum Harbor
Cut and Run (coming Winter 2012)

The Honeymooners Trilogy (thriller/suspense)
Jekyll Island – Book 1
Napa Valley – Book 2 (coming Fall 2012)

**The Hollywood Hills Series (romantic comedy)**
Special Delivery
Split Decision

# As You Sow, So Shall You Reap

by Tim Ellis

# Tuesday

Verona Izatt wanted to scream as she watched the man's hands forcing the thick curved needle and catgut through the skin of her lips like a demented tailor, but her throat wouldn't work. In fact, nothing worked anymore. Her whole body was paralysed, but she could feel everything. He had slipped something small inside her mouth, but she had no idea what. Now, he was sewing her lips together, and the pain forced her to peer through the gossamer veil separating sanity from insanity.

Above her was the full-length mirror that had hung on the wall by the door. He had strung it up from the light fitting and positioned it just right, so that she could watch everything he did to her. The bedside light was on. She was naked, and could see a pool of blood had formed between her open legs.

She'd been asleep when the needle had pierced the skin of her neck, and a hand had smothered her scream. The drug had acted within a handful of seconds. She became a petrified witness to her own demise.

He laid out his instruments on her dressing table. Prepared everything for his work. Using a pair of long, thin scissors, he had slashed up the front of her nightdress, and then raped and sodomised her for what seemed like hours. At last, he grunted like a pig as he ejaculated into a condom, and saliva dripped onto her face through the mouth of the evil clown mask he was wearing.

Was that it? Please let him leave now. But he hadn't left. He had all the time in the world to take a shower. She lived alone in the cottage her aunt had left her in the village of Little Haven in Wales. It was situated on a hill overlooking the beach. Each morning, before breakfast – come rain or shine – she would follow the winding path down to the beach, and walk along the beautiful sand. In the summer she went barefoot, and paddled in the sea. In the winter she wore the pink wellies that she kept by the back door. Little Haven was meant to be her slice of paradise. She had left her job behind, and was trying to earn a living as a writer. Had nearly forgotten the past, and begun to believe her own lies.

Water dripped from his white, flabby body as he came back into the room, and she thought it strange that he was completely hairless. It was then that he had threaded his needle and begun the task of sewing her mouth shut. He pulled the last stitch through, knotted the end, and stood back to admire his handiwork.

Was he finished? What was he going to do to her now?

He left the room. She heard him padding downstairs in his bare feet. After a while he came back with a mug of something hot.

It must be thirsty work, she thought. She didn't want to think that. In fact, it was probably the last thing she ever wanted to think, but it had popped into her head all the same. What she really wanted to do was focus on the scalpel in his right hand, and what he planned to do with it.

**\*\*\***

# Wednesday

'Jesus,' Detective Inspector Inigo Morgan said, turning away to catch his breath and to stop his breakfast of poached egg on toast from regurgitating.

The pathologist, Dr Jess Reese, looked up, a strand of black hair falling from the hood of the white zip-up suit. 'Didn't they tell you downstairs what to expect?'

He heard the bitterness in her voice. 'Yes, but you never really believe it's going to be as bad as it always is.' He and Jess had history – a failed marriage and a twenty-three-year-old daughter – but this was neither the time nor the place to re-visit the ghosts of his past.

'Well, if you're going to puke, go outside. This is bad enough without the stench of your vomit.'

'I'll be all right. It was just the initial shock.'

He'd known Verona Izatt; she'd been trying her hand at crime fiction to pay the bills and used him as a so-called expert to bounce ideas off. He turned back, glad that he had a mask covering most of his face. The body lay on the bed in an ocean of blood. Her lips had been sewn together, and she'd been opened up like a fish for gutting.

'What have you got for me?'

'I've never seen anything like this.' She stood up straight and stared in his eyes until the guilt made him look away. 'Apart from what you can see with your own eyes, she's had her heart torn out. And when I say 'torn out,' we're not talking about a nice neat job for organ transplant, I mean ripped from her chest.'

He pointed to the splinters and jagged edges. 'What about the ribs?'

'I'd say a bolt cutter, or something of that nature.'

Morgan shook his head in disbelief.

'She's been sexually abused front and back, but the

scary thing is that she was conscious while all this was going on. Whoever did this is a real piece of work.'

'Conscious?'

'I know, don't ask me how she could just lie there while he did this to her, but that's what appears to have happened. More than likely a drug, but I don't know what yet.'

'Time of death?'

'Early hours of this morning. I'd say about four thirty when he'd finished with her, and ripped her heart out. I'm going to get the body back to the mortuary now. Post mortem about four this afternoon. I'll let you know more after that.'

'Thanks, Jess. I'll be there.' He checked the time as he wandered from the bedroom. It was eleven fifteen.

*** 

'Tig?' he called as he walked down the stairs.

'Here, Sir.'

Detective Constable Tigris Griffiths was his partner, had been for eleven months. He knew that she was originally from London, but had called Pembrokeshire her home for a number of years. He didn't think the name Tigris suited her. Told her it was the name of a river, so he decided to call her Tig instead, but sometimes he called her Tigger just because he could. She didn't seem to mind when he'd given her the news, merely shrugged her shoulders and said, 'Whatever.'

'Well?'

'The window cleaner came today. He found her. Saw her through the window. Nearly fell off his ladder. Phoned us.'

'Did he come inside?'

'No.'

'Entry?'

'Open kitchen window. Climbed in. Let himself out through the back door.'

Shortly after she'd first arrived, he had asked her why she spoke like a notebook.

'Saves time,' is all she'd said.

'It makes you seem like a cold fish.'

She'd shrugged, and that was as far as he'd got. After eleven months, he didn't really know much about her past.

He'd had no input into her appointment, but if he had, he would have chosen her anyway. She was extraordinarily beautiful with thick, bouncy, blonde hair past her shoulders, a fabulous smile, and a body made for Hollywood blockbusters. The trouble was, she didn't like men in any shape or form. She had a thing for women – although that didn't stop every man she met from trying to get her into bed.

'Anything else?'

'Made coffee. Washed up afterwards. Had a shower. Forensics examining plug hole for hair. Footprint outside could be the killer, plaster cast taken.'

'You're looking good this morning.'

She dismissed his compliment with a toss of her head. 'I always look good.'

'Yes, you do, but I thought I'd mention the fact this morning.'

'No need. I have a mirror.'

He gave up. 'I don't suppose anyone saw anything?'

'Unlikely. House on its own up here. Plods asking questions in the village.'

He wandered through the open front door and stared out over the bay. The cottage was perched on a grassy hill overlooking the village, which enclosed the beach in a semi-circle. The sky was a clear blue, the sun had nearly reached its zenith, and the sea lapped lazily against the sand. To his right, the hordes of holidaymakers were already pressing the sand in search of the perfect tan; some were swimming in the cold Atlantic to ward off heat stroke. Was the killer a holidaymaker, or a local? He couldn't believe it might be someone local. Even though he worked out of the Divisional Headquarters at Haverfordwest, this was his patch, had been for twenty years. It was a short trip up and down the B4341. He lived here and knew everyone, for God's sake.

What had Verona Izatt done – or not done – to attract the attention of a killer? Why had he sewn her mouth up? Why had he ripped out her heart? Was there some symbolic reason behind the barbaric way he had killed her?

'Thoughts, Tig?'

'Someone from her past. Came here three years ago. What do we know about her?'

'Good. We'd better find out who she was before.'

Tig wore a cream satin top tucked into her black trousers. If he'd strained his eyes, he would have been able to see the lace pattern of her bra and the gentle curve of her breasts, but he didn't. For one thing, she was twenty-seven and he was fifty-nine – one year away from retiring. Also, she was his partner, and partners were a protected species. There were other reasons as well, which the monster on his shoulder would have recounted in lurid detail had he even thought about Tig in a non-partner way.

Tig had her notebook out. She was the flip side of him. He rarely wrote anything down anymore. 'What was she working on?' she said. 'Could have upset someone.'

'We've taken her notebooks and laptop into custody?'

'Forensics examining them. We'll get them this afternoon.'

He stretched his neck, closed his eyes, and bathed his face in the sun. 'You don't think it's someone local?'

'Didn't say that. Could be. Depends what she was working on. Everybody's got a past.'

He certainly had. The landscape of his past was littered with the rotting carcasses of failed relationships, and resembled a Salvador Dali painting. After he and Jess drifted apart seven years ago, he had tried dating again. It didn't last long. Now, he preferred not to look backwards into the darkness. 'What's in your past, Tig?'

She ignored him as she always did. Wouldn't let him in. They were partners at work, and that was all. They fitted together like two jigsaw pieces when they were working on a case, but beyond that they were ships passing in the night.

'So, we're looking at her past, and what she was working on. What else?'

'Random.'

He thought about the possibility of it being a random killing. Little Haven had a population of 807, soon to be 809 when Vic and Nicola Trowell's twins were born. Yes, there were villages and towns all around, but the killer had come prepared. Knew exactly what he was going to do before he set foot in the cottage. That wasn't random, it was pre-planned. 'Random doesn't fit what we've got here. If it is random, then we're wasting our time.'

'Maybe victim is random, but killer isn't.'

His eyes narrowed. 'A serial killer? Have you been drinking?'

'You know I don't drink.'

'Why don't you drink, Tig?'

'Even serial killers need a holiday.'

It didn't matter how many personal questions he asked her, she never answered any of them. She'd told him a while ago – in no uncertain terms – to keep his nose out of her private life. Tig was definitely an enigma. On the one hand, the detective in him wanted to investigate her thoroughly, so that he knew everything about her. On the other hand, he wanted to respect her privacy, as he hoped people would respect his.

'We can check for similar killings, but I'm betting a pint of lager you're wrong.'

As well as not drinking, she didn't bet either. As far as he knew she had no vices... if, of course, one believed that a woman having a relationship with another woman was normal. He thought the prudent course of action in that respect was to sit on the fence until his arse hurt so much that he fell off.

A half-smile wrinkled her freckles. 'Tempted, but you know I don't bet.'

He saw Jess come out of the cottage. She followed the

paramedics carrying Verona Izatt's body on a stretcher and headed towards her car as the paramedics slid the corpse into the back of the ambulance and shut the doors. They would take the body to the mortuary at Withybush Hospital on Fishguard Road, which was only a hop, skip, and a jump from the police station. She still looked good. Mind, she was ten years younger than him, so she should. But, even after all this time, he would have gone running if she'd clicked her fingers. The sad fact of the matter was that he still loved her, but there was a universe between them now – a universe that neither of them had the technology to cross.

'Let's get back to the station then,' he said.

**\*\*\***

Tig had put out a call for similar murders across England and Wales, and sent a request to Interpol for them to carry out a database search.

They were sitting in the incident room either side of the table. Forensics had finished with Verona Izatt's notebooks and laptop. He had the notebooks, and Tig had the laptop. She'd been brought up on gadgets. Whereas he was an old dog trying to learn new tricks, but failing miserably.

'No memory stick.'

He knew what a memory stick was – barely. 'I'm sorry?'

'Thankfully, no password. Word processor, click on last document, not there. Says, 'Path not found.' She used a memory stick.'

'Haven't forensics got her memory stick?'

She shrugged, stood up, and left. Not only did she speak in notebook form, but also if there was no need to say anything, she didn't. Inigo knew where she was going, and she knew he knew.

In her absence he rifled through the notebooks. There were seven of them, and Verona Izatt had written her notes in another language. When he examined them more closely, he realised he'd seen the lines and squiggles before.

He got up, opened the door, and walked along the corridor to the clerical office. There were seven women and a man in there, who all looked up when he entered.

'Who can read shorthand?'

Three hands went up.

One hand belonged to the man – Declan Munro, his identity tag stated. The world could call him a dinosaur, but Inigo wasn't comfortable with a man who could read shorthand. Another hand belonged to a middle-aged woman with a green streak in her hair. She looked like a badger from Mars. Her ID tag stated that she was Emma Harris. He also didn't feel comfortable with a woman who found it necessary to spray-paint her hair green.

'Sheila,' he said to the woman in possession of the third hand. He knew Sheila Cooper, had spoken to her a few times before. She'd been doing the Clerical Manager's job for a number of years. 'Can you come and help me?'

She followed him back to the incident room.

Tig had returned and was interrogating the laptop. 'No memory stick.' She smiled and said, 'Hi Sheila.'

He guided Sheila into a chair. She was probably in her mid-fifties with brown-grey, frizzy hair falling to her shoulders, dark bags under her eyes, and an upside-down smile. Her mouth made him think of other people's mouths. How – at rest – a mouth probably reflected a person's personality. He guessed Sheila was a miserable person – maybe she had good reason to be. If he'd had a mirror, he would have examined his own mouth to see where it came to rest. Was he an old misery like Sheila, or maybe a wishy-washy, sit-on-the-fence type of person with a straight mouth? He doubted he was the life-and-soul-of-the-party guy with a mouth that said, 'Eat me.'

'Hello, Tigris,' Sheila said, but there was no smile in return.

As he shuffled round the table to sit down, he said to Tig, 'What's on the hard drive?'

'Rubbish.'

He didn't question Tig's interpretation of rubbish. She knew what she was doing, which was more than he did.

He directed his gaze at Sheila. 'I've got these seven notebooks belonging to a victim, which appear to be written in shorthand. Can you take a look?' He slid one of the notebooks across the table to her.

The notebooks were what an old stereotypical reporter might have used, with the ring binding at the top of the page and a thick card for the back cover. Now, of course, they used electronic devices. He'd seen them in the press briefing, tip-tapping with tiny sticks onto tiny screens and muttering into small boxes like crazy people.

Sheila opened the notebook and began to read aloud. 'The post mortem of Hilary Weekes revealed...' She put the book down and peered at Inigo. 'Are they all like this?'

He hadn't really looked, simply assumed they were. He laid them side by side and opened each one up at a randomly selected page. One after the other revealed shorthand symbols similar to the notebook Sheila had in her possession. 'Yes, they're all the same.'

'Well, I could sit here all day reading to you, but I don't think the Chief would be very happy with either of us. Let me take the notebooks away and type them up in plain text for you. I have a mountain of work, but I'll try and fit you in somewhere. '

He could understand the logic of what she was saying. 'You'll guard them with your life?' he said closing each notebook and putting one on top of the other.

'I hope that won't be necessary, Inspector, but I'll certainly keep them safe.'

He slid them across the table as if they were the only copies of the Dead Sea Scrolls in existence. 'I'll trust you.'

'Most generous.'

'Can you...?'

'No, I don't know when I'll have them done by. As I said...'

He held up his hand in submission. 'I'd be grateful if you could get them to me as soon as possible.'

'Grateful? How grateful?'

'What do you mean?'

'Well, there's probably about ten hours work all told in these notebooks. That's a day and a half. I'm all for doing people favours, but this is a bit more than a favour. So, when you say grateful, what exactly do you mean?'

'I see, you want money?'

'No, I don't want money. Although a pay rise would be very welcome, but I don't think you have the power to do anything about that.'

'No, I'm a minor cog in the bureaucratic machine. So, what is it that you want?'

'You could take me out for a meal?'

His eyes narrowed and his heart rate increased. 'What, you mean like a date?' A date with miserable-faced Sheila would be a step too far in the wrong direction, and what the hell would she want him to do after the date? God forbid!

'No, I don't think my husband would approve of that. Just a meal will do.'

Relieved, he said, 'I could manage a meal.'

She thrust an outstretched hand towards him. 'Deal.'

He was about to grip the hand when he had a thought. 'By tomorrow lunch time?'

'As you saw, there's three of us in the office that can read shorthand, I'll have to give each of them two notebooks to be able to complete the job by then. It'll mean three meals with puddings.'

He shook her hand. 'Deal.'

Sheila scooped up the notebooks and left.

Tig had a wry smile on her face.

'What?' he said.

'Should have been a hostage negotiator.'

***

'So there's nothing on the computer?'

'No.'

'What was the document called?'

'WIP.'

He didn't say anything, but rested his chin on his balled fist and stared at her.

'Work In Progress.'

'Very informative. So, you think it was on a memory stick, and the killer took it?'

'Yes.'

'Which would suggest that the motive might be about what, or who, she was writing about.'

'If there is a motive.'

'Even serial killers have motives. Have we found out what she did before she came here?'

'Do that now?'

'That would be good.'

Tig left.

He stretched back, put his hands behind his head, and interlocked his fingers. He ignored the stabbing pain in his left shoulder, and hoped he was going to last a few more years into retirement. He had no idea what he was going to do when he had nothing to do. Maybe he'd do nothing.

What the hell did he have here? A thirty-one-year-old woman named Verona Izatt arrives three years ago after her aunt dies and leaves her the cottage. Why didn't he know what she did before? Usually, it would have cropped up in conversation, but it hadn't, and that was strange in itself. He'd only been conversing with the woman for a little over three months. Bumped into her in the village, because that's where he lived. It wasn't by accident; she'd found out he was a murder detective and wanted to pick his brains. He'd been flattered – old fool – so he'd answered her questions. She'd been particularly interested in what the police procedures were when there was a murder, and he'd been more than helpful.

Tig came back. 'Name's not Verona Izatt.'

He squinted at her.

She shrugged. 'Better have another look in the

cottage.'

'Why isn't her name Verona Izatt? I don't understand. That was what Kathryn Brinck's niece was called.'

'Verona Izatt died three years ago.'

His mind began racing with a hundred and one questions. 'So, this woman, whoever she was, became Kathryn Brinck's niece? Why? Did she murder the real Verona Izzat? We need to get hold of Verona Izzat's post mortem results. Was there a post mortem? How did she die? And how...?'

'Don't know any of that.'

He stood up. 'Okay...' He checked the time on the wall clock. It was twenty past three. 'Meet me at the cottage at nine o'clock tomorrow morning. We'll go through the place with a magnifying glass and see what we can unearth. In the meantime, I want you to find out everything you can about Kathryn Brinck and Verona Izatt. I'll...'

'Post mortem.'

He looked at the clock again – of course, four o'clock. Maybe he needed to start writing things down again. 'Crap. I'll go along to the post mortem then. You visit forensics and see if they've found out anything. Even if the footprint does belong to the killer, it won't be of any use until we have something to compare it against.'

'Foot size indicates height.'

'That's not the way I heard it.'

'Don't be dirty.'

He grinned.

'Find out whether anything came back from the house-to-house, but we probably need to re-visit that now that Verona Izatt isn't Verona Izatt. Maybe we'll have a chat with a few villagers tomorrow after we've been back to the cottage.'

'Post mortem.'

The clock showed eighteen minutes to four. He'd be out of breath by the time he got to the mortuary. 'I'm going. Ring me if...'

She pushed him out of the door.

***

Chief Superintendent Paul Northfield collared him as he was hurtling along the corridor towards the stairs.

'Inspector Morgan, I've been looking for you.'

Inigo wondered how a boy – barely out of his teens – could be a Chief Superintendent. If it weren't for the uniform and the shoulder tabs with the crown and pip on them, no one would give him the time of day. He was thin and pale, with spiky hair, and a know-it-all attitude. Inigo was sure that he used gel, but proving it without actually touching the hair was another matter.

'I've been around, Sir.' There should be a law about old people calling young people 'Sir.' It lodged in his throat like a chicken bone. He wanted to cough it up and spit it out.

'Well, anyway...'

'I'm in a rush at the moment... Sir. On my way to the mortuary...'

'You don't want to be rushing there at your age, Inspector.'

'Very droll.'

'The murder at Little Haven. How's it going?'

'Confusing at the moment. Can I brief you when I come back from the mortuary?' He checked his watch. It was five to four. Jess would give him a hard time. She'd use it as an excuse to wax lyrical about his unreliability.

'We need to talk about your pension as well.'

His brow furrowed, and a wave of nausea washed over him. 'Oh?'

'Not now, when you come back. I'll be leaving at six though, I have a dinner engagement this evening.'

As he reached the door to the stairwell, he said over his shoulder, 'I'll be back long before then.' Why didn't the Chief say there was nothing to worry about? A year to go, and now there's a problem with his pension. There'd better not be, that's all he would say. Well, that wasn't strictly true. If there were a problem, he'd say a hell of a lot more.

Jess had already started the post mortem when he reached Withybush mortuary at nine minutes past four. The killer had done some of her job for her, and all she had to do was cut the top V of the Y-cut.

'Never could be on time. I say four o'clock, and you translate that as ten past, or some other God-forsaken time.'

He wasn't going to get drawn in like a trout. In the past he would have swallowed the hook, line, sinker, and fishing rod, but he'd learned his lesson at last. 'Well?'

'Here.' She passed him a plastic evidence bag with a small, silver object inside. 'It was in her mouth.'

'What is it?' He said out of habit. Hadn't even noticed that she'd removed the sutures from the victim's mouth.

'I could tell you, but then I'd be denying you the pleasure of finding out for yourself.'

Sometimes, when he didn't love her, he hated her. She wound him up like a cheap watch off the market. He lifted the object up to the light and examined it. 'Two hearts entwined.'

'The obvious is usually the right answer. See, you can do it when you really try.'

She was good; he had to give her that. A lesser man would have crumpled under the weight of her sarcasm. 'Have you heard from Marielle recently?'

Jess stopped rummaging around inside Verona Izatt's abdomen and stared at him. 'Why don't you ring her?'

'Why doesn't she ring me?'

'Same old Inigo. She's your daughter.'

'Daughters ring their fathers. She doesn't ring me because she's ashamed.'

'Of course she's ashamed; you're her father.'

'She's ashamed because of what she does.'

'You're just a prude. She likes what she does.'

'A father should not have to open up a newspaper and see his daughter naked in front of him. Nor should he have to listen to men making lewd comments about her over coffee and biscuits. She could have been anything she wanted. Instead, she flaunts herself like a whore.'

'Do you know how much money she makes as a model?'

'Money isn't everything.'

'When you haven't got any, it is everything.'

'We could have given her money.'

'You've never had any money to give her, but she wants to make her own way in life.'

'She could have finished university – something to fall back on.'

Jess laughed behind her mask, but there was no humour in the laugh. 'You know nothing about her, do you? Our daughter is a millionaire. She's beautiful, and she's using what we've given her to make her own way in life. Times have changed, Inigo.'

'Not for the better.' When they discussed Marielle's career choice, he always felt as though he came out second best. A millionaire! Surely an exaggeration, but even if she had half of that, what else was she doing to earn that kind of money? He knew he shouldn't be thinking that way about his own daughter, but she'd broken his heart, and he couldn't help himself. He had become everything he despised in his own father – a bitter and twisted old man.

An uneasy silence filled up the chasm between them like a fog that had drifted in from the sea.

Once she had completed the post mortem she said, 'The drug he used is called Tetrodotoxin, or TTX for short. It's a neurotoxin, and there's no known antidote. It's extracted from pufferfish, toads, and the blue-ringed octopus, but it has also been synthesised. At near-fatal doses it can leave a person close to death, but they remain conscious. You might try and find out where he got the drug from.'

He gave her a begrudging thanks, and left. In another year he would never have to see her again. He didn't know whether that would please him, or destroy him.

He forced himself to think of the two hearts entwined.

Unbidden, a quote from Suzanne Chapin jumped into his brain: All that is worth cherishing begins in the heart, not the head. As he was walking through Reception towards the main entrance, he realised he was a fool, turned around, and returned to the Mortuary.

She was cleaning her instruments, even though she had technicians to do that for her. When she turned to see who had entered, he saw that she'd been crying.

'You do have a heart then?' As soon as he said it, he knew he shouldn't have. Force of habit, a defence mechanism. Throw the first barb and then run. 'Sorry, I didn't come back for another argument.'

'But you thought you'd start one anyway?'

'No, I came back to apologise, and to tell you I'll ring Marielle.'

She stared at him as he left, stunned into silence by his softening.

***

'There's a shortfall,' the Chief said.

They were sitting in the boy-Chief's plush office. Behind the Chief stood a bookcase full of books that Inigo wondered if he had ever read. Probably for show, he thought. On the walls were framed awards, certificates, and photographs – the type of things thirty-year officers collected during an illustrious career. What had this boy ever done?

'What do you mean, a shortfall?' He knew exactly what the boy-Chief meant by a shortfall, but he wanted him to explain it anyway. It would give him time to think.

'You've applied to leave at sixty – five years earlier than usual. When you first applied for early retirement three years ago, the market was buoyant. Now... well, you know as well as I do what the economy is like.'

'Let's get to the bottom line. What are the figures?'

'You'll lose £500 a month, £6,000 a year, and your lump sum would be reduced by £10,000.'

'The bastards.'

'It's hardly anybody's fault, Inspector Morgan.'

'It's somebody's fault, and I'd like you to bring the bastard who is responsible here, so that I can torture him for a very long time.'

The Chief ignored his outburst and passed him a piece of paper. 'This letter explains the changes in detail as it affects you. You're not the only one, you know. There have been thousands of officers affected. Also, the changes have been backdated to 2010.'

'Somebody should be shot, Sir. Tell me a firing squad is being organised?'

'Unfortunately, unless the changes are put in place, the pension fund would become insolvent. Do you still think you can take early retirement with the reduced benefits?'

'Don't worry, Sir, I'm still going. If necessary, I'll work down the coal mines.' He was being facetious, since they both knew there was no coal mining in Pembrokeshire anymore. He stood up to leave.

'You were going to brief me on the murder in Little Haven?'

'I'm not in the mood now, Chief. Can it wait until the morning?'

'I suppose so, but make sure you leave your phone on tonight in case I'm asked some awkward questions at the dinner party.'

'I'll try and remember,' but they both knew he wouldn't.

He left the Chief's door open, and felt guilty about ignoring Sharon Richards' smile. The Chief's secretary had always been pleasant to him.

After he'd paid his bills, he wouldn't be able to live off what was left. At that moment, if he'd come face to face with the person responsible for his predicament, he would have murdered them with a smile on his face. Her Majesty could have had the pleasure of paying for his board-and-keep in his dotage.

He trudged up to forensics and tried to push the

retirement disaster into a dark corner of his mind. Why people referred to 'corners' in the mind he had no idea. Nobody had a square brain or right angles in any shape or form. A recess or a fold would be more appropriate. Anyway, wherever the pension news was, he wished the Chief hadn't told him. He stopped outside the connecting door into forensics and kicked the wall. 'Shit.'

'I've often said that wall deserves a good kicking, Sir.'

He didn't realise there was anyone in the corridor with him.

Constable Christine Walsh was leaning against the opposite wall, smiling at him.

He'd heard about football being a game of two halves. Well, Christine Walsh had a body of two halves. The top half was lovely – lustrous black hair, a shapely attractive face, and breasts that would fit snugly into a swimming hat. The bottom half, though, belonged to someone else. Hips ballooned out from her waist, and her legs resembled thick, knotted tree stumps.

'You've heard about the pension changes?' he said.

The smile disappeared. 'You obviously have. There's a meeting tomorrow lunchtime to decide what we're going to do about it. I don't think wall kicking is on the agenda.'

'I didn't know you were so funny.'

'I have many talents, Sir.'

'Well, it's been nice talking to you, Constable Walsh, but I have places to be and people to see.'

'Have a nice life, Sir.'

'And you, Constable.'

He opened the door into forensics, and left another embarrassing moment behind him. So, they were having a meeting. Mind, they could have meetings until the sheep came home, it wouldn't make any difference. Some bastard had mismanaged the pension fund, and now Inigo Morgan had to pay for it – all very simple and straightforward. They'd never know the complete truth behind the catastrophe. It would be covered up. The money that had been siphoned off would be sitting in a bank in the Cayman Islands, while the bastard responsible for re-allocating Inigo Morgan's pension fund would be sunning himself by a heart-shaped pool, and drinking Black Widow Martinis to the sound of 'Mr Saxobeat.'

*** 

Dr Alexis Walker was the Chief Scientific Officer in charge of Forensics, and Inigo didn't like her. In fact, there weren't many people he did like – in forensics or otherwise.

'Are you lost?' Dr Walker asked.

Lynda Phillips – the bottle-blonde receptionist – had been flirting with a deliveryman when he'd arrived, so he'd hunched his shoulders into his jacket and aimed himself in a purposeful manner along the corridor.

'Lost is such a depressing word. I prefer to think of myself as drifting between unknown points on the landscape.'

'Your partner's already been up here annoying me. Now, I'm busy, so go away.' Alexis Walker was in her late forties and overweight. She had dark brown hair past her shoulders, the split ends making the last couple of inches frizzy. She was at that time of life when her hair colouring should have been getting lighter, not darker.

'I bring you the find of the century, and you treat me like a plague victim.'

She held out her hand. 'You with the plague! We should be so lucky.'

He passed her the evidence bag with the silver interlocking hearts inside. 'Dr Reese found it inside the victim's mouth, usual tests.'

'Are you still here?'

'I always enjoy the welcome I get up here.'

He ambled back along the corridor, and smiled at a surprised-looking Lynda Phillips. 'You were sleeping,' he said.

'You'll get me into trouble.'

'I think I'm a bit old for that.'

'Charlie Chaplin was eighty-two.'

'There's still hope for me yet then, doctor?'

'Next time, don't sneak past me like a criminal.'

'Would you have let me in if I'd have stopped?'

'No. I have strict instructions from Dr Walker not to let you in under any circumstances.'

'There you are then. No point in me stopping if you're going to treat me like an unwanted guest.'

'But that's what you are.'

'Have a nice day, Lynda,' he said, as he pushed open the door.

***

Tig was at her desk talking on the phone.

'Well?' he said to her when she'd finished.

'Verona Izatt died in a hit-and-run. Never caught driver. Have to go to London to talk to her friends, find out what happened.'

'Why London?'

'Worked at the Transmarine Shipping Company as an Insurance Broker. Offices at 121 Westminster Bridge Road, which used to be the station and terminus of the London Necropolis Company.'

His back was aching, so he perched on the side of her desk to ease it. 'Okay, let's deal with this Necropolis Company first – what is it?'

'Used to transport the dead of London to Brookwood Cemetery in Surrey using own railway line.'

'But they're not operating now, are they?'

'No, 1852 to 1927. Found it interesting.'

'It's not. Tell me about the Transmarine Shipping Company.'

'They insure ships.'

'Is that it?'

'Yes. LNC was more interesting.'

'So, the hit-and-run driver could have been the woman who's been masquerading as Verona Izatt?'

Tig shrugged. 'Possible.'

'Something for you. When Doc Reese unpicked the sutures in the victim's lips, she found two silver interlocking hearts inside the mouth.'

Tig's eyes narrowed. 'Old lover?'

'Could be. Maybe someone she rejected. First, we need to find out who this woman was. Okay, here's what we'll do. I'll go to London tonight and stay at my daughter's place. In the morning I'll visit the Transmarine Shipping Company offices and find out as much as I can about Verona Izatt. I'll take a picture of the victim with me, show it around, see if anyone recognises her. I'll come back tomorrow night, and we'll go from there.'

'Not been to London for a long time.'

'And you're not going tonight either. You go back to the cottage in the morning and turn it inside out. Question the villagers about the woman they knew as Verona Izatt. Anything from the house-to-house?'

Tig shook her head.

'Any similar murders in the UK or abroad?'

She shook her head again.

'Are you not talking to me?'

Her head shook vigorously.

He stood up. 'Well, I'm going home to pack then. I'll ring you about lunchtime tomorrow, and we can update each other. That doesn't mean you can't ring me at other times if something important comes up. I also don't want you shaking your head over the phone when I do ring.'

***

'Hello.'

'It's your father.'

He'd just arrived at London Paddington. It had taken him over five hours so far. After catching the quarter-to-seven train from Milhaven, he'd had to change at Swansea. Now, he needed to descend into the bowels of London and catch the tube to Knightsbridge.

'Mum said you'd be ringing. Everyone else has a dad,

I have a father.'

'I'm on my way to London.'

'Mum didn't say you were coming to see me. I'm not sure that's a good idea.'

The last time they'd met was three years ago. It had ended in disaster, and they hadn't spoken to each other since.

'I didn't know I was.'

'You're coming because of work, not to see me?'

'I could have sent someone else. I'm coming to see you. The work is something I have to do as well.'

'So, you feel obligated to see me while you're here doing your work?'

Marielle was her mother's daughter all right. When they'd all been living together as a family, the two of them used to gang up on him until he didn't know which way was up, and which way down.

'I'll be arriving at Knightsbridge tube station at quarter to midnight. Can you pick me up?'

'You want to stay with me?'

'Where else would I go?'

'I don't think...'

'Would you prefer your father to sleep in a cardboard box with a bottle of methylated spirits for company?'

There was half a laugh on the other end of the phone. 'We have hotels in London now, you know.'

'I don't have money for posh London hotels.'

'You're already here, aren't you? Why didn't you ring me before? Why wait until quarter past eleven?'

'Can I stay with you, or not?'

There was a long silence. 'I have some rules.'

'Oh?'

'You're not to mention what I do for a living.'

'Okay.'

'You're not to mention my lifestyle, or the way I live my life.'

'Okay.'

'And you're not to pick on my boyfriend.'

'You have a boyfriend?'

'I said you weren't to mention him.'

'No, you said I couldn't pick on him.'

'You're not to mention him either.'

'Is there anything I can talk about?'

'No, not really. I don't want to argue with you.'

'I didn't come all this way to have an argument.'

'That's not what mum says.'

He smiled. 'I promise, I'll be good.'

'You'd better be.'

***

She was sitting in a black taxi outside Knightsbridge tube station waiting for him.

When she opened the door and called his name he wanted to cry. What in God's name had he been doing with his life? Three years wasted. Even at five minutes to midnight, Marielle looked like an angel. Her long, dark hair had been hastily tied back. Her face without makeup was that of his five year-old daughter chasing butterflies.

He threw his overnight bag on the floor and climbed in. 'Hi,' he said. He was embarrassed, and didn't know whether to kiss her, hug her, or shake her hand. In the end, he did nothing.

She said, 'Okay,' to the driver, who obviously knew where he was going.

'You look older.'

'I feel older.'

'How was your trip?'

'Long and boring.'

'Are you hungry?'

'A bit. I forgot to eat before I set off.'

'Max is cooking you steak, chips, and salad.'

'Max? Isn't that a dog's name?'

Her lips turned white and pencil-thin. 'You said...'

He grinned. 'I'm joking. I still have my wicked sense of humour.'

She rolled her eyes. 'Yeah, I'd forgotten about that.'

The taxi pulled up outside a large block of expensive-looking flats.

'Forty-seven pounds,' the taxi driver said.

'Bloody hell!' He began rummaging in the inside pocket of his jacket for his wallet. 'Are you sure you didn't come via India to get here?'

Marielle put her hand on his arm. 'It's all right, dad, I've got it.' She passed the driver a fifty-pound note. 'Keep the change.'

'Hey, don't bankrupt yourself, lady.'

She put her hand out again. 'You can give me the change back, if you want.'

He grunted and pulled away.

'I don't know how you can afford to live in London.'

'I manage.'

He looked up at the block of flats. 'Which one's yours?'

'The third floor.'

'You'll have to point to it.'

'All of the third floor.'

'All of it? Is it Max's?'

'No, dad, it's mine. Come on, we don't want to stand out here all night in the dark.'

She led him through the reception area where a tall, grey-haired man in a uniform was standing behind a desk. 'Goodnight, Walter.'

The man nodded his head. 'Goodnight, Miss Morgan.'

He wished he wasn't such a good detective. She didn't say, 'This is my father' to the night porter. He must be used to her bringing back old men at all hours of the day and night. God, she was a prostitute. He'd known it all along, and that was merely confirmation.

She used a key in the lift, and it took them up to the third floor.

The lift doors opened first, and then his bottom jaw dropped open shortly afterwards. He stepped into a gigantic, open-plan living room with a white and beige colour scheme. Off the living room was the dining room in the same colours. His ex-Council house would have fitted at least six times into the space.

'I'll show you where everything is first, then you can eat.'

He followed her through the living room, along a hallway, and into a bedroom with a double bed. The room had been decorated in a potpourri of grey shades. There was a huge LCD television screen on the wall facing the bed.

'Very nice,' he said, throwing his green holdall onto the bed.

She led him out into the hallway again. 'That's our bedroom,' she said pointing to a door on the left. 'That's the bathroom,' pointing to a door on the right, 'And this,' she said opening the door, 'is the swimming pool.'

He walked through the door. Sure enough, it was a swimming pool – about twenty-foot long and eight-foot wide. 'A swimming pool?' he said squatting to dip his finger in the chlorinated water. 'On the third floor?'

'Yeah, it's amazing, isn't it?'

'It certainly is, and I didn't bring my trunks with me either.' He hadn't been swimming for as long as he could remember. In fact, he didn't even own a pair of trunks.

'You don't need trunks, dad. Max and I swim naked.'

He pulled a face. 'Of course you do.'

'It's fine if you want to have a swim in the morning. Nobody will come in and surprise you; we usually swim at night.'

'I don't think so, but thanks anyway.' The thought of what might be in the water would give him the heebie-jeebies.

They walked back along the hallway, and turned right just before the dining room into a large kitchen. A man – like the Colossus of Rhodes – was standing against the kitchen worktop looking at the messages on his mobile phone. He had short, black hair like a US Marine, wore a red apron that stated 'The Cook is Hot', and had a physique which resembled a young Arnold Schwarzenegger.

Inigo stood a head shorter, and had to tilt his neck backward to look at Max.

'I'll be back in a minute, dad,' Marielle said and left.

'Hey, Mr Morgan, I've heard a lot about you,' Max said. He offered a hand that looked more like a crushing machine.

Inigo took it, but wished he hadn't. 'Then you have me at a disadvantage, because I know nothing about you.'

'Well, first off, take a seat at the table, I'll serve your meal.'

He did as he was directed, and Max put a plate of steak, chips and salad in front him.

'Medium rare, help yourself to the condiments.'

While he did that, Max turned a chair round and sat opposite him at the table. He crossed his arms, and Inigo could see that the biceps were as thick as his own thighs.

'I'm a fashion designer, Max Allsopp Designs. I have my own company.'

'I'm really pleased for you.' All male fashion designers were gay, weren't they? What would a man with a body like a brick shithouse be doing designing women's clothes if he wasn't gay? That would explain how Marielle could bring all the tricks back. He was probably using Max's bedroom. He hoped the sheets had been changed. Max was probably bunking in with Marielle just for tonight. Maybe he was Marielle's pimp.

'You have a wonderful daughter, Mr Morgan.'

'Thanks. Did you cook the steak?'

'Sure did.'

'Not bad for a fashion designer.'

'Used to be a trainee chef until I reached for the stars.'

Marielle came back in wearing a long pink dressing gown and old slippers.

'Good to see you, Mr Morgan.' Max stood up. 'I'll probably see you before you go, but if not, you take care.'

Marielle poured herself a glass of milk. 'Beer?'

He nodded.

She sat down in Max's vacant chair after she'd turned it round to face the table.

'He's a good cook,' Inigo said between mouthfuls.

'Max is good at a lot of things.'

'So, this is all yours?' he said waving his knife around in the air.

'Yes.'

'Not Max's?'

'No. He's renting out his flat.'

'How could you possibly afford something like this?'

'I get paid a lot of money.'

'Doing what?'

'Modelling.'

'I see.'

'Mum still loves you, you know.'

'Don't be ridiculous, we've been separated for seven years.'

'Why do you think she's never applied for a divorce?'

'Because she's been too busy.'

'She told me about your pension.'

'What does she know about my pension?'

'She knows you're not going to be able to retire next year.'

'I'll retire, even if I have to work down the coal mines.'

'Doesn't that defeat the purpose of retirement? I can help, you know?'

'Help, in what way?'

'With money.'

'I don't think so. I'd feel as though I was living off immoral earnings.'

Her face went white. 'What do you mean?'

He put the last chip in his mouth and placed the knife and fork in the centre of the plate. 'You've got to do more than a few modelling jobs to be able to afford something like this.'

She stood up, shaking. Her fists were clenched, the knuckles white. 'I offer to help, and you throw it back in my face. Get out.' Tears streamed down her cheeks. 'GET OUT.' She shoved him through the living room and into the lift. 'I never want to see you again. NEVER.' She pressed the button for the ground floor, and the lift doors closed.

Now I've done it, he thought. His bag was on the bed. Crap, what now?

In the lobby the night porter said, 'Going out at this time of night, Mr Morgan? Anything I can help you with?'

'You know who I am?'

'Yes, Marielle said she was picking up her father from the tube station when she first went out.'

'No, I don't need any help, I'm just going to get a bit of fresh air.' He looked at his watch. It was ten past one. After turning right and walking up the road a short distance, he sat down on the edge of the pavement. God, he was probably the worst father in the world... in the universe. He put his head in his hands and sighed.

'You're a jackass, Mr Morgan.'

'It's probably a crime to verbally abuse a Detective Inspector.'

'You're lucky I haven't ripped your head clean off your body.'

'I bet you could as well.'

'You need to know some things about your daughter. For one, she's beautiful. For two, she has a brain. And for three, she and I are getting married as soon as our schedules ease off a bit. You don't really think she's a hooker, do you?'

'I just wonder where she got all that money.'

Max grabbed a fistful of Inigo's jacket collar and lifted him up. 'Come with me, Mr Morgan, let me show you how Marielle makes her money.'

'I'd rather not.'

Max propelled him back to the building and into the lift. Back in the living room he told Inigo to sit.

After an hour of watching Marielle in television commercials for perfume, hair colour, hair spray, make-up, anti-ageing cream, beer, cars, and a dozen or more other consumer items, he realised Max was right – he was a jackass.

'Marielle is one of the hottest models around. Everyone wants her, and they're willing to pay millions to get her. And you know what else?'

'What?'

'She does her own accounts, and she looks after her own investments. Marielle is one smart cookie.'

'Why didn't she tell me?'

'Would you have believed her?'

'Probably not. Any chance of a beer?'

'And then you have to make things right with your daughter. She's devastated. All she wants is for you to be proud of her.'

***

# Thursday

He stood outside 221 Westminster Bridge Road. The narrow four-storey building looked odd wedged between a 1990s block of flats and a two-storey house. At ground level was a wide arch with a driveway that now led to a car park for staff. The car park exit was some streets away off Hercules Road. For many – between 1852 and 1927 – this would have been the start of their last journey to Brookwood Cemetery. The portal was the entrance to the London Necropolis Company railway station.

The second and third floors had pillars in front of the windows like the Athenian Parthenon, and the fourth floor was topped with an elaborately decorated arch. He thought it was very impressive, and guessed the building was listed for protection, and that was why it was still standing.

It was three thirty before he'd climbed into bed exhausted. After being shown how stupid he'd been by Max, he had tapped on the door and entered Marielle's bedroom. She was lying on the bed, sobbing.

'Max says I'm a jackass. I was going to arrest him for verbally abusing a police officer, but I have to agree with him – I've been a jackass for a long time.'

The sobbing began to subside, but she didn't acknowledge him.

He continued. 'I don't blame myself though, that wouldn't be right. I blame you and your mother. Somebody should have hit me over the head with the truth.' He sat down on the end of the bed with his back to her. 'You've let me live in my own little world for over three years, believing something that I'd made up in my head like a crazy person.' He began to cry himself. 'I've wasted all those years thinking the very worst of the only two people I love in the world, and those two people have got a lot to answer for.'

She snuggled up behind him, and put her arms around his neck. 'You wouldn't see beyond what you believed to be true.'

He squeezed her hand. 'Yes, I knew you'd make it so it was my fault. If I'm going to apologise for being a complete jackass, then you and your mother have to take your share of the blame, which I've calculated as at least ninety-nine percent. And unless you agree, I don't think we can move forward on the reconciliation thing.'

'I agree, dad.'

'What about your mother? She's played a major role in this little fiasco.'

'She agrees as well.'

'Okay then.' He stood up. 'I think we should let Max get to bed, but you need to fill me in on those missing three years... if you're not too tired?'

And that's what they did until three thirty. They were father and daughter again. He was still a jackass, but he kept that for other people now.

He crossed the road towards the entrance to the Transmarine Shipping Company. The London Necropolis Company was in the past like his erroneous beliefs about his daughter.

At seven thirty he decided he would have that swim, and crept along the hallway in his pyjamas with a towel slung over his shoulder. He wasn't keen on swimming naked in his daughter's swimming pool, but Inigo Morgan was a new man this morning and he thought he'd give it a go.

He swam breaststroke for ten lengths, and felt ten years younger. He climbed out, and when he was in no-man's land between the pool and his towel, a woman walked in and saw him.

Under normal circumstances, and with a normal person, she would have turned away embarrassed, but she didn't. And he was caught like a rabbit in the glare of headlights. He didn't know whether to jump back in the pool, or make a dash for his towel. In the end, he froze as rabbits do.

She walked towards him. 'Ah, Miss Morgan said she was having one of those Greek statues installed, but I didn't expect it to look so real, or so old.' She put a hand on his chest and began to move it downwards.

He made a dash for his towel.

She laughed. 'I am Tracey Carter, your daughter's cleaner.'

He gave her a lopsided grin. 'Marielle said there would be no one about.'

'You're lucky this week only. I swapped my days because of the school holidays, and I'm glad I did. I like surprises.'

He made his way out to take a shower. Later, when he ambled towards the kitchen with his overnight bag in his hands and clean clothes on, he heard laughter. It was Marielle and Tracey the cleaner.

'Sorry, dad, I forgot Tracey had changed her days.'

He shrugged. 'Maybe I should become a Greek statue to supplement my retirement income.'

***

'Good morning, Sir.'

He produced his warrant card, which he really shouldn't have done. Yes, he was a copper as much here as he was in Haverfordwest, but it was common courtesy to tip your hat to the local constabulary. He hadn't done that, didn't have the time. A phone call would have done the trick, but it was too late now. He was a loose cannon operating in someone else's area.

'I'd like to see the person in charge, please. It's about Verona Izatt.'

'Just one moment, Sir. Please take a seat.'

The reception was bright and airy with a parquet floor and brown leather sofas for visitors. He preferred to stand and gaze out of the window at the passers-by.

'You're here about Verona Izatt?' a female voice came from behind him.

He turned and showed his warrant card again.

'Detective Inspector Morgan. Yes, if it's not too much trouble? I won't keep you long.'

The woman was probably in her early forties, but trying to pinpoint a woman's age – with all the help they get in trying to disguise their age – was akin to aiming at a moving target. She wore a dark blue skirt and jacket with a red blouse. Her hair was skewered at the back of her head like a peacock's tail.

'Susie Gillott, how can I help?' She began to move to a lift.

He followed. 'Were you employed here at the time?'

'Yes, very sad. Verona was one of our better insurance brokers.'

'You insure ships?'

'Yes.'

'No international conspiracy, or a front for the Colombian drug cartels, or...'

They arrived in an office that looked as though it belonged to a shipping magnate. Pictures of ships adorned the walls.

'Coffee?'

'Strong and black, please.' He wasn't exactly tired yet, but he knew he would be later. Normally, his head was clear, but this morning it felt as though someone had stuffed it with candyfloss using a long stick.

'I'd certainly like a bit of conspiracy to break the monotony, but no – unfortunately, all we do is insure ships.'

'How long had Miss Izatt worked here?'

'Seven years. She was a rising star until the accident.'

'What do you know about that?'

'Hit-and-run as far as I'm aware, but I read something a couple of weeks ago...' She picked up the phone. 'Judy, have you still got that article about the hit-and-run driver? Can you bring it in, please?'

A much younger woman in a plaid skirt and lime-green blouse came in carrying a newspaper, which she handed to her boss, and left.

'Yes, here it is.' She began to read: 'John McGregor of

no fixed abode... blah, blah... among a number of other crimes, he admitted to a hit and run accident on St George's Road during the evening of 4<sup>th</sup> October 2009...' She put the paper down. 'That accident was Verona Izatt. She was walking down St George's Road to the Elephant & Castle at seven thirty at night on her way home when a Porsche Carrera mowed her down.'

'Is there any indication in that article that she was killed on purpose?'

Susie Gillott's brow furrowed. 'You need to get out more, Inspector. John McGregor stole cars to feed his drug habit. Verona was in the wrong place at the wrong time. What's all this about? Why are you here after all this time?'

He pulled out the photograph of the victim. 'This woman has been living as Verona Izatt in Little Haven, Pembrokeshire. Kathryn Brinck – Verona Izatt's aunt – died three years ago and left her niece a cottage at Little Haven. Now, this woman has been murdered.'

'How strange.'

'Yes it is, and that's why I'm here asking questions.'

'No, of course, that's strange, but I know the woman in the picture.' She picked up the phone. 'Me again, Judy. Can you get Verona Izatt's file and bring it in.'

Judy appeared with the said file and left.

Susie opened the file and withdrew a double page from a newspaper. 'Yes, here it is. This is the original article about Verona's accident. Look here...' She thrust the paper towards him and pointed at a tiny photograph. 'That's her, isn't it?'

Inigo squinted. He really needed to do something about his eyesight. He leaned closer. 'It certainly looks like the same woman.'

'Her name's Emily Blake. She was the journalist who wrote the original article on Verona's accident. She came here, said she was doing background research for the article.'

'Which paper is that?'

'The Westminster Gazette, at Stamford Hill.'

'Can I get a copy?'

She passed it to him. 'You can have this. Why we've still got it after three years I have no idea.'

'You've been most helpful. I now have a name for my murder victim, and it doesn't appear as if this Emily Blake killed Verona Izatt so that she could take her place. Rather, I think she saw an opportunity to disappear for whatever reason.' He offered his hand. 'Thanks very much for your time, Miss Gillott.'

***

Outside, he tried phoning Tig, but was directed to voicemail. 'Weren't you meant to be ringing me? I know who the victim is, ring me.'

The Westminster Gazette wasn't actually located in Westminster. He had to travel to Stoke Newington to find out that the building didn't exist anymore. Once it did, but where it used to be was a pile of rubble.

He found a cafe opposite called The Kinghorn, which was run by obese twins Josie and Lucy. Josie cooked, Lucy served, and neither smiled. He asked them about the Westminster Gazette, and they snorted like pigs at a trough.

'Yer crackers, Mister,' Lucy said.

'It ain't existed since 1928,' proclaimed Josie through the serving hatch.

'Became the News Chronicle in 1930,' said Lucy.

Josie snorted some more. 'Until it was stuffed into the Daily Mail in 1960.'

'Yer gotta go to the Daily Mail, Mister,' Lucy told him.

'That'll be five pounds fifty,' Josie said.

Lucy leaned towards him. 'Unless, of course, you order something, and then you get the information for free.'

He checked his watch. It was five to twelve. He ordered steak and kidney pie, chips and peas with a cup of tea up front, which cost him seven pounds thirty-five.

What the hell was going on? If the Westminster Gazette didn't exist anymore, then it was more than likely that the name Emily Blake was false. What about the newspaper – he'd forgotten about that? He pulled it out of his pocket and opened it up. It certainly looked real. He took it up to the counter.

'I have part of the Westminster Gazette for...'

'You never heard of spoof newspapers, Mister?' Lucy said.

'Hold it up to the light, Lucy,' Josie hollered through the serving hatch.

Josie took it from him and held it up to the light. 'There, Mister,' she said pointing to the white border at the bottom. 'A watermark of the company's name.'

'That'll be five pounds fifty,' Lucy said.

He happily paid.

***

The company – MakeTheNews – was located on Aylesford Street in Pimlico. It took him thirty-one minutes on the tube from Stoke Newington, and during the journey he phoned Tig again. He was directed to voicemail.

'Where the hell are you, Tigger?' He was getting annoyed.

She should have phoned him, or at least have been available to take his calls. Where the hell was she? All she'd been doing was searching the house again for clues about who the victim was, and questioning a few of the locals to see if they knew anything about the woman known as Verona Izatt.

He phoned Detective Sergeant Tony Saunders.

'Do you know where DC Griffiths is?'

'I thought she was with you, Sir?'

'I'm in London following up on a lead, she went back to the cottage in Little Haven to have another look at things, and then she was going to question a few of the locals.'

'And she's not answering her phone?'

'No, I keep getting re-directed to voicemail.'

'Maybe her battery's dead.'

'I didn't phone you for stupid suggestions, Tony.'

'Yeah sorry, Sir. I'll make some phone calls, and call you back.'

'I'm not going to get back until very late tonight, so I'd appreciate it, Tony.'

'Oh, by the way, the Chief has been looking for you. Something about a briefing you were going to give him.'

He'd forgotten about briefing the Chief. 'Tell him you haven't seen me.'

'I haven't.'

'Well, there you are then.' He ended the call.

MakeTheNews had two operations. Customers could walk into the shop and order a newspaper – created to their specifications, but based on a template for weddings, stag and hen nights, educational, job and football success – there was a long list. The second part of the operation was much larger and took up the second and third floors of the building. It consisted of their online operations, which contributed seventy percent to the business income.

He flashed his warrant card. 'Who can I speak to about an order placed three years ago?'

'God,' the thin pale young man said. He had short black hair that was long on top and fashioned into a point at the front. It hung down over his eyes, and he kept tossing his head to the right to remove it. Inigo wanted to cut it for him, because no matter how much the young man tossed his head the hair slid back down over his eyes.

'Can you get me someone who talks sense?'

'You just happen to have struck lucky; I own the business.'

Inigo was reminded of his daughter. What was the world coming to? Young people were turning away from education, and becoming millionaires at the drop of a hat. It had become an upside-down world. There was no place for crustaceans like him. It was time he retired, but how could he retire now? The bastards had pulled the rug from under him.

'I need to know who ordered this three years ago.' He pulled out the newspaper and unfolded it on the counter.

'I said God before, because the person who used to run the business back then is dead.'

'I see, so can you help me?'

'We have financial records in the basement, but no staff to look through them.'

'If you show me where they are, I could look?'

'Okay, I can do that, but don't mess the records up.'

He was deposited in the basement with the financial records, which were contained in filing cabinets – one for each year. He didn't think it would take him long to locate a credit card receipt if there was one. He went straight to October and found what he was looking for within half an hour. The name on the credit card receipt was Joy Lawson, and he hoped he'd found his victim.

Upstairs, the young entrepreneur – Syd Field – copied the receipt for him.

'Thanks for your time, and if you'll take my advice, you want to go to the barber's shop and get that cut.'

Syd laughed. 'Yeah, old people always say that.'

Outside, he rang Dawn Kellett in database enquiries.

'Long time no see, Inigo?'

'Yeah, what can I say? I've got a name. Can you run it through CrimInt for me?'

'It'll take...'

'Ten minutes?'

'That's not what I was going to say. There's a queue, you know?'

'There's always a queue, but this is important.'

'With you, it's always important. What's the name?'

'Joy Lawson, used to live in London, probably around Westminster.'

'There'll be a few.'

'I'll know the one I'm looking for when I see her.'

'Okay, I'll ring you back, but you'll owe me a meal.'

'And I'll look forward to that.'

The call ended.

He found another cafe, and waited with a mug of coffee. It wasn't worth starting off anywhere because he didn't know where he was going. If Joy Lawson was a dead end, then he may as well go back to Marielle's, pick up his overnight bag, say goodbye, and then make his way back to Wales.

Had Tony found Tig yet? Why hadn't she rung him? He had a sinking feeling in his gut.

His phone vibrated on the table.

'Yes?'

'Joy Lawson was reported missing in November 2009. She lived at number seven Leinster Mews. I've checked, and it's close to Lancaster Gate tube station, postcode W2 4EY.'

He wrote the address down in his notebook. 'After three years, I doubt I'll find much there. Where did she work?'

'The Pentonville Mercury on Pentonville Road in Pentonville. You want the Angel tube station.'

'Thanks, Dawn. Any news on Tig?'

'What do you mean?'

'She's missing.'

'Sorry, I didn't know.'

'Okay, don't worry. I owe you.'

'I have it marked in my diary. I'll be in touch when I find the most expensive place near here.'

'I'm sure you will.'

He ended the call, finished his coffee, and made his way to the tube station. He was beginning to feel a bit the worse for wear. According to the large station clock, the time was five past two. Pimlico was on the Victoria Line. At King's Cross St Pancras he had to change to the Northern Line, and Angel was the next station.

The Pentonville Mercury was a local newspaper run, in the main, by a husband and wife team called Dawn and Whitfield Cothay, and eight other staff. Inside, the offices were open plan. Apart from a few partitions, nobody had any privacy, and everyone could see what everyone else was doing.

'Joy Lawson?' Dawn Cothay said. 'Now there's a name I haven't heard in a while.'

Her husband, so she said, was out gathering the news.

He showed her the picture of the dead victim.

'Yes, that's Joy.'

'Can you tell me what happened?'

'Not really. One minute she was here working, the next she wasn't. I was the one who reported her missing. As far as I know, she didn't have any family.'

'No idea why she disappeared?'

'None, she loved being a reporter, wanted to make it big one day.'

'Can you remember what she was working on at that time?'

'Bridget?' she shouted.

A young girl appeared chewing gum. She had piercings in her left ear, bottom lip, tongue, right eyebrow, and belly button. A tattoo of a blue snake slithered up her left arm. Inigo guessed she must be on work experience.

'Don't get creeped out by Bridget,' Dawn Cothay said. 'Behind the insane decorative artwork, she's really a very nice person.'

The girl shot her arm out. 'Bridget Knight, IT guru.'

'A guru?' Inigo said shaking the hand.

'Ain't nothing I don't know about IT.'

Yes, Inigo was sure that the world had turned on its head. Here was a self-proclaimed genius with computers, who couldn't speak the Queen's English. Time to step aside, and make way for this new species of human being.

'Detective Inspector Morgan wants to know what Joy Lawson was working on before she disappeared three years ago.'

'Yeah, got her files zipped up, encrypted, and tucked away. You want me to open 'em up for the 'spector?'

'Yes please, Bridget.'

'Can do. Come with me, 'spector Morgan.'

Dawn Cothay offered her hand. 'I've got to go out soon, but I hope you find what you're looking for.'

'Okay, thanks for your help.'

She whispered to him. 'If she offers you sex, decline politely.' Then she turned to her IT guru. 'You be nice to the Inspector, Bridget?'

'Will do, Mrs C.'

Inigo followed Bridget to a space cluttered with gadgets and sat down in an orange plastic chair.

Bridget worked quickly and then said, 'You want it on a stick?'

He guessed she was talking about a memory stick. 'Yes please, but I'd also like to have a quick look at what she was working on in the last month before she disappeared.'

'No probs.' She passed him a memory stick. 'That's all her records decrypted and unzipped.'

'Thanks.' He slipped the stick in his pocket.

'Now we wait.'

'Oh?'

'Done a block print. There's a bit of stuff. It'll take about five. You want to have sex with me while we're waiting?'

'That's very nice of you to offer, but I had a late night last night.'

'Hey, don't sweat it.'

She shot off, and came back with a stack of paper. 'There you go, 'spector. Anything else I can do for you?'

'No, I don't think so. Thanks very much for being a guru.'

'Hey, nice of you to say so.'

He caught the tube back to King's Cross St Pancras, and switched to the Piccadilly Line for Knightsbridge. Between Holborn station and Green Park he found out that Tig couldn't be found anywhere. She wasn't at home, in the station, or at the cottage in Little Haven. They were a bit concerned, and had begun a minor manhunt. Her mobile had been switched off, or the SIM card removed, but her last recorded location had been in

Little Haven. They were focussing the search in the village, but nothing had turned up yet.

'It'll take me at least six or seven hours to get back, Tony.'

'We're doing everything we can to find her, Sir,' DS Saunders said. 'The Chief Super's heading up the operation. If nothing materialises in an hour, we're escalating the search to a full manhunt. We'll find her, don't you worry.'

But he was worried. Chief Superintendent Paul Northfield was a boy. He didn't have Inigo's experience, didn't know the lay of the land, and the people. He doubted the boy-Chief could find his way out of a wet paper bag.

Crap! He was in the wrong place at the wrong time. He wanted to be there. Tig was his partner for Christ's sake, and he wasn't there to watch her back.

'I'm relying on you, Tony.'

***

He made his way back to Marielle's flat.

'I have to go.'

'That's always been the way, dad.'

'It's who I am, Marielle, for good or evil.'

'I know, and I still love you.'

'What a difference a day makes.' He told her about Tig going missing.

'Two things. First, you don't have to spend six hours on a train.' She took her mobile from her bag on the floor next to the sofa, found a number, and dialled. 'Hobb, it's Marielle. My dad needs to get from London to Wales to save someone's life. I know, but for me? You're priceless. Yeah, half an hour.' She ended that call, and made another one for a taxi to come for them immediately. 'We have to get you to the Westland Heliport in thirty-five minutes.'

'Heliport?'

'Hobb Whitley will fly you to Withybush Aerodrome in forty minutes in his helicopter. I often use him to beat the traffic.'

'I can't afford a helicopter flight.'

'Don't be dense, dad. Also, here's the number of my stockbroker, her name is Marilyn Atkins. I asked her to invest £25,000 for your retirement fund, and the value of those shares has already risen to £37,500. And if I hear anything about immoral earnings, or you couldn't possibly take money from me, you'll be investigating your own murder.'

Tears welled in his eyes. 'A father is meant to give his daughter money, not the other way round.'

'I read something once: Some people earn millions investing in themselves, and some people give of themselves investing in society for very little reward. I'm grateful, not only for all the help you gave me when I was younger, but also for giving what you had to give, so that I could live in a safer society. Think of it as payback, and believe me when I say that to me it's a piddling amount that I'll recover before the day is out. Right, shall we go?'

He wiped his eyes. 'Look what you've made me do.' He hugged her, then bent down and grabbed his bag. 'Lead the way, daughter of mine.'

At the heliport they hugged again.

'Remember, you have to give me away soon.'

'I don't know if I want to give you away anymore.'

'And be nice to mum, you never know what might happen.'

'She'd die of shock that's what would happen.'

'See you soon, dad.'

'Yeah.'

***

At four-fifteen Hobb Whitley landed at Withybush Aerodrome. Inigo had dozed off for most of the flight. Under normal circumstances he would have given him a tip, but he thought that ten percent of a helicopter was probably beyond his resources, so he just waved goodbye instead.

He'd left his car at Milford Haven train station, which was along the coast in the opposite direction, so he caught a taxi to Little Haven. It was five past five when he arrived, and found they'd set up an incident room in the hall of Little Haven Primary School.

'DS Saunders said you wouldn't get back until late tonight,' the Chief said as soon as he entered.

'Helicopter.'

'I hope you don't think I'll sanction that expenditure?'

One of his people was missing, and all the Chief was worried about was a few pounds out of the budget. 'Have you found DC Griffiths yet?'

'No, we're still searching.'

'What have you done so far?'

'The cottage, the surrounding area, a house-to-house in the village.'

'What's your next move?'

'Well, I suppose we'll have to move further afield.'

'How many officers have you got on the ground?'

'Thirty-one now that you're here.'

'Thirty-one, is that all?'

'Unfortunately, that's all the manpower available.'

'What about getting people from neighbouring forces?'

'Do you know how much that would cost?'

'How much is DC Griffiths' life worth, Sir?'

'Be careful, Inspector, you're treading on very thin ice.'

He walked away then. If he'd stayed, he would have put his own neck in the guillotine, and that wouldn't have done Tig any good at all.

At the place set aside for refreshments, he made himself a black coffee. He didn't normally take sugar, but there wasn't a lot of fuel left in the tank, so he spooned a couple of sugars into the treacle-like liquid. What he needed was to stay awake, and for his brain to be operating at maximum efficiency. Tig had been missing for at least six hours. Where was she? There was no sign of her at the cottage, or in the local area. Had they retraced her steps? If the killer had taken her, maybe he was a local, or at least staying locally. Maybe she'd knocked on his door, he'd invited her in, and then overpowered her. Were they already too late?

'You must be on the take if you can afford a helicopter, Sir.'

'There's got to be some perks to the job, Tony. Listen, have you retraced her steps?'

'As far as we were able.'

'What do you mean?'

'Well, we relied on eyewitnesses who saw and spoke to her as usual.'

'And where does it end? Where do the sightings tail off? What times did people see her?'

'We haven't collated all the information yet.'

'Put more people on it, Tony. It's been over six hours now.'

'Okay. Was London any help?'

He remembered the sheets of paper Bridget Knight from the Pentonville Mercury had given him. 'Maybe, but I need to do some reading.' Where had he put his holdall? 'Oh crap! I've left my holdall in the boot of the taxi.' He shook his head. 'I can't even remember the name of the Taxi Company.'

'I'll get people onto mapping out Tig's last known movements.'

'Okay, the sooner the better, Tony.'

What an idiot! He was tired, and tired people made mistakes. He needed to get onto the taxi companies in Withybush, phone around, try and find... The stick! He rummaged in his jacket pocket and found the memory stick.

Six computers had been set up in the hall. Four of them were in use. He sat at a free computer and slotted the memory stick into the USB port, but even as he was doing it he knew it wouldn't work, and it didn't.

'I need a computer technician,' he said in a rather loud voice.

Constable Anne Sanderson was sitting at the computer next to him and shook her head. 'I'm sorry,

Sir, there are none here.'

He raised his voice again. 'Somebody must know how to access a memory stick?' He wondered if his feelings of desperation manifested themselves in his voice.

'Try the Chief, Sir, he's a computer whiz.'

Wouldn't you know it, he thought? The last person in the whole world he wanted to ask for help. 'Chief?'

'Yes, Inspector?'

'I need to get into this memory stick, and I hear you're the man who knows how.'

'It's against regulations, you know?'

'There might be something on here that can help us find DC Griffiths. This is what I went to London for.'

The Chief held out his hand. 'Just this one time, and don't watch what I do.'

Inigo passed him the memory stick, stood up, and turned around.

'What did you find out in London?'

'The victim's name is Joy Lawson. She used to work at the Pentonville Mercury as a reporter. In October 2009 she disappeared, which was shortly after Verona Izatt's aunt died and left her the cottage here in Little Haven. Around the same time, Verona Izatt was killed herself in a hit-and-run accident. Joy Lawson then found out everything she could about Verona Izatt under the guise of writing an article about the accident, but it was a fake. She then became Verona Izatt, and came here to start a new life. What I don't know, is why. I'm hoping the answer to that question is on that memory stick.'

The Chief stood up. 'Okay, but in the future, remember I'm the Chief Superintendent, not a computer technician.'

'If there's information on that stick that will help us find Tig... DC Griffiths, then you can be anything you want to be, Sir.'

Inigo sat down and began wading through Joy Lawson's files. The majority of articles related to local news in Pentonville and the surrounding areas. Man

robbed by gang, dog rescued from tree, the Cultural
Minister visits, and computer scam hits local businesses
– to name but a few, but there was one folder entitled
'Research', which contained one document and three
images. He opened up the images first. Each image was
a grainy black-and-white photograph of a man in his
late fifties, or early sixties, hunched into a donkey jacket
taken on the same day. His hair was unkempt, he was
unshaven, and his whole face sagged. Inigo didn't
recognise him as a local.

Next, he opened up the document. There was only
one paragraph:

*Arthur Morris is a serial abuser of children who has
escaped the attention of the authorities and the police.
The first person he abused was his daughter when she
was just five years old. Since then, as a registered carer
of looked-after children with his wife Mary, he has
abused hundreds of vulnerable children between 1987
and 2009.*

That was all there was. Inigo sent the three images
and the paragraph to the printer, and then stuck them
on the incident board.

'Who's that?' the Chief asked as he came to stand
next to Inigo.

'Arthur Morris, but I have no idea whether he's
connected to DC Griffiths' disappearance, or not. It was
the only item in Joy Lawson's files that could be
considered remotely interesting and out of the ordinary.'

'A child abuser?' DS Tony Saunders said.

Inigo shrugged. 'So it would seem, but there's no
evidence to support Joy Lawson's claim that he is.'

'What about putting his name through CrimInt and
giving copies of one of those photographs to the officers
on the ground. Let's see if anyone recognises him?'

'Good idea, DS Saunders,' the Chief said. 'It's not as
if we've got any other leads to pursue.'

Tony Saunders called over one of the Constables. He
pulled the best picture of Arthur Morris from the

incident board, told her to put his name through the CrimInt database, and to organise the copying and distribution of the photograph.

'What's happening with the collation, Tony?' Inigo said.

'Over here.' He led them to two tables pushed together. There were three Constables hovering over a large-scale map of Little Haven. 'Okay, we've mapped out where she went based on the approximate times of the reported sightings, and identified where the reports ended. She started off by calling at the nearest houses to the cottage on Point Road and St Brides Road and went as far as the Post Office.' He pointed to the roads on the map. 'She then retraced her steps and travelled along Grove Place to Walton Hill. At the Y-junction she turned left along Settlands Hill. The last confirmed sighting of her was by Marian and Andrew Pearson at Number 107. They also said they saw her go to Number 109.'

'That's old Pam MacRuary's Guesthouse, isn't it?' Inigo said. He lived on Wesley Road, but he knew Pam and her sister very well.

Tony nodded. 'Yes, but there was no answer when officers called at the house earlier.'

Inigo scratched his head. 'That can't be right, Pam – or her sister Janet Barr – are always there. Come on, Tony, you can drive.'

The time was quarter to seven, but it was still light outside. Tony Saunders had a Ford Mondeo from the motor pool, and they were there within ten minutes.

Tony knocked on the front door, but there was no answer. Inigo peered through the windows, but couldn't see anything out of place. Tony went left, and Inigo went right. They met round the back. Inigo banged on the window and shouted, 'Pam? Janet?' but there was no response.

'Look on the table,' Tony said.

'Keys.'

'People don't go out and leave their keys on the kitchen table.'

'That's enough for me. Contact the Chief, and get permission to break in.'

Tony moved away and rang the Chief. After a few minutes he came back and said, 'Do it.'

Inigo picked up a chunk of stone from the rockery, smashed the window in the back door, and put his arm through the hole. He turned the handle, but the door wouldn't open. 'One of those keys on the table must open the door,' he said.

'Watch yourself, Sir.'

Inigo moved out of the way.

Tony aimed a kick at the lock. The door splintered, burst open with a crack and the sound of smashing glass on the kitchen floor.

There was nothing downstairs, but they found Pam MacRuary and her sister Janet Barr in an upstairs bedroom. Their throats had been cut, and they were lying in a pool of their own blood. Tig was nowhere to be found. Tony rang the Chief and told him what they'd found.

'Dr Reese and forensics are on their way,' Tony said.

'The guest bedrooms are empty.'

'Maybe Marian or Andrew Pearson saw something.'

They went next door and questioned the Pearsons, who confirmed that a male guest had been staying for a few days.

Inigo showed them the picture of Arthur Morris.

'Aye, that's him,' Marian said. 'Got shorter hair, and uglier, but that's him all right.'

An All Points Bulletin was issued for Arthur Morris, but if he had gone to ground, Inigo knew it was as much use as a concrete parachute.

***

Who was Arthur Morris? How did Joy Lawson find out about him abusing children? She must have threatened to reveal his dirty little secret, and then he came after her. She used Verona Izatt's misfortune to disappear, but after three years he'd found her. Now he's got Tig, but where? And more importantly, why?

It was twenty-five past ten before the results of the database search came back. Inigo was on his last legs, and he ached all over from swimming ten lengths of Marielle's swimming pool like a crazy old man. All he wanted to do was lie down and close his eyes.

'No formal charges were brought against him due to a lack of evidence,' Constable Jane Whitfield said.

Inigo tried to concentrate, but he kept hallucinating.

'But his wife left him in October 2009, and he was removed from the Local Authority's list of registered carers.'

'Joy Lawson must have notified people about what she knew,' Tony said. 'Including his wife.'

'Maybe Joy Lawson was one of Morris' victims,' Tony suggested.

'That would explain a lot,' Inigo said. 'What about the daughter?'

'There's nothing on the database, Sir, except that her name is Sarah.'

Inigo stood up and began pacing. 'We need to find the daughter, and his wife should be brought down here to help us. Has Morris been down here before? Is there somewhere he might have taken DC Griffiths? We're at a dead end. We have no idea which way to turn next. He could be in a different country by now. Tig could be lying dead somewhere with her heart ripped out. Fuck!' He didn't normally swear, but he was frustrated at the lack of progress. 'Sorry,' he said to Constable Whitfield. 'I need to lie down before I fall down. Tony, we need more information about Arthur Morris. We need to know where to direct our energies next. When I wake up, I want to see his wife and daughter here waiting for me to question them.'

'I'll do my best, Sir.'

Inigo found a dark spot in the hall, curled up in a ball like a dog, and fell into a dreamless sleep.

***

# Friday

'What time is it, Jane?' he said to Constable Whitfield after she'd shook him awake.

'Half past four, Sir.'

'Coffee?'

'Here.' She held a steaming mug towards him.

'Thanks.' He sat up and took the coffee in both hands. 'I didn't do anything I shouldn't have, did I Jane?'

She smiled. 'I'm sure I wouldn't know anything about that, Sir.'

'The story of my life.'

He stood up and walked over to the incident board. The Chief was nowhere to be seen, but Tony Saunders was sitting at a table staring into space.

'Any news, Tony?'

'All bad.'

'Go on?'

'Arthur Morris' ex-wife had married again. They found the two bodies in the bedroom when they went to get her. He'd had his throat cut, and she resembled your first victim. Mouth sewn shut, silver hearts inside, heart ripped out.'

'Seems to be about revenge. Sewing the mouth shut is probably because they talked. Ripping the heart out could be because that's what they did to him. Joy Lawson tore his family apart when she spoke out, and his ex-wife did the same when she left him.'

'And the silver hearts?' Tony asked.

Inigo shrugged. What did he know? It was all speculation anyway. He wasn't a profiler, or a criminal psychologist, but he had a good idea what went on in a killer's mind even so. He felt much better after five hours of sleep. His brain was functioning again. Now, he had to find Tig.

'What about the daughter?'

'Disappeared. From about the age of fifteen, there's no record of her.'

'Ran away from home because of what he did to her?'

'Could be.'

'Okay, so what are we doing? Tig's been missing seventeen hours now.'

'We've been extending the search in a semicircle from the village, but nothing yet.'

'Let's do some speculating, Tony. Let's say Tig knocked on the old sister's guesthouse. He invited her in, and then disabled her. We know they're not there, so where did he take her? He obviously didn't carry her over his shoulder through the village, so he must have put her in a vehicle. Did he have a car? Have we checked?'

'Army green Landrover. It belonged to...'

'...the old sisters. Yes, I recall. And we can't find it?'

'No, and it hasn't been spotted once.'

'In which case, he's hidden it. Even if he'd switched vehicles, and he was on the move, we would have caught him by now. He's gone to ground, and I think he's still somewhere local.' He turned to the map on the incident board. 'I want all the farms checked again, but this time the barns and outhouses are to be searched. That Landrover is somewhere near. He's hiding until things quieten down.'

'What about the people further afield?'

'Bring them in. The farms are our priority now.'

'You could be wrong, Sir.'

'You know very well that telling a senior officer he could be wrong is not something that will enhance your promotion prospects, Sergeant.'

'I'm tired, and probably a bit reckless, Sir.'

'If I'm wrong, Tony, then...' He left the sentence hanging. If he was wrong they both knew the consequences of failure. Tig would probably die – if she wasn't dead already, and he'd be retiring a year earlier than planned.

Tony began organising the new search pattern, bringing in the officers and cars that had gradually travelled out to Broadhaven, Haroldston West, Talbenny, Ratford Bridge, Hasguard Cross, and a number of the other surrounding towns and villages.

The only thing that Inigo could do was pace and drink lots of coffee. He was bereft of ideas. If this didn't unearth Arthur Morris then Tig was lost, and a serial killer would have escaped.

***

At nine twenty-three, Constable Sanderson shouted across the hall, 'They've found the Landrover, Sir.'

Vindication, he thought. He crossed his fingers. Please let Tig be alive. 'Where?'

'Inglenook Farm, just past All Saints Church on Walton Hill.'

He knew the owners – Terry and Rose Wilson. 'Come on, Tony.'

'You'll wait until CO19 arrive,' the Chief said.

Inigo had forgotten all about the Chief. Where had he been? He looked dishevelled, but didn't they all? 'We haven't got time to wait for an armed response unit.'

'I'll put your confusion concerning the chain of command down to your tiredness, Inspector. We wait for CO19.'

God, he hated jobsworths – it's more than my job's worth to let you go out there without backup, Inspector – he mimicked the boy-Chief inside his head. 'How long will they take to get here?'

'Three quarters of an hour.'

'Too long, Sir. I'm going. You can sack me afterwards, if you want. Are you joining me, or staying here, Tony?'

Tony shrugged. 'In for a penny...'

They made their way out to Inglenook Farm. There were already two patrol cars and four officers there.

'Have you knocked?' Inigo asked.

'No, Sir. We thought it best to wait until you got here.'

'Okay, here's what we'll do.' He explained what he

had in mind, and then sent Tony and two officers round the back. He headed towards the front door with the other two officers behind him.

'Names?' Inigo asked over his shoulder.

'Alexandra Hudson...'

'...and Calloway Martin.'

'Nice to meet you. Now remember, no dithering.'

Inigo banged on the door. 'Police, open up.'

He did this twice more, and after a handful of minutes the door opened a crack. He could see the Wilson's fifteen-year-old daughter, Sophie, in the gap. She looked petrified, but there was no time to think about that. He barged forward. He wasn't a great believer in negotiation. The government had it right: 'No negotiation with terrorists.' Criminals were simply local terrorists with a different agenda. Morris wasn't going to be reasonable, nor was he going to release his hostages for a plane and a million pounds. He had absolutely nothing to lose by killing a few more people. A quote came to Inigo's mind as his shoulder crunched against the door: As You Sow, So Shall You Reap. The only thing that would stop Morris from doing what he'd set out to do, was death.

Hudson and Martin pushed him in the back to add more weight to his forward momentum. The door flew open. He went sprawling, and fell on top of Sophie Wilson. She began screaming. He could hear dogs barking, cows mooing, and pigs grunting in response to the noise. Hudson and Martin trampled him underfoot as they'd been instructed to do. Inigo gently put his hand over Sophie Wilson's mouth to stop her from screaming in his ear, and said, 'Sshhh.'

Morris had fallen backwards. He still gripped a knife in his hand, but had released Sophie Wilson's neck as he fell. He crab-walked backwards until he had space to stand.

Tig was tied to a hard-backed chair. There was fear in her eyes, and a gag tied round her mouth.

Morris stood behind her, put the knife to her throat

and said, 'Don't come any closer.'

That would have been going against Inigo's instructions, so Hudson and Martin continued to rush forward. They ploughed into Morris. The chair Tig was tied to crashed sideways to the floor. Morris flew backwards on his backside again. He still clutched the knife in his hand.

A crash came from the kitchen. DS Saunders and the two officers burst in.

Morris scrambled across the floor towards Tig, with the knife raised. 'If I'm going, my daughter's coming with me.'

Tony Saunders dived on his back. He grabbed Morris' wrist holding the knife, and they rolled together across the floor locked in a deadly embrace.

Morris managed to work his wrist free, and slashed Saunders across the side of the neck, but before he could do any more damage, Constable Martin smacked him round the back of the head with a poker he'd found in the hearth. Morris collapsed on top of Saunders like a marionette with its wires cut.

Inigo bent and righted the chair Tig was strapped into. 'Anybody got a knife...?'

Constable Anderson passed him a Swedish penknife.

'Stupid question really, thanks.' He took it and cut through the plastic restraints at Tig's wrists and ankles. She pulled the gag off herself.

He helped her up, and held her as she cried. 'Call an ambulance and forensics,' he said to no one in particular.

Tig pushed herself away from him and aimed a kick at Morris' head. 'Bastard. Fucking bastard. He was going to rape me again, you know.' She gave him a second kick for good measure, before Inigo pulled her away.

Morris didn't move.

Martin turned him over. Morris' knife was embedded in his chest. 'He's dead.'

'Good,' Tig said.

'Come on, let's go and wait outside for the

ambulance.'

'I don't need an ambulance.'

'You'll do as you're told, Detective Constable Griffiths,' he said.

She broke down sobbing. 'Oh God, I thought I would never have to see him again. I ran away when I was fifteen years old, and changed my name. How did he find me?'

'He didn't find you, he found Joy Lawson.'

'I remember her. She was one of the looked-after children he and my mum fostered.'

'Well, three years ago Joy Lawson told everyone about him, and although she became someone new like you, he found her. I'm not a great believer in coincidence, but I think that's what it was when she decided to hide in the same place you were hiding.'

'Thank God it's over.'

Inigo bit his lip then said, 'I'm sorry, but he also killed your mother.'

'Good riddance to her as well. She knew exactly what he was doing to us, but pretended it wasn't happening. And I remember now, he used to give those silver hearts entwined to the children after he'd had sex with them. Mum wore one, and then he gave one to me after...' She broke down again. 'I'd buried it in my memory.'

***

Jess arrived at the same time as the ambulance. The paramedics put Tig, Sophie Wilson, and Tony Saunders in the back.

Inigo said to Tony before the doors were slammed shut, 'Once I've done the write-up, you'll get a medal and a promotion for what you did in there.'

'I'm just glad Tig is OK.'

'Yeah, aren't we all?'

Tig was staring into space. Her wrists and ankles had livid lines around them where the plastic restraints had dug into the skin. It also looked as if she'd fractured her right upper arm when the chair had fallen over. Inigo knew she'd need a whole bucketful of therapy before he got her back in one piece, but she was still young, and he'd help her.

Forensics arrived. They found the Wilsons dead in the kitchen. Sophie Wilson was now an orphan.

As the ambulance disappeared up the driveway, he realised Tony had the keys to the car in his pocket. He asked Hudson and Martin to give him a lift back to the Primary School, but before he could leave, Jess caught his attention.

'Come to my house tomorrow night at seven.'

His brow furrowed. She'd never invited him to her house before. 'Because?'

'I'll cook you a meal, and we can talk about Marielle.'

'Are you sure you want to do that? It could end in disaster.'

'I'm willing to take a chance, if you are.'

He rubbed his two-day-old beard. 'I suppose I'll get a decent meal out of it.'

'Hey, don't do me any favours.'

'I thought we weren't going to argue.'

'When I don't love you, I hate you.'

'The feeling's mutual. See you tomorrow night.'

## About the Author of *As You Sow, So Shall You Reap*

**Tim Ellis** is a retired soldier, bean counter, and teacher. He has been writing fiction for five years and is the best-selling author of a number of crime novels. He has also written historical fiction, science fiction, and fantasy.

# *Rum Shot*

## by Lawrence Kelter

# Chapter-1

## 1963

John Angel swung the steering wheel on his cherry red Thunderbird convertible and turned heads as he made his way onto Collins Avenue in Miami Beach, Florida. The T-Bird was waxed up brighter than a shiny new dime. The chrome front bumper blinded the valet as he pulled up in front of the Fontainebleau Hotel.

The valet recognized Angel and raced around the car to open the door. "Good afternoon, Mr. Angel. So nice to see you again."

Angel swung his legs out of the car and dusted the lint off of his sharkskin slacks before he stood up. His jacket shirt was crisply pressed and flawless. He stuffed a few bills in the valet's pocket. "Park her in the shade, Sonny."

"Very good, Mr. Angel. I'll find a nice spot for her."

Angel strode through the hotel's massive open-air lobby—his slipstream hair was impervious to the strong winds that blew off the Atlantic. The sixty-five-hundred-square-foot pool area stretched out in front of him. Beyond the pool, the turquoise water of the Atlantic sparkled as if it was filled with emeralds. Tito Puente was playing on the Fontainebleau's outdoor sound system. Angel spontaneously broke into a cha-cha as he stepped into the sunshine.

A pretty brunette in a calico bikini looked up from her lounge chair and caught a glimpse of Angel as he tripped the light fantastic. "You're light on your feet." She smiled and held up a bottle of baby oil. "Would you?" she said. Her expression was an invitation to apply the baby oil and more.

Angel flashed his pearly whites. He knelt so that he could look directly into her eyes. "What's your name?"

She smiled sweetly. "Honey."

"Really?"

"Uh-huh."

"Well, *Honey*, it's so hot down here the lizards carry parasols. Baby oil is the worst thing you can put on your skin."

"It is?" she said, with an air of helplessness in her voice.

"*It is*, but if you give me your room number, I promise to stop by later and show you a good use for it."

She gasped.

"You seem shocked," Angel said.

"I am," she said and then brought forth a devilish smile. "Room 710. What time should I expect you?"

"Hard to say; I'm working right now."

"I'll be waiting. "

"That's a good girl," Angel said. He gave her cavalier pat on the butt as he walked off.

He pulled out a roll of cash. The sound of the crisp bills stopped a waitress dead in her tracks. "Can I help you, sir?"

"Where can I find Roger Hollister's cabana?"

"It's on the ocean side. I'll take you."

Angel dropped a few bills on her serving tray. "Bring me a seven and seven. Back it up in exactly ten minutes."

She took note of the bills on her tray and smiled. "My pleasure. Follow me."

Angel followed the waitress as she zigzagged through the sunbathers and lounges to Hollister's cabana.

A dark-haired woman almost knocked Angel over as she burst from the cabana.

"Get out!" Hollister bellowed. His voice was resentful and filled with indignation, "Gypsy! Charlatan! Get out!"

The fortune teller rushed through the pool area and disappeared into the lobby.

"What the hell was that?" Angel said. He looked at Hollister as if he were crazy. He entered the cabana. "I can't believe you're still into that mumbo jumbo. I guess she didn't give you any good news."

"Not even the winning horse at Hialeah." Hollister's voice sounded more normal. His heavy English accent was once again discernable.

"You know it's all bullshit. Why did you get so mad at her?"

"Ah hell, Johnny, the gypsy was spot on," he said with frustration in his voice. "Washington's been pressuring 10 Downing Street for months now. America will be in the Vietnam War by this time next year. Officially, the Labour Party is against going to war in Southeast Asia but that doesn't mean that MI5 won't be involved. We've been discussing the situation for months."

"And Her Majesty's Secret Service wants you up close and personal?"

"Correct. England has to do something to endear itself to the White House."

"Well, do you want to live a long, happy life, or do you want to die a hero?"

Hollister broadcast a dashing smile reminiscent of Errol Flynn. "I'll take a hero's funeral anytime."

"And the gypsy knew all that?"

Hollister shrugged and then patted Angel on the back. "There's nothing like a cold war to keep everyone on their toes."

"It's still hot here in Miami."

"Indeed, the Bay of Pigs Invasion, Russian missiles just ninety-miles off shore—you Floridians must sleep with one eye open."

"I sleep just fine."

Hollister smiled. "Glad to hear it. Thanks for coming."

They sat down at a bridge table within the cabana just as the waitress returned with Angel's drink. She stirred it with a swizzle stick while it was still on her tray and then handed it to him. "Another bottle of water for you, Mr. Hollister?"

Hollister winked. "Straight away, Love."

The waitress walked away immediately.

Hollister admired her as she moved off. "She's got a

lovely bum, that one. I might ask her out for a drink."

"Forget the broad. You actually pay for water?"

"You must try this, John. It's called Perrier. The Fontainebleau is the only place in the states that has it. It comes from France and has bubbles."

"Around here we call that seltzer."

"It's lovely; really, you must try it."

"How much?"

"It's not cheap."

"Someone should talk to the prime minister about your expense account, Roger. Who in their right mind would spend big bucks on water?"

"Take pity on me, I'm here on a hazardous assignment," Hollister said playfully. He sounded as if he were begging for sympathy.

Angel took a long sip of his cocktail. "Yeah, I guess. So what does British intelligence need from a local guy like me?"

"Read the papers much, Johnny?"

"Every morning."

"What do the words *ich bin ein Berliner* mean to you?"

"I just told you that I read the newspaper. It's a quotation from the speech JFK made in Berlin last month. It was an endorsement of the West Germans."

"Correct. What a lovely piece of oration that was and so heartfelt. He's a great speaker, that one . . . Jack Kennedy loves Berlin, did you know that?"

"No."

"Well, he does; he likes it a great deal, especially the female population, savvy?" Hollister tapped a cigarette out of a fresh pack and gripped it between his lips. "Care for one, Johnny? They're Turkish."

"No, thanks. So, what does the First Lady do while JFK is out satisfying his cravings for pretty German women?"

"She has tea with the German chancellor's wife, cuts ribbons, and does whatever else dutiful wives do if they want to ignore their husband's indiscretions and continue to be the First Lady."

Angel finished his drink. "I'm listening."

"Her name was Kristina Braun, an absolutely stunning little blonde with lovely legs."

"You said, 'was.'"

"That's right, she's dead, and that's why I asked you here."

"Roger, I'm just a local PI. International politics and the president's dead mistress are a little over my head. Now if you need someone to track down a bail jumper, I'm your man."

Hollister tapped Angel on the knee. "Forget the high-level stuff; that's not why I need your help."

The waitress returned with Angel's second drink and Hollister's bottled water. Angel had asked for a second round to remind him that ten minutes had passed—to cut the meeting short if he wanted to. Now, however, he felt himself intrigued with Hollister's tale. He tasted the fresh cocktail. It was much stronger than the first. He waited for the waitress to leave. "You've got an audience; go on."

"Kristina wasn't German. Her actual name was Christine Kersey. She was a Brit from Manchester, in fact. She was one of ours. We positioned her in Berlin and made her accessible to old Jack. He took a fancy to her straight away." Hollister poured his bottled water into an ice-filled glass and drank without removing the unlit cigarette from his mouth. "As we figured he would."

"All right, Roger, it's time for you to connect the dots for me."

"Well, don't you see, Johnny, women who don't object to putting out for the Crown, don't object to putting out at all. Jack arranged for her to make a trip stateside. He set her up down here and . . ."

"And what?"

"Well, all that sneaking around must have worn thin on old Jack. In no time at all, he stopped taking the midnight flight to Miami."

"Really, he got tired of her that fast? DC to Miami is only ninety minutes in the air."

"A high-functioning man like Jack Kennedy? I'm not surprised. I suppose Kristina got bored just as fast. So, here she is, a beautiful, young woman in Miami; her last lover was the President of the United States, and well . . . hell, man, how do you follow an act like that?"

"I'm clueless, Roger. Tell me, what did she do?"

"She found someone with money and power, someone who could make her feel like she was on top again. Figuratively speaking, that is."

Angel smirked. "So who was the lucky guy?"

"Sal Bobano."

Angel's mouth dropped. "Ah, shit. . . really? She goes from the commander-in-chief to a Cosa Nostra boss?"

"It wouldn't be the first time. JFK seems to travel in those circles. I mean when he's not busy fronting for the colonies, of course. No doubt you've heard the rumors that he and Momo Giancana were both diddling Judy Exner?"

"So, JFK has a healthy appetite for the lovelies. Judy Exner's still alive. Why is Kristina Braun dead?"

"That's exactly what we want to know. We don't fancy our agents turning up dead, and we like it even less when we don't understand what's happened to them. I arrived here from the UK last night for the purpose of debriefing her. We were to meet this morning for just that reason. Unfortunately, someone preempted our meeting."

"Roger, come on; you've got a mobster and the president of the United States playing footsie with the same woman, and you want to know why she's dead? I can see where her death could be the solution in any number of scenarios. You don't need a PI; you need the FBI, CIA, and the Secret Service. You don't take a Rolls Royce to Earl Scheib for a paint job. Bring in the big guns and throw a little money around; you'll get results."

"American intelligence doesn't know that Kristina worked for us, and we'd like to keep it that way—on the QT, if you will. We had our reasons for putting that pair together, and we'd like the secrecy of our little plan to remain intact. I can't afford to have American intelligence become interested in this. Do a little checking around and report back to me if you find anything you think might be useful. It pays five hundred a day."

"*Wow*. That's a big chunk of change. So why *did* you put an agent in JFK's bed?"

Hollister stood up and walked to the wide entrance of his cabana. The brunette waitress was bent over, placing a drink on a lounge table. Hollister had an excellent point of view. "That, my dear boy, is a Crown secret. We simply want to know the details of her death." He reached into the pocket of his cabana set and handed Angel an envelope. "One week in advance."

"This is a lot of cash, and I'm not ignoring it, but you're going to have to tell me more before I take the case. This isn't exactly a minor-league assignment." He tried to hand the envelope back to Hollister, but Hollister's arms were folded across his chest. He was still admiring the brunette.

"Look here; hold onto the money, Johnny. You see the room key lying on the table over there?"

Angel picked up the key and examined it. The key fob was imprinted with the Fontainebleau's banner. "It happened here?"

"Yes, old boy, it happened here. Go have a sniff around, and let me know if you get hungry. Worst case scenario, you and I take a puddle jumper over to Puerto Rico for some late-night gambling on the Crown's tab." He turned to face Angel. "As I said, this all happened early this morning. I've managed to keep this under wraps, but we'll have to move quickly. I won't be able to keep it quiet for long."

Angel nodded. "What about the body?"

Hollister reached into his pocket and withdrew a lighter. He finally lit the cigarette that had been clenched between his lips. "Oh, I'm saving the best for last. Go have a look around. I'll be waiting here."

# Chapter-2

Angel swung the room key on his finger as he approached the concierge's desk. "Santo, what's shaking?" Angel said. He was already reaching for his wad of cash.

"Mr. Angel, what a lovely—"

"Yeah, yeah, yeah, look, Santo, I'd love to chat, but I just don't have time for pleasantries." He had a folded twenty in his palm as they shook hands. Santo didn't even flinch as he stashed the bill in his pocket. "The doll staying on the top floor, Kristina Braun: I need a list of her phone calls, incoming and outgoing . . . the whole enchilada."

"Done, John. Anything else?"

"Anyone visit her that I should know about?"

Santo made a face that said, "Are you kidding? You mean other than John-fucking-Kennedy?"

Angel chuckled. "What was I thinking? Tough to keep something like that quiet, I guess."

"They're talking about it from here to Palm Beach. I mean we get celebrities in here all the time: Sinatra, Sammy Davis Jr., you name it, but the president, I mean that gets attention. I'm surprised you haven't heard."

"How long did that go on?"

"Often, from what I've been told. I leave at eight, but I get an earful every morning from the boys on the night shift . . . Cadillacs rolling in late at night, black suits and sunglasses . . . They used the freight entrance, but the president's the president. Everyone knows who he is."

"Did she have any other *special* visitors?"

"Why, JFK's not special enough?"

"Anyone else I should know about is what I'm

asking."

Santo shrugged. "I don't remember anyone else."

"Did she go out a lot?"

"She was in and out of here all the time. I must have called her a dozen cabs myself."

"No idea where she went?"

"No."

"How did she dress?"

"Smart: nice dresses, nude stockings, and black pumps. Great legs, man. The kind that makes a guy want to whistle."

"Do you remember any of the cabbies?"

Santo rubbed his eyes, while he struggled to remember. "Ah, I don't know. It's Miami; there are hundreds of cabbies in and out of this place every day. I'm here less than a year—I'm still trying to get used to the palmetto bugs."

"Oh yeah, I forgot. You're a California boy—where'd you say you worked before this?"

"The Beverly Hills Hotel," Santo said proudly.

"Nice place?"

"Hell yeah. You think this place is fancy? The Beverly Hills Hotel has movie stars up the wazoo: Doris Day, Bob Hope, John Wayne, Natalie Wood—I've got souvenirs and autographs from some of the biggest names in Hollywood."

"Sounds great. So why'd you give up a sweetheart setup like that?"

"Family . . . you know how it is."

Angel sighed. "Okay, look, how long for the phone list?"

Santo shrugged. "I don't know. How often do you think I get asked for something like that?"

Angel was already reaching into his pocket for a fresh twenty.

Santo smiled. "Give me an hour."

# Chapter-3

Angel caught the elevator up to the top floor. Kristina Braun's room key was once again spinning on his finger as he approached the door. The *Do Not Disturb* sign was hanging from the doorknob.

It was a nicely appointed suite with linen furniture and a large credenza. The Atlantic was visible through the open patio doors. Angel watched the powerful surf land on the beach for a moment before he began to look around the room. The suite had a full kitchenette with an electric cooktop, sink, and a full-sized refrigerator.

It was mid-afternoon, and the room was unbearably hot. Angel closed the patio doors and switched on the air conditioner. He did a three-sixty to quickly take in the sitting room. *Nothing has gone on here,* he thought. Everything was in its place—the room looked as if it had been freshly made up.

A short alcove led to the bedroom area. The bedroom looked normal. There was no sign of a struggle and no blood. Nothing had been smashed or broken. An empty bottle of rum was lying on the carpet next to the bed. Angel examined the indentations in the mattress and opined that two people had slept in it. *Where the hell is the body?*

Angel checked the carpet for bloodstains and then walked into the bathroom. *Nothing out of order,* he observed.

As he walked back into the bedroom, he inspected a side chair to make sure it was evidence-free. He plopped down and took a moment to gather his thoughts. *A hot broad, a horny gangster, steamy sex . . . Why did he kill her?*

The hotel room was still dreadfully hot. He began to sweat. *What am I looking for?* He sat for minutes before he began to search for clues.

He got up and walked into the kitchen. "Christ," he grumbled. "I hope there's something cold to drink." He yanked open the refrigerator door. *"Holy shit!"* His arms shot out just in time to catch the naked body of Kristina Braun as it tumbled out of the refrigerator and into his arms.

# Chapter-4

Angel dragged the body a few feet and placed it gently in the center of the kitchen floor. He noticed that her skin was coated with a sticky substance that felt tacky on his fingertips. He stepped back and looked her over from head to toe. *What a body!* She wasn't much more than five feet tall. *Not an ounce of fat.* There wasn't a mark on her. Her skin was smooth and perfect without any apparent bruises or swelling. There were no punctures or stab wounds.

A thought hit him like a mule's kick. He left the body and began to yank open all of the kitchen cabinets, one by one. There wasn't much to see, only some basic utensils, dishes, and a coffee pot. He raced into the sitting room and opened the large credenza drawers. One of the drawers was filled with the refrigerator shelves. "Oh, that's beautiful," he said. "Come to daddy."

# Chapter-5

Angel walked to the kitchen sink and turned on the hot water. He smelled his fingers before he washed them and detected a sugary smell. He licked his fingertips. "Rum?"

He washed his hands and dried them. The telephone was only a few feet away. "Operator, please connect me with Roger Hollister's cabana." He heard the phone ring on the other end of the line.

Hollister picked up quickly, "You're slowing down, Johnny. What took you so long?"

"You're a real jerk, Roger. Why did you leave the poor little thing in the refrigerator?"

"*Because, Johnny*, I couldn't call the police, and I didn't want her to rot. I wanted you to find her in the same condition that I did."

"You scared the shit out of me."

"Lily-livered Yankee," he chuckled. "Find anything?"

"I have the refrigerator shelves that the murderer removed to make room for the body. If we're lucky, they'll have prints all over them."

"Clever lad."

"Do you know anyone discreet who can dust for prints?"

"Yes, I believe I have just the right fellow. He'll check for prints and make arrangements to move the body."

"Great, so what do I do with the body for now? I can't just leave her lying on the kitchen floor."

"Do what I did, Johnny. Stuff her back in the fridge."

# Chapter-6

Angel rode the elevator back down to the lobby. Santo gave him the "high sign" as soon as he stepped out of the elevator. Santo walked out of the lobby and past Sonny the parking attendant. He lit a cigarette.

"What have you got?"

Santo reached into his pocket and handed Angel a sheet of paper that had been torn from a legal pad. "I was surprised. She didn't make many calls."

"Thank God," Angel said. He took the phone list and folded it in quarters without examining it. "I thought that women like to talk."

Santo took a drag on his cigarette. "You ever meet a woman who didn't?"

He handed Santo an extra twenty. "Nice work."

"Thanks." He looked Angel over. "You don't look like your usual cool, calm, and collected self. I didn't think a guy like you had any sweat glands."

"Yeah, I could use a shower."

"No problem. I can fix you up with an empty room— have your shirt washed and pressed in under an hour."

"Thanks, but I've got it covered."

Santo nodded, "Okay," and then took a heavy drag that burned the cigarette paper down to the filter. "So why are you interested in her? She do something wrong?"

"Everyone's done something wrong, Santo. It's all just a matter of degree." He placed the list of phone numbers in his pocket. "Stay cool."

Angel reentered the lobby and took the elevator up to the seventh floor. He found room 710 and knocked on the door. Honey answered wearing a towel. "I didn't expect you so soon. I just got out of the shower," she said.

"You look good to me." Angel's gaze traveled down to

her long, tan legs which emerged from the bottom of a white bath sheet. Her toenails were polished cherry red, the same shade as Angel's convertible.

Honey blushed. "You scared me with all that talk about the baby oil being bad for you. I figured I had better wash it off." She gave Angel a knowing smile. "Come on in."

"Thanks, got anything to drink?"

"Rum and Coca-Cola. Would you like me to fix you a drink?"

"I'd love one." He noticed that the bottle of rum was the same brand as the empty bottle he had seen in Kristina Braun's room. It was a local favorite named *Dos Cristo*. "Mind if I rinse off?"

"Go right ahead. It'll give me a chance to change."

"Don't go to any trouble for me," Angel said as he swaggered into the bathroom.

Honey began humming "Runaround Sue" and filled two glasses with ice.

~~~

Angel awoke with Honey nuzzled comfortably against his arm. He looked out through the glass patio doors and saw that the sun was now low in the sky. He checked his watch. It was almost 6:00 p.m. His mouth was pasted shut. He reached for his glass of rum and Coke. All that was left in the glass was melted ice and water. He downed it quickly and then slid his pinned arm out from under Honey. He dressed quickly and left the room.

# Chapter-7

By the time Angel got home, it was after 7:00 p.m. There wasn't much daylight left in the sky. He could see the sun setting over his rooftop as he pulled the T-Bird into the garage.

He made himself a fresh drink and sat down with Santo's phone list. As Santo said, she had only made a few calls. He picked up the phone and dialed the first number.

He heard the sound of an answering machine. "Thank you for calling *Caña de Cuba*, the home of *Dos Cristo*, the world's finest rum. Our offices are closed. Please call back during normal business hours."

Dos Cristo? Again?

Angel grabbed the Yellow Pages from under his coffee table and looked it up. He checked *Dos Cristo* first and found nothing listed. He flipped back a few pages and found *Caña de Cuba.* The phone number was listed along with an address that Angel knew was near the port. The listing also said *See Our Full Page Ad.* The ad contained a sketch of a bottle of *Dos Cristo.*

He circled the phone number on his list and jotted the address down next to it along with the company's name. The next phone number on the list caused him to become alarmed. It was his.

# Chapter-8

Angel swallowed his drink and then raced back to his car. He was back on the road in a minute flat. The tires smoked as the T-Bird fought for traction. He had only made it to the corner when a car skidded into the intersection in front of him. He slammed on the brakes and brought the T-Bird to a hard stop. He watched as the door opened, and a detective he recognized got out and walked up to his car. "Rojo, what the hell? You could have killed me."

"What's your hurry, Angel? I heard your car burning rubber."

"Just checking to see if the T-Bird still has the goods."

Rojo was a slight Cuban with greasy hair and a goatee. "Don't be rude, Angel; get out of the car and talk to me." Rojo walked to the front fender and lit a cigarette. Angel shook his head and then reluctantly joined him.

"So what's going on?" Angel asked. "I'm on a case."

"A case that involves Kristina Braun?"

"No. Why?"

"She's missing and may be dead. We got an anonymous tip from someone at the Fontainebleau saying they saw a body getting rolled out of her room. We checked and found the room empty."

"Did you find anything suspicious?"

"Nothing much, only that the shelving had been removed from the refrigerator and that there were traces of rum smudged on the inside of the refrigerator and the kitchen floor."

"No blood? No signs of a struggle?"

"No, nothing."

"What does all this have to do with me?"

"We questioned the staff and checked her phone

calls. I recognized your phone number right away. Are you working for her?"

"Working for her? No, I'm not working for her. Lots of people call me—I must have missed her call. You know that I don't have a secretary. Listen, why are we beating around the bush, Rojo? I'm sure you know what I know."

"And what's that?"

"That Kennedy was seeing a pretty German broad at the Fontainebleau. You have no idea where to look for her?"

"Not yet."

"Well, let me know when you do. Now, can I get back to work?"

"You were at the Fontainebleau this afternoon. You mean to tell me you don't know anything about this?"

"Sorry, Rojo, I was on a date with a pretty brunette with a smile like Annette Funicello. She's in Room 710—you can check it out if you don't believe me."

Rojo threw his cigarette on the ground and crushed it with his heel. "All right, Angel, I know you're smooth, but if I find out that you're lying to me . . ."

"Don't give it a second thought, Rojo. I always cooperate with the police. Now if you'll excuse me . . ."

"I don't like being conned, Angel. Don't piss on my boot and tell me it's raining."

"Look, man, you're looking for a German doll who was having an affair with the president of the United States. I can think of all kinds of people who might want to get to her, and I know that you can too. Does this sound like a case for a local PI like me?"

Rojo walked away without answering.

Angel got back into his car and drove south in the direction of the port. He was familiar with many of the warehouses near the Port of Miami and their customary hours of operation. The offices of *Caña de Cuba* may close at five o'clock, but the shipping department works all night.

# Chapter-9

Salvatore Bobano looked down at the warehouse floor through the window of his mezzanine office. Cartons of rum were stacked in aisles as far as the eye could see. Bobano oversaw alcohol distribution in Miami for the Giancana Crime Family. They controlled all the major labels and their distribution throughout southern Florida.

He sat down at his desk and poured two fingers of *Dos Cristo* into a tall glass and threw it down. He smacked his lips and poured another. He pulled out a nylon duffle bag from beneath his desk and unzipped it. He checked the contents: a clean change of clothing, ten thousand in cash, bullets, and a Makarov PM pistol, a Russian automatic. He unclipped his waistband holster and locked his Colt in the desk drawer.

The phone rang. Bobano let it ring twice before answering. "Hello?"

"Sal, that you?"

"Yes, Momo, I'm getting ready."

"Do you have the Russian piece?"

"Yeah, I'm checking it now. It's seen better days, you know. I hope it don't jam. Can I bring my Colt just in case?"

"No. You know you can't. Don't you think you should have checked the Russian gun before now? What time are you leaving?"

"After midnight. We've got an independent charter plane waiting for us. We should land well before dawn."

"I don't have to tell you that there's a lot riding on this—no mistakes, Sal. Got it?"

"Yes, Momo, I understand. I'll oversee it personally."

"Good! Call me when you get back. We'll celebrate."

"Sounds good, Momo." Bobano hung up the phone. Giancana was getting paid one hundred thousand and

Bobano's cut was forty percent. He smiled as he thought about the money. He ejected the clip and checked the slide on the Makarov pistol.

"No mistakes, Sal."

Bobano was startled by a mocking voice. He instinctively reached for the clip but in his panic knocked it off the desk. He looked up and saw a gun pointed at him. "Who the fuck are you? How long have you been standing there?"

"No mistakes, Sal," the stranger repeated.

"What are you, a fucking parrot? You'll never make it out of here. I've got men—"

"Down at the pier? Unloading the ship? The warehouse floor is empty." He pushed the door closed. He rapped on the glass panel that overlooked the warehouse floor. "This is double-thick plate glass to keep the noise from the warehouse out of your office."

"Look, I don't know who you're working for, but I've got ten grand that says it ain't worth all the trouble my death is going to bring you. It's right here in the duffle bag."

The gun spat twice—two bullets in the chest. Bobano wheezed as his last breath sailed past his lips.

Bobano's murderer unzipped the duffle bag and checked the contents. "Your money won't undo your insolence, but it will come in handy." The Makarov was still in Bobano's grip. He pried it free and dropped it in the duffle bag along with the clip that had been lying on the floor. He was on his way to the door before he noticed the open bottle of rum on Bobano's desk. He replaced the cap and put it in the duffle bag. "Thanks," he said. "Killing makes me thirsty."

# Chapter-10

John Angel saw two bright flashes of light come from the mezzanine window as he pulled up in front of the *Caña de Cuba* warehouse. He opened the glove box and grabbed his gun. He could see the forklifts moving freight at the far end of the pier. He could just make out the sound of their engines.

The warehouse was quiet. Cases of alcohol were stacked ten-feet high in aisles from one end of the warehouse to the other. From his vantage point at the entrance, he could see that there was no movement in the mezzanine office, but a man was slumped over in a chair by the desk. He held his gun at the ready as he made his way to the staircase that led to the office.

Angel moved slowly and cautiously up the stairs. The office door was open. He walked in and checked to make sure that he was alone. A dead man was sitting in a desk chair. There were two bullet holes in the man's white shirt, which was stained with blood. Angel checked the man's pulse just to make sure that he was gone. He pulled the man's wallet from the pocket of his slacks. The wallet contained lots of cash and a Florida driver's license. The victim's name was Salvatore Bobano. A partially filled drinking glass contained an amber-colored liquid. Angel sniffed the glass. *Rum.* "This stuff will kill you," he said to Bobano. "You're the second one today."

He picked up the phone and dialed. It rang four times before the operator at the Fontainebleau answered. "Roger Hollister's room, please."

"One moment," the operator said.

"Hollister."

"Bobano's dead."

"You're covering a lot of ground, Johnny."

"Did you hear me? I said that Bobano's dead."

"How do you know?"

"I'm standing over his body as we speak. I'm at his warehouse. I saw the muzzle flashes in his office window as I pulled up, but his killer took off—I missed him."

"Interesting."

"I don't find murder interesting. I find it frightening. That's two related deaths in one day. I want to get clear of this case before I become number three. My life is worth a hell of a lot more than five hundred bucks a day."

"I completely agree. Do you have any idea who shot him?"

"None. I also don't know who dialed my home phone number from Kristina Braun's hotel suite. Any ideas, Roger?"

"None, Johnny. How do you know about this?"

"A Miami detective named Rojo stopped me for questioning. He said that he received an anonymous tip. Someone saw Kristina's body being rolled out of her room. Whoever you used to remove her body was sloppy. Rojo checked the hotel telephone records just as I had and saw that a call was placed to my home. I tipped the concierge for a list of Kristina's calls."

Hollister was quiet for a moment. "That doesn't make sense, Johnny. Who would call you?"

"I don't know; someone who's trying to set me up for the murder, maybe."

"I understand what you're inferring. It wasn't me, Johnny. You've known me a long time. I don't operate like that."

"You're a spy, Roger; you'd do anything to protect the Crown. That story about setting Kristina up with Kennedy falls a little short too. I know there's more to it than you're telling me."

"I don't set my friends up as patsies, Johnny. I—" Hollister heard a thud on the other end of the line. "Johnny? Johnny? Are you there? Johnny?"

# Chapter-11

Angel awoke to see Detective Rojo staring at him. "What the hell is going on?" he said. His head ached. He touched the back of his head where his hair was damp and then examined his fingers—they were covered in blood.

"You were cold-conked," Rojo said. "The phone was hanging off the desk. It looks like someone came up behind you while you were on the phone."

It took a moment for Angel to put his thoughts together. "Sounds about right." He sat up and winced. "I thought I was alone."

"Guess not," Rojo said. "So while we're on the topic, what are you doing here with a dead mobster?"

*Guess I have to give him something.* "I got a copy of Braun's phone calls, just like you. This was the first number on the list. That's why you're here, right?"

"That's right. You should have come clean when I stopped you before. I could have your license pulled for that."

"It's a sensitive case. My client wishes to stay anonymous." Angel got to his feet.

"Screw your client, Angel. You'd better spit out some information. You were found alone with a dead man. Your leverage is pretty weak. What do you know?"

"The girl is dead. I went up and checked her hotel suite this afternoon. Someone had stuffed her into the refrigerator."

"So where is she now?"

"I left her where I found her. I don't know who moved the body. I was hired to find out who killed her and why. I'm running down leads just like you."

"Any idea why Bobano took two in the chest?"

"I've got nothing for you, Rojo."

"Who are you working for?"

"You know I won't tell you."

"I can get a subpoena and force you to tell me."

"Sure, go ahead. In the meantime, I've got a case to work on. You're not holding me, are you?"

"No. Your gun hasn't been fired, and I'm reluctant to believe that you were able to knock yourself out cold after you shot Bobano. No one is going to miss Bobano. He was a slug." Rojo stuffed a business card in Angel's shirt pocket. "I want a call if you come across anything, and I'm not kidding."

A case of rum was lying on the floor near the door. Angel pulled out a bottle, uncapped it, and took a swig. "That's two dead today. I wonder how many more bodies we'll find before midnight." Angel toasted Rojo with the bottle of rum. "See you around."

# Chapter-12

Sonny was still on duty when Angel pulled up in front of the Fontainebleau. "Long day," Angel said. "Pulling a double shift?"

"Management asked everyone to stick around. Someone robbed the office."

"Really, what was taken?"

"I'm not sure. They found the door lock busted about an hour ago. I think they're still taking inventory."

"Are the cops here yet?"

"Haven't seen them. I guess they'll be here soon. You've got some blood on your shirt collar."

"Yeah, I bumped my head. It's nothing. Can you leave the car out front? I won't be here very long."

"Sure thing, Johnny. No problem."

Kristina Braun's hotel suite was not yet an official police crime scene, but it would become one as soon as Rojo returned. Angel had confirmed for Rojo that Braun was, in fact, dead. It was now an official homicide investigation. He unlocked the door to her room and switched on all of the lights. *There's got to be something that I missed. Something killed that girl.* Angel spent the next fifteen minutes going through the room, examining the contents of the drawers and closets. He went through all of her clothing and checked her suitcase and pocketbook. *Nothing. I guess a spy knows better than to leave information just lying around.*

The bottle of rum was still lying on the floor near the bed where he had first seen it in the afternoon. He lifted the bottle using the bed sheet to prevent leaving his fingerprints. He sniffed the rum but did not detect an unusual odor. *There's nothing else,* he thought. He replaced the bottle in the same spot it had originally occupied. He stepped back and felt something under his shoe. His toe was under the bed. He got down on his knees and found a large, burgundy-colored pill buried in the pile of the carpet. "What's this?" He examined the pill. It was an oblong tablet that was marked *B-080.*

# Chapter-13

Angel found an unoccupied payphone in the lobby and inserted a dime. He pulled out his "little black book" and dialed his friend Stan Belsky.

"Hello?"

"Stan, it's John Angel. I'm sorry to call you so—"

"John, it's almost eleven. I'm in bed."

"I know. I'm sorry."

"You know the next time you need some penicillin, you'll have to go to a doctor. You can't call me every time your piss burns. I could lose the pharmacy."

"My johnson is just fine. Is it worth fifty bucks for you to look up a pill for me?"

"Fifty bucks?"

"Yeah, fifty bucks. Can you help me?"

"Hold on. I'll grab my reference book." Angel pictured Belsky fumbling in the dark for his glasses. "Okay, describe it for me."

"It's distinctive. It looks like a small, burgundy football, and it's marked *B-080.*"

"Did you say *B-080?*"

"Yeah."

"I don't need my desk reference for that. Any pharmacist worth his salt knows what a chloral hydrate tab looks like."

~~~

Angel was on his way out of the hotel when Detective Rojo's car pulled to a stop outside the lobby entrance. "Angel, you seem to be one step ahead of me all day. What were you doing inside?"

"I paid my girlfriend another visit. I usually like a late-night pop before I go to bed."

"Fine," Rojo said dismissively. He checked his watch. "Not quite midnight. I hope you don't become the third fatality of the day." He tossed his keys to Sonny. "Leave it right there. Got it, kid?"

"Sure, detective," Sonny said.

Rojo walked into the hotel without looking back at Angel.

"Ready for your car, Mr. Angel?"

"Sure am." Angel pulled out a pair of twenties. "You think you can help me out with a little information?"

Sonny's eyes lit up. "You bet."

"Who would I talk to at the hotel if I wanted to score some drugs?"

"Drugs?" Sonny replied nervously.

Angel gave Sonny a playful slap on the cheek. "Hey! This is me you're talking to—don't play cute. Uppers and downers, where can I get them? Who's dealing?"

Sonny looked around nervously.

"It's okay, kid, we're the only ones out here."

Sonny was only five-foot six. He stood up on his tiptoes and whispered into Angel's ear.

# Chapter-14

Hollister parked his rental car a quarter mile down the road and made his way through the dark using a pen flashlight. The house he was looking for was in a rough area of Dade County on a gravel road without street lamps.

The house was dark when Hollister came upon it. The driveway was empty. He crept up to the window and used his flashlight to look inside. The living room was unoccupied. He used a pocketknife to shimmy the window lock and went inside.

He kept the lights off and used his flashlight to search the house. He didn't want to alert anyone that he was inside. Hollister was a well trained agent. He knew that he had to get in and out as quickly as possible. The fact that the house was currently empty did not mean that it would be empty for long. He went from room to room, quickly and efficiently checking each one. He found several prescription bottles in a dresser drawer in the bedroom. The ceiling fan had been left on. Hollister found the breeze refreshing, but the noise of the fan was loud and distracting. He put the flashlight beam on a prescription label and was about to read it when a bullet hit him in the back and passed through his chest.

~~~

Angel heard the shot. He pulled his gun and scrambled out of the car. A Chevy Nova was parked in the driveway. He could feel the residual heat from the engine as he squeezed past it in the driveway and knew that it had just been turned off. The house was dark. He listened attentively for a sound that would disclose where the shot had come from, but the house was now silent. He checked the side of the house. A window was open. He climbed through it without making a sound.

Angel's eyes quickly adapted to the dark. He was silent as he peered through the living room doorway down a long corridor that led to one of the bedrooms. He could hear the sound of someone in distress, someone injured. The sound of labored breathing reached his ears. He could just barely distinguish the large, shadowy figure of a man pointing a gun at someone on the floor. The breathing of the man on the floor was becoming more erratic.

"Be a man. Pull the trigger."

*Hollister?* Angel recognized the Brit's accent.

"You're English?" the other figure said. "This is not your fight."

"Any good fight is my fight," Hollister said. "Why did you kill the girl?"

"Why did I kill the girl? It was a warning, like the last time. Maybe this time our warning won't fall on deaf ears."

"Like the last time?" Hollister said.

"Don't play stupid. You know what I'm talking about. That was my work too. How close do we have to get before the message is understood? How many have to die?"

"How many will Castro kill with Russian missiles if he's not stopped?"

"He won't be stopped. We proved that when we defeated the American forces in the Bay of Pigs Invasion. Here is the bullet you asked for."

Angel heard the rotating of the gun cylinder as the hammer was cocked. He aimed at the shadowy figure and fired. He heard a thud as the man hit the floor.

Angel flipped on the light switch and raced forward to cover the fallen assailant. His bullet had found its mark. It hit Santo near the left shoulder and had severed the brachial artery before exiting his throat. Blood was gushing from the wounds.

"He's a Cuban revolutionary," Hollister said. "He killed Kristina; probably Bobano too."

Life was fading in Santo's eyes. He tried to speak but

was choking on blood.

"Why, Santo?" Angel asked.

"Tell Kennedy," Santo said, "the next time America comes for Castro, Cuba will come for Kennedy." His mouth froze while it was still open, and then he was gone.

# Epilogue

Angel found Roger Hollister's hospital room at the far end of the critical care ward of Jackson Memorial Hospital. Hollister had been hanging on by a thread when Angel left the hospital the night before. He was surprised to hear Hollister's strong voice echoing in the hallway as he approached his room. It allayed any fears he had about his friend's serious condition.

"Tomorrow, and tomorrow, and tomorrow, creeps in this petty pace from day to day . . ." Hollister noticed Angel standing in the doorway. "Johnny!" he boomed in a hearty voice. Hollister's hospital gown was pulled up, exposing his chest wound. A bed sheet covered him from the waist down. A young candy striper was giving him a sponge bath. Hollister's chest was heavily bandaged. The candy striper was carefully cleaning around the bandages.

"*You* look well," Angel said with surprise in his voice.

Hollister smiled heartily. He lifted the candy striper's chin. "This angel of mercy is nursing me back to health."

"Then why in God's name are you punishing her with that painful Shakespearian soliloquy?"

"Why, Johnny, she adores my accent. Don't you, Carmen?"

Carmen squeezed out the sponge and looked up at Angel. "*Si*, he speak *muy* beautiful." She gave Angel a pretty smile and pointed to a chair. "You sit?" Carmen blotted Hollister's chest with a towel. Angel pulled the chair next to Hollister's bed and sat down. "All done," she said. "I go."

"Will you be back soon?" Hollister asked in a needy voice. "I can't possibly manage without your tender care."

Carmen blushed and picked up her supplies. "*Mañana*." She waved to Hollister and left.

Hollister watched her until she was gone. "Had I known that Spanish women are so lovely and caring, I would have taken a bullet much sooner in my career."

"She's probably fourteen, Roger," Angel said in an admonishing tone. "This isn't feudal England—we enforce statutory rape laws here in the colonies. How are you feeling?"

"Other than the gaping hole in my chest?"

"Yes."

"Surprisingly good. Must be all the morphine they've given me for the pain. I think I may be hallucinating."

"You were lucky. The doctor said the bullet missed your heart by a hair."

"I've got nine lives, Johnny. I'm like a cat."

"Oh yeah? Which life are you on now?"

Hollister counted on his fingers. "Eleven, I think—at least eleven, maybe twelve." Hollister laughed and then stopped abruptly. He placed his hand over the wound. "God that hurts."

Angel noticed Hollister's pained expression. "Take it easy. I hope that you're feeling well enough to fill in some of the blanks."

"Well enough, yes, but you know I can't divulge official information. I've sworn an oath to the Crown."

"And I saved your worthless hide. That should be worth something."

"Worth something? You know that I favor a hero's funeral. That's where the glory is. You threw a spanner into the works last night. Now all I have to look forward to is another twenty years of service to the bloody Crown."

"Sorry that I disappointed you, but I need to know, and this time don't bullshit me with tales of British agents picking up with mobsters because Jack Kennedy got bored with them."

Hollister turned serious. "God help me. If I'm found out, I'll tell them that I was delirious from the bloody morphine."

"I don't care what you tell them. Besides, how well do

you know me?" Angel said.

Hollister considered Angel's question. "Bloody well enough, I suppose. What do you want to know?"

"Let's start with what Santo said last night. What's England's involvement in the feud between America and Cuba?"

"England is America's ace-in-the-hole ally. We were assisting the CIA. Kristina was the go-between for the CIA and the mob. She brought Bobano a Russian-made Makarov pistol, which was to be used to kill Castro. As a Brit posing as a German, Kristina was above suspicion by the Cubans. Cuba has been circumspect of CIA agents ever since the Bay of Pigs Invasion . . . American intelligence can't get near the place, but a mobster who imports rum can get in and out of Cuba without a problem. And by using a Russian pistol . . . Well, you understand. We were asked to insert one of our people so that there were no ties back to your intelligence community. Your government has been trying to remove Castro for years."

"By remove, you mean assassinate. I think that's pretty obvious from what Santo said yesterday. 'The next time America comes for Castro, Cuba will come for Kennedy.' Who was Santo and how did you find him?"

"I was disturbed when you told me that someone had called your home from Kristina's suite. You said that you tipped the concierge for a list of her phone calls. More importantly, the last thing out of your mouth was a grunt."

"You figured that Santo was trying to set me up for Kristina's murder, and you broke into the hotel's office to look for Santo's personnel file?"

"Guilty as charged. I obtained his home address and full name, which was Santo Bayo. I made a call to 10 Downing Street and was able to identify Santo Bayo as a member of Castro's Revolutionary National Police. I went to pay him a visit last night. I was examining some prescription bottles when I was shot. You know the rest."

Angel chuckled. "You didn't have to break into the office for Santo's address. All *I* had to do was tip the valet. So the CIA enlisted the mob to kill Castro? How does that wash?"

Hollister shrugged. "All I can say is that it wasn't the first time they've tried that angle—I guess they were going back to the well. I already mentioned Momo Giancana and his relationship with Judith Exner and JFK. That was the same dynamic. Apparently JFK wants Castro dead and doesn't want to get his hands dirty. "

"Sounds like his hands are already filthy."

"And I've said far too much. Have I satisfied your infernal curiosity? There's only so much I can blame on the morphine."

"One more thing, Roger. If Kristina was above suspicion, why was she killed? Santo was ranting about warnings. Was Kristina's death a warning?"

"I believe so, old boy. Kennedy was sleeping with Kristina. By killing her, the Cubans were demonstrating that they could get as close to Kennedy as they wanted to—close enough to kill."

"Santo said that the first warning was his work too."

Hollister averted his eyes. "I feel the morphine wearing off."

"Avoiding eye contact, Roger? That's your tell."

"My tell?"

"You avert your eyes when you want to avoid a subject."

"What the hell are you talking about, Johnny?"

"It all adds up. Santo worked at the Beverly Hills Hotel until about a year ago. I found a pill in Kristina's room just before I went to Santo's house. It was under the bed, buried in the carpet. It's a sedative. I don't know why Kristina allowed Santo into her room, but it seems pretty clear that he fed her lots of rum to mask the taste of the sedatives."

"Perhaps she invited him up for some Latin love—he *was* a big, strapping fellow."

"You Brits, so goddamn droll."

"Sorry."

Angel shook his head sadly. "I guess she never saw it coming—the thing with barbiturate overdose is that you fall asleep and then your heart stops. She was yawning one moment and dead the next. You said that you were looking at prescription bottles just before you were shot." Angel reached into his pocket and showed Hollister the pill he found in Kristina's room. "Did you find any of these?"

"I didn't have a chance to look at the actual tablets. What is it?"

"Chloral hydrate."

"Yes. One of the prescriptions was for chloral hydrate. The other was for Nembutal."

Angel's mouth dropped. "Nembutal? Now there's no doubt." He blew out a deep and troubled sigh. "Santo was living in Los Angeles last August, and he said that he was responsible for the first warning. I called a pharmacist friend of mine last night to help me identify this pill. He knew what it was immediately. He knew what it was because chloral hydrate was found along with Nembutal in the autopsy of a celebrity. You know who Kennedy was seeing."

"You'll have to take this one to the grave, Johnny."

"Just say it," Angel demanded.

"I don't know what you want me to say except . . ." Hollister paused, examined Angel's unwavering expression, and knew that he had to divulge the answer. "Last night you shot and killed the man who murdered Marilyn Monroe."

# About the Author of *Rum Shot*

**Lawrence Kelter** is the best-selling author of the Stephanie Chalice Mystery Series and other works of fiction. A resident New Yorker, he often uses Manhattan and Long Island as backdrops for his stories. He is the author of three novels featuring street savvy NYPD detective, Stephanie Chalice: *Don't Close Your Eyes*, *Ransom Beach*, and most recently, *The Brain Vault*.

Early in his career, he received direction from best-selling novelist Nelson DeMille, who put pencil to paper to assist in the editing of Kelter's first book. DeMille said, "Lawrence Kelter is an exciting new novelist who reminds me of an early Robert Ludlum." Kelter was also a member of a private writer's workshop led by the late soap opera legend, Ann Loring. His novels are quickly paced and routinely finish with a twist ending.

Novels by Lawrence Kelter

*The Stephanie Chalice Mystery Series*
*Don't Close Your Eyes*
*Ransom Beach*
*The Brain Vault*

*Palindrome*
*Kiss of the Devil's Breath*
*Season of Faith*
*Saving Cervantes*
*By Executive Order*

# *Jinxed*

## by Rebecca Stroud

# PROLOGUE

## Monday, September 19 - 7AM

For an officer of the law, Scott McBride had no qualms about breaking it on a regular basis.

But he was also a born and bred beach boy. So when the sun started to peek over the eastern horizon, he and Jinx, his seven-year-old German shepherd, crossed the street, crossed the dunes, and headed to the sea.

Glancing up and down the shoreline, Scott made sure the sand was virtually empty of humans. Sighting a lone fisherman up towards the pier, far enough away to pose no problem, he threw the tennis ball as far as he could and grinned as Jinx bounded after it with unbridled enthusiasm.

He hadn't bothered to bring his surfboard, as he knew the waves would be nonexistent, which they were. So he simply squatted and waited for his girl to return the ball for another toss...or ten.

As this part of the beach was a "no dogs allowed" section, Scott nevertheless risked the wrath of one of his fellow officers so that he could give Jinx some much-needed exercise—and joy—before he started another long day at work. Another long day she would spend alone. Besides, he felt the ordinance was silly anyway, especially when he noticed a feral feline slinking through the sea oats.

*Ah, bureaucracy...ain't it the cat's meow*, he thought, as he threw the ball again.

* * * * *

Erin Gray stood on her tenth-story balcony, sipping coffee. Leaning on the rail, a soft breeze blew her long, red hair behind her in a gleaming trail of gold. She lifted her face to the morning sun, then returned her gaze to the beach...and smiled at the sight of the man tossing a ball for his dog. Sparkles of light glinted off the water, dancing around the pair below.

From her bird's-eye view, they both looked like gorgeous creatures. The man: tall, tan, and lanky. Sun-bleached hair. The dog: a huge black-and-silver shepherd with perfect conformation. Her smile widened at the picture-postcard scene.

Although Erin was well aware that dogs were not allowed on "her" beach, she couldn't care less when she saw canines romping with their people along the shore. A recently ordained veterinarian, Erin loved all animals and she had the lineage to prove it.

Raised on an Ocala thoroughbred farm, she'd been surrounded by various domestic and wild creatures while growing up. Her natural inclination to protect those who could not do so themselves had steered her straight to the University of Florida's veterinary program, where she had excelled. A part-time opening at the new SPCA clinic in Cocoa Beach had lured her in without a second thought as she didn't need the money. She came from tons of it, so it was a win-win situation for her: Erin helped and she healed and she donated over half of her earnings to various local humane organizations.

Plus, she had the additional bonus of the glorious view below her and she wouldn't trade this early show for anything. Besides, Erin was just as guilty as the man. Every evening, right before dark, she took Bo—her ancient mutt—for a short stroll along the water's edge. She took another drink of coffee and thought she just might have to change her routine. Dogs were, after all, a great conversation starter.

# CHAPTER ONE

**Six Months Later...**

**Thursday, March 22 - 1PM**

Luki Hasan tuned out the perky real estate agent as he surveyed the penthouse. Way more space than he'd ever need—or use—but this was all a ruse anyway. All he wanted was to get in, get his revenge, and get out before his brain exploded with the rage that had been building since last week's call from his father.

Born in Saudi Arabia to a richer-than-rich oil man, Hasan had come to the United States six years ago to attend Embry-Riddle in Daytona Beach. He'd graduated with honors and a pilot's license and decided to hang out in Florida for a while, contemplating where he wanted to go, what he wanted to do with his life.

Part of the answer came when he received the news that his twin sister had committed suicide. Raped at eighteen by one of his father's American cronies, Lana had paid a hefty price for her perceived adultery. A strict Muslim, Amir Hasan had beaten his daughter senseless, leaving her with disfiguring physical scars and emotional wounds that never healed.

His father's message had been short and succinct. According to him, Lana had shed her burka, written "whore" across her breasts with charcoal, and hung herself—stark naked—in the grand salon of her father's mansion. End of a sad life and an embarrassing story. *Praise Allah,* Daddy had said with a soft sigh of relief that Luki heard quite clearly thousands of miles away.

\* \* \* \* \*

Florida's fickle weather was behaving itself by providing warm temps for the onslaught of spring breakers flocking to Cocoa Beach. Because of the less frantic pace surrounding this small beach town, it was fast becoming popular with college kids from all over the country. Especially around the pier which housed bars and restaurants and shops and, best of all, the aura of a happening place. There was also a plethora of inexpensive motel rooms to be had where partying could go on into the wee hours of the night.

"It sounds perfect!" gushed 22-year-old Christy Anderson to her roommate, Wendy Stephens, as they sped down I-95. "I know you're skeptical but, trust me, my parents come down here every winter and just love it! Love it, love it!"

"We shall see," Wendy said as she stared out the Corvette's window, hoping Christy was right.

"Oh, Wen, come on. I mean, just think of all the cool dudes we might meet." Christy glanced at her friend. "Really, if we don't have a fabulous time, I'll pay for your trip."

"In that case, I hope you got us a suite at the Hilton."

### Thursday, March 22 - 8PM

Twilight was upon them as they walked hand-in-hand in the gathering darkness, content to watch the dogs splash in the water, having a grand time.

Distracted, Erin glanced up at her penthouse. "Looks like I have a new neighbor," she said.

Noticing the change in tone-of-voice, Scott asked, "And does that bother you?"

"Not really. Other than I came home for lunch to take Bo out and saw the guy getting a suitcase out of his car. I don't know, he seems kinda spooky. But he is very good-looking." Erin grinned.

"Well, I'm glad you think he's spooky since I really don't need any competition this early in the game."

"Not to worry." Erin's big brown eyes met the emerald green of Scott's, and she planted a light kiss on his lips. "Not to worry at all. Let's go in now, and I'll prove it."

* * * * *

Hasan watched the pair from his fully-furnished

condo, part of the reason he'd been so quick to pay the exorbitant rent. All he'd had to do was bring his clothes, and not many at that, as he had no intention of living here very long.

His head started to throb, and he turned away from the sickeningly sweet view. He could think of little else but that his innocent sister had died for no reason while the "unclothed, unclean, and unholy" women of this country paraded around, blatantly flaunting themselves.

Swallowing his intense anger, he checked his watch. Time to shower, shave, and get to work.

* * * * *

After 85-year-old Lenore Rosenberg saw the happy couple return to the building, she moved to her front window. A recent widow who was also stricken with severe arthritis, her sleeping habits were sporadic at best. So, by day, she sat in her rocker and watched people on the beach; by night, she monitored the parking lot. Therefore, she had a front row seat to any action surrounding SeaSide condominiums. Not for the first time, she mused how it beat the hell out of the idiot box.

* * * * *

Amy Blair was working her ass off. A waitress at Bananas on the Beach, she absolutely despised the month of March. Although only twenty-three herself, she never could get used to how much her peers drank when they were on spring break. Not to mention that said peers weren't exactly huge tippers.

*Oh well,* she thought, as she filled another tray with four pitchers of beer. At least she had a job, which was more than she could say for a lot of people. Turning to deliver the order to yet another table full of college students, she almost dumped the whole thing down the shirt of one of the best-looking men she'd seen in ages.

"I am *so* sorry!" Amy said and backed up a few feet. "Did I spill any on you?"

"No problem, darlin'...may I ask your name?" He flashed a dimpled smile of perfect white teeth and Amy felt her heart skip a beat. Four hours later, she was in his arms.

# CHAPTER TWO

**Friday, March 23 - 7AM**

Scott awoke to the bleating of his cell phone. Glancing at the lady asleep beside him and the two dogs snoozing at the foot of the bed, he answered the necessary-but-noisy contraption so as not to awaken any of them.

"McBride here."

"Scott, it's John. I need you up at the pier, pronto."

"Okay." He paused a few seconds. Nothing. "Uh, any more info than that?"

"You'll soon see for yourself," said Cocoa Beach's lead detective. "Don't dally." Click.

Scott slid out from under the covers and, as he dressed, thought about his boss. John Patterson was a former New York City cop who looked like he'd been on the losing end of multiple barroom brawls. But he was one helluva police officer and Scott admired him to the max. So knowing Patterson would never summon him unless it was a dire situation, he grabbed his keys, pecked Erin on the cheek, tapped Jinx on the head, and motioned her to follow. They were both out the door within minutes.

Jabbing the button for the ground floor, he wondered what was up this early in the morning but had no time for further contemplation as the elevator arrived...and Jinx went ballistic.

* * * * *

Lenore stared at the black-clad man as he hurried towards the front entrance. She'd seen him yesterday carrying a few suitcases inside, so figured he was a new resident. Yet there was something very fishy about this guy and she leaned closer to the window to get a better look. Watching his head swivel from right to left—as if he was being chased—she frowned, thinking maybe she should call the police. But what would she say? The man who just moved in looks suspicious? And, more to the point, who would believe that an elderly woman who sat up all night staring out at the parking lot ever had anything worth reporting? Sighing, she settled back in her rocker. It sucked being older than dirt.

* * * * *

Luki's eyes went wide with fright when he saw the snarling dog, fangs bared. "What the fuck!? Get that thing away from me!" he snarled in return.

"I'm sorry, man," Scott said as he grabbed Jinx by her collar and commanded her to sit/stay and shush.

"Yeah, well. Good thing I'm too fucking tired to kick his teeth in."

Frowning, Scott said, "He's a she and, again, I'm sorry. Come on out, she'll be okay." Starting to get a bit pissed, he laid his hand on Jinx's head to calm her down.

"Fucking better be! And since when were dogs allowed here?" Luki glared at the dog.

"Since they were built, over ten years ago. So, if you have a problem with that, guess you moved to the wrong place," Scott spit out the words. "Oh, and by the way, they're allowed on the beach now, too, so better watch out," he added.

"Yeah, well, whatever. I know I'll be filing a complaint with management about dangerous animals roaming the halls."

Scott was now thoroughly pissed. "You do that, pal. Now, for your own good, hurry your ass out of there so we can be on our way."

Luki skirted around the pair as they entered the elevator and Scott watched his receding back with disgust.

"Lovely new neighbor Erin has. A certified asshole," he muttered to Jinx. She growled in response.

* * * * *

Scott reached the pier within fifteen minutes of John's call. Leaving Jinx in his Tahoe, he hurried down to the water's edge and was glad he hadn't eaten breakfast when he saw the woman's body. Or what was left of it.

Splayed on the sand like a petrified starfish, arms and legs spread-eagled, her face was obliterated by stab wounds that the sand crabs had found too enticing to resist. The woman's lips were gone, leaving nothing behind but a death's head grimace. Breasts were gone, too...the word "whore" etched in blood above the gaping holes in her chest.

Scott approached John and asked, "So what do we know so far?"

"A surfer found her. Came out to check the waves and saw her hair wrapped around a piling. Thought it was some weird kind of seaweed. Poor kid's in shock, I think. Anyway, she was sodomized with a sharp instrument—probably the same knife—then strangled...with her hair. Must be at least three feet long." Patterson ran his hand over his face. "And there's so much damn blood, it's a wonder the sharks haven't had a feast yet."

Scott shook his head. All he could think of at the moment was, thank God, he'd left Jinx in the SUV.

...Five years ago, Scott McBride's wife—Debra, by name—had decided that being married to a cop was the absolute pits. So she'd packed her bags, cleaned out the savings account, left a scribbled note that sort of said she was sorry, and split for parts unknown.

Scott didn't bother looking for her. He knew the marriage was a mistake from Day One, especially when Debra started whining about his job on Day Two. But as he had become accustomed to having another living being in the house, he decided to get a dog.

And along came Jinx. Serendipity smiled on both of them when the former Military Working Dog came up for adoption. She'd been severely injured in Afghanistan while trying valiantly to save her handler, who had bled to death in the skirmish.

Because she was so traumatized, Jinx was taken out of commission soon after and returned to the states, where the MWD adoption program began seeking a suitable home. A friend of a friend told Scott her story and he knew then he had to have her.

Her arrival on his doorstep was an instant success. The two floundering souls bonded immediately and Scott knew he'd do anything to protect Jinx...and vice versa.

Over time, Jinx seemed to completely recover from her nightmare. Except for one small detail: she absolutely went berserk at the sight and smell of blood.

* * * * *

Luki was almost hyperventilating after the unexpected encounter with the beast from hell. Fucking dirty animals. Fucking dirty women.

He stripped out of his clothes as fast as he could and jumped in the shower, hoping to rid himself of the repugnance of the last few hours. Praise God, he had the foresight to wear dark colors or else the copious amount of blood would've been a dead giveaway to the man waiting for the elevator.

As he lathered himself from head to toe, he wondered who the guy was. Then he remembered. It was that guy fucking the brazen redhead next door. Slut. All of them, sluts. Luki let the hot water wash away some of his anger...that and the fact he had rid the earth of one of America's hussies allowed him a modicum of peace. Yet he knew in his heart that this was just the beginning, his rage nowhere close to being appeased. Maybe he'd get a few hours sleep, then go hunting again. This time in broad daylight.

### Friday, March 23 - 11AM

Hanging up the phone, Erin looked up as Scott entered her office. Listening to his staccato account of the gruesome sight he'd encountered earlier, her freckled face paled.

"Oh my God! How horrible!" She hugged him tight and gently touched his cheek. "Are you okay??"

"Well, I have to tell you, sweetie, I never in a million years thought I'd see something like that." Scott held her close. "Not here, anyway."

Pulling away, she walked over to the window and hung her head. Her shoulders started to shake. "Jesus, Scott. What kind of freaking monster could do such a thing? Do you know who the girl is?"

"We're trying to find out both identities, babe. Techs are still working on the victim. Again, this kind of shit doesn't happen very often, thank God." He went up behind her and rested his head on top of hers. "Which means, I'll probably be out of pocket a lot until we do catch the bastard. So I wonder if you'd do me a favor?"

Erin whirled around and said, "Anything you need me to do. Anything."

He smiled at her. "Actually, it shouldn't be too hard...would you keep Jinx with you since I'll be gone a helluva lot longer than usual? She'd be good company for Bo and..."

Erin interrupted him. "Of course, I will!" She gave him a rueful grin. "Just wish I could keep you with me, too."

"Well, while you have me, want to grab an early lunch? I finally got a little appetite and I have a feeling this day is going to last a week. How about we go down to Bananas?"

* * * * *

Bananas on the Beach was hustling and so was Suzy Kramer, but her mind was definitely not on the job. Her best friend hadn't shown up for her shift. Neither had repeated phone calls, text messages, nor voice mails yielded a response so Suzy was becoming increasingly worried. *Where the hell was Amy?*

The couple at the corner table briefly took her mind

off her angst as she tried to pick up the slack and hurriedly scribbled their order before being summoned to the back by her boss.

"Suzy. Do you have any idea where Amy is?" The bar and grill's manager looked as frazzled as she felt.

"I'm sorry, Dave, I don't. I've tried everything to get in touch with her but no luck. And I'm getting really concerned."

"Yeah, I know. Amy's never late. Or not without letting me know anyway." He blew a huge sigh and said, "Just hope everything's okay."

"You and me both. I gotta get movin' now."

"Sure. And thanks for pulling the extra weight."

Suzy grabbed the double order of the cheeseburger combo and nearly ran to the couple by the window. "Sorry, we're shorthanded, so it's been a little hectic."

"I can tell," Scott said. "But, hey, you're doing great."

"Thanks. Just hope Amy is," Suzy muttered under her breath.

Noticing the look on the server's face, Scott asked, "Something wrong?"

"Oh, it's just that my friend is supposed to be here, and I don't know where she is. Hope she didn't get snatched by a rapist or anything," Suzy said with a forced laugh.

Scott went on high alert with her words. "Uh, what does your friend look like? I mean, I'm with the Cocoa Beach Police so maybe I can help."

"Really? You're a cop? Anyway, Amy—that's her name, Amy Blair—has really long, blond hair, big blue eyes...beautiful, she is. Just turned twenty-three last week."

Scott's facial expression hid his alarm. "Well, I tell ya what. Here's my cell number. If you don't hear from her by this evening, give me call."

"Gee, thanks. I'm really hoping she just overslept. Maybe had a hangover since she usually goes out after we get off work at night." Suzy hesitated, then said, "I'm married so..."

"Okay, well, don't worry too much. You're probably right. Partying at spring break can be overdone sometimes."

"Hey, thanks again." Suzy glanced over her shoulder. "Gotta go now. Enjoy your lunch."

*Yeah, right,* Scott thought as he punched John's number into his cell. He glanced at Erin and said, "I think we may've just identified our victim."

\* \* \* \* \*

Lenore had nodded off in her perch beside the front bay window and awoke with the sun blazing into the room. Rubbing the sleep from her eyes, she yawned and thought about making something to eat when she saw the creepy new neighbor emerge from the lobby.

Settling back down in her rocker, she watched him climb into a black Cadillac Escalade just like her dear, departed Bernie's, may he rest in peace. She kept watching as he pulled out of a parking space, wondering why he hadn't used his garage yet. Well, waltzing in at the crack of dawn and flying out at noon...must be in one helluva hurry, this one.

Lenore got up and went to the kitchen, the man still on her mind.

\* \* \* \* \*

Christy Anderson slathered on the Coppertone, put on her sunglasses, then plopped a hat on her head. Sitting up to survey the scene, her shining blond hair hung to the sand like a golden cape.

"Isn't this the coolest, Wen?" she asked her roommate who was already lying prone on the blanket, trying to get a tan as fast as she could. "I mean, this place is packed!!"

"Yeah, so I noticed. A little too much for me, but I guess this is what spring break's all about."

"Oh, you're such a party-pooper." Christy's head was jerking in all directions like a drunken marionette and her smile was a mile wide. "Come on, Wendy. Get with the program. Don't you want to meet people? Or at least one person? Like a really cool guy?"

As Wendy Stephens was already engaged to her high school sweetheart who was currently serving another term in the futile Afghanistan war, her entire reason for being in Florida was to take her mind off his deployment.

"Christy. I know you're hot to trot but, duh, remember Mike? My fiance?"

"Okay, okay. Don't get huffy. Just thought you'd at least like to *talk* to someone of the opposite sex. I mean, that's not exactly going to violate your vows, is it?"

Wendy rolled her eyes, then closed them. "No, Christy, it won't. But unless it's someone who's more interested in conversation than a screw job, I'm perfectly fine working on my tan."

"You are no fun, Wen. But, hey. Don't look now. Here comes someone who just might be."

Christy glanced up at the muscular guy looking down at her with a smile that made hers seem like a weak imitation. Shaved head, brilliant white teeth, deep dimples, fathomless black eyes...

"Hi there, pretty darlin'...may I ask your name?" Luki dropped to the sand beside her and Christy Anderson was a goner.

\* \* \* \* \*

After Wendy's half-asleep blessing, Christy scampered off to the pier's open-air Tiki Lounge for a drink with the dark and dashing stranger. A few wine coolers later, she found herself feeling the heat of more than Florida's blazing sun.

"So, Larry, would you like to go out dancing tonight?" Christy batted her eyelashes and grinned, hoping she appeared sufficiently sexy to the hunk across the table who was definitely so.

"Uh, what did you say, darlin'? I was lost in your eyes." Luki had almost forgotten that he'd given this bimbo a false name.

"I said, do you want to go out with me tonight? We could have a really super time," Christy repeated, thinking maybe she'd come on too strong.

"You know, that sounds great. But what I'd really love to do right this minute is ravage your body." Luki winked and flashed his dimples, praying she'd agree.

Christy felt her pulse flutter and took his hand. "If you promise to be gentle, I'd love that, too."

"Cross my heart and hope to die," Luki said as he plunked down a twenty-dollar bill on the table and stood up. "But where can we go? I walked down here, plus my brother was still sleeping when I left the room so we sure as hell don't want to go there, do we?"

Christy laughed and said, "No, we sure don't. So let's go to my motel." She jiggled the Corvette's keys in her purse. "Wendy is stuck for now. But she'll be fine. All she wants to do is bake to a crisp anyway."

Luki pulled out her chair and said, "In that case, after you, my princess. Let's go make magic."

* * * * *

Hot and sweaty from the humidity and the anticipation of "Larry's" body against hers, Christy went right to the thermostat and cranked up the air-conditioning. Turning to him with what she hoped was her most sexy smile, she froze in fright and stammered, "Larry, why on earth did you put your shirt back on? And what's with the rubber gloves?"

Luki's eyes glazed over as he punched her in the mouth. "Shut the fuck up or I'll slit your throat."

Christy's front teeth shattered. She gagged and tried to run for the door. Yanking on her long hair, Luki pulled the switch blade from his jeans pocket and flashed it before the girl's terrified eyes.

"You're all whores. Nothing but dirty whores," he whispered in her ear as he jammed the knife through her neck.

Blood gushed onto his shirt and, disgusted, he continued to ram the knife through Christy's cheeks, mouth...and breasts. Flipping her over, he repeatedly shoved the blade up her shithole in a grisly imitation of intercourse and felt an amazing sense of release.

Panting heavily, Luki stopped and swallowed hard. Taking just a minute to calm himself, he flipped her again and started carving on her stomach.

## Friday, March 23 - 5PM

Beer in hand, Scott joined Erin and the dogs on the balcony. "So, how was your day?"

"Lousy, to be honest. After we had lunch, I had to euthanize two very old dogs and it broke my heart." Erin looked down at Bo, who had just turned twelve. "But, you know, they at least lived good, long lives and their owners loved them dearly. Not like the son-of-a-bitch who dumped Bo just because he didn't want to deal with 'old age' issues. Ain't that right, baby?" Her beloved mutt thumped his tail at the sound of her voice.

Scott draped his arm across her shoulders and said, "Don't know how you do it. I mean, I realize it needs to be done but that has to be really tough."

Erin brushed her hair away from her face along with a tear. "It is and it isn't. We know they can't live forever." She turned and said, "But what about your day? Any progress?"

Scott sighed and took a swig of his Bud Light. "Yeah. The victim was that girl from Bananas, Amy Blair. After what Suzy told us at lunch, I kind of figured that. But still don't have a friggin' clue about her killer. Salt water does an awesome job of diluting evidence if there was even any to begin with."

Erin hugged him. "God, I sure as hell hope you find that it was someone she knew. I mean, we definitely don't need a random rapist here, especially with all the college kids visiting now. Talk about a smorgasbord of flesh, to put it bluntly."

"My thoughts exactly." Scott put his empty can in the garbage, kissed Erin, stroked the two dogs, and headed for the door. "Back to work, babe. Call ya later."

* * * * *

Wendy looked at her watch. "Where the hell are you, Christy?" she mumbled to herself. "Oh, screw it." She packed up their stuff, which amounted to only two towels and a small cooler, and trudged towards the pier, dialing Christy's cell at the same time. No reply.

"Damn! I'm going to kick her horny ass!" Wendy said aloud and kept moving. Thankfully, their motel was within walking distance. Fifteen minutes later, she noticed the Corvette parked in front of their room so she banged on the door, not giving a shit what she might be interrupting. No reply.

Tired and hot and pissed, Wendy fumbled in her purse for her key, shoved the door open with her foot, and dumped the beach baggage on the floor. "Christy! Are you here?" No reply.

Feeling a twinge of alarm, Wendy decided to get a shower, get something to eat, and then try her friend's cell phone again. She walked into the bathroom...vomited, then ran screaming into the parking lot.

* * * * *

Blinds open to let in the afternoon light, Lenore was feeling pretty chipper so was watching TV when, out of the corner of her eye, she saw her weird new neighbor trotting towards the lobby, again looking in all directions as if being chased...

...Erin decided to take the dogs down to the beach for a walk. Maybe work out some of the lingering sadness she still felt about her day on the job. Both Jinx and Bo were anxious to get out in the fresh air so Erin held their leashes close as she waited for the elevator.

The bell dinged and she started to go in as Luki Hasan flew out...right into the snarling face of the huge German shepherd.

Scared shitless, Luki kicked at Jinx and, instead,

connected with the side of Bo's leg. The old mutt let out a yelp of pain and that's all it took for Jinx to go into attack mode.

Pulling back on the leash as hard as she could, Erin screamed, "You goddamn jerk!"

Luki responded with a "Go to hell!" and hurried to his front door, never noticing that Jinx had ripped a hole in his bloody sweatshirt.

Erin was shaking like a leaf as she tried in vain to calm the dogs. Bo was limping in circles and Jinx was frozen in place with a piece of cloth clenched in her jaws.

"Come on, kids. Let's go back inside and settle down." Erin herded them into her living room, sat on the couch, and took deep breaths. As a vet, she knew Bo wasn't hurt too badly, but she was livid. "It's okay," she whispered to the dogs and patted them both, telling them how good they were. She held her hand under Jinx's mouth and said, "Drop it, girl." Jinx did...but not before she started growling again.

* * * * *

Scott sat down next to Wendy Stephens and placed a blanket over her quivering shoulders. "Hey there. I want you to come with me downstairs. Can you do that?"

Wendy nodded but didn't move an inch.

As the small room was filling up quickly with cops, emergency personnel, and the motel's manager, all waiting for the medical examiner and all chattering like hungry squirrels, Scott needed to remove the girl from the scene as soon as he could.

So he asked her again and, this time, Wendy rose and—like a zombie—walked out the door, Scott hovering like a protective father. He'd seen the horrifying mess in the bathroom so he couldn't even imagine what she'd felt upon discovering her roommate strung up—twisting and bleeding—like a butchered hog.

Hanging from the shower curtain rod by her hair, Christy Anderson's face and breasts were hacked to pieces by knife wounds. "Whore" was carved across her belly, mingling with the lower intestines that had emerged from the deep cuts. Blood poured down the back of her legs from where she'd been brutally sodomized and Scott almost got sick thinking about it.

He gently guided Wendy to the motel's courtyard, got her seated at a table by the pool, and said, "If you're up to it, please tell me what you know. Every little detail."

## Friday, March 23 - 10PM

Scott sat down in the lounge chair and gazed at the dark ocean. *What a crap day*, he thought as he rubbed Jinx's ears.

Having already seen the evening news, Erin brought him a beer. "You okay, honey?"

"Christ, babe, this is almost unbelievable. Two dead women in two days, the media is already crucifying us because we haven't caught the shithead yet, so John's tearing his hair out, and with spring breakers coming out of the woodwork..." Scott shook his head and pulled Erin down beside him.

"Need I ask if you're home for the night?"

"Let's put it this way. I'm *planning* on it, but I guess it depends upon our perp." Scott squeezed her hand. "But there's nothing I'd rather do than get a hot shower, curl up beside you, and sleep."

"Sounds fine, but do you want something to eat first?" Erin asked.

"Not really. Guess I should, though. Got any nachos?"

"Sure. I'll be right back. Oh, and I hate to stress you out any more than you already are, but wait till I tell you what happened with that creep next door."

# CHAPTER THREE

## Saturday, March 24 - 7AM

Kaitlyn Prentice packed her Toyota with all the stuff she'd need over at the beach. The 17-year-old daughter of Orlando's mayor was not about to miss out on the spring break action, even if it meant sneaking out of the house before her parents woke up.

Knowing they'd be seriously pissed off—especially her dad—Kaitlyn left a note, texted five of her friends and told them she'd be at the Cocoa Beach Pier in an hour or so.

Cruising the highway, she amped up the CD player and sang merrily along with Lady Gaga. *This was going to be such a super day,* she thought, as she reached the county line.

\* \* \* \* \*

Scott woke up with a massive headache after tossing and turning most of the night. He'd kept thinking about the murdered young women, about the killer still running loose...and about the second encounter Jinx had had with Erin's new neighbor. Something had burrowed into his brain and stayed there.

Dressing quickly, he motioned to the dogs and headed for the beach, hoping Erin didn't wake up. He needed to sort his thoughts the only way he knew how...he'd have a talk with his God while the sun rose over his beloved ocean.

\* \* \* \* \*

Erin was sitting at the table reading the gory details of the two murders in the morning paper when Scott returned with the hungry dogs, who immediately dashed over to their breakfast.

"Morning, sweetie," she said without taking her eyes off the printed page. "Get yourself some coffee, then come read this before you go."

Scott sat down. "Just tell me the bottom line. Are they calling in the militia yet?"

"No, but they're making noises about the FBI, for God's sake."

"Well, ya know. We probably could use the help." Scott frowned, then said, "But, I was thinking...that weirdo next door. He moved in what? Thursday?"

Erin nodded. "Yeah, pretty sure that's when."

Scott continued, "And Amy Blair was killed sometime overnight Thursday. Then yesterday, Christy Anderson. And I know there are a gazillion strangers in town now, but Jinx has really gone nuts the two times she's seen this dude."

Erin took off her reading glasses, a quizzical look on her face. "Honey, where are you going with this?"

Scott held up his hand. "Bear with me a minute. What did you do with that piece Jinx tore off the asshole's shirt?"

"I threw it in the laundry room wastebasket 'cause she was very upset. Honestly, I had a really hard time making her give it to me." Erin's big brown eyes got bigger. "Oh, God, are you thinking what I think you're thinking?"

Scott got up and said, "I'm going to go look at that cloth, but I'll close the door, so Jinx should be fine. Just stay here with her and Bo for a sec."

Five minutes and a cell phone call later, Scott poked his head out from the laundry room and told Erin he needed a couple Ziplocs. Another minute later, he came out and said, "Babe, I gotta go. Like, now, before Jinx gets a whiff of this. I'll call you from the lobby and explain."

Before Erin had a chance to say a word, he was out the door.

* * * * *

Luki pulled out of the parking lot and drove toward the pier. He knew he was probably a bit early but his adrenaline was pumping. Until he'd totally released his inner anger over the useless death of his sister, he would not—could not—rest. Gunning the engine, his tires squealed down Ocean Beach Blvd.

* * * * *

Lenore watched the Cadillac roar down the road. Thinking that she really should tell someone about what she'd seen in the past few days, she fell asleep.

* * * * *

Scott called upstairs and Erin answered before the second ring.

"For starters, I'm glad you don't have to work today because I want you to stay close to home, okay?"

Erin stood on the balcony, staring at the ocean, and said, "I can do that. But mind telling me why? I mean, you're scaring me." A pelican flew right over her head and she jumped like she'd been shot.

"The reason Jinx went bonkers over that cloth is because it's covered in blood and I need to get it to John ASAP." Scott's headache was getting worse. "So not only do I not want to worry about you, but neither do I want that freak to hurt Jinx if y'all were to run into him again. Got it?"

"I got it. Loud and clear."

"Good," Scott said. "Another thing. Do you have your property manager's number? I don't want to talk to anyone yet, but I'd like to have it handy."

"Hold on." Erin rummaged through her files and found her leasing agreement. "Here it is."

Scott wrote down the information, started the Tahoe, and told Erin again to stay put. Gunning the engine, his tires squealed down Ocean Beach Blvd...in the opposite direction from the one Luki Hasan had taken in search of his next piece of ass.

* * * * *

John Patterson was exhausted. But he sat at his

desk and listened patiently to Scott's theory that the murders and Erin's new neighbor were connected.

After his best detective had spilled his guts, John said quietly, "I don't know, Scott. Kind of a flimsy thread but we'll definitely check out the blood type. Yet, if you think about it, Jinx could very well have bitten the guy and that's where the blood came from." He sighed and shook his head. "Hard to say, as we certainly can't go ask this man to give us a sample."

"Damn it!" Scott pounded his fist on the desk. "I know Jinx didn't bite him, not from the way Erin described what happened. Damn it! Damn it!"

"Hey. Don't give up yet. Let's just take this one step at a time. I got the lab tech working on it, even though she's bitching up a storm because it's Saturday and she wanted to go down to the pier."

"Well, on that cheery note, here's an idea." Scott fingered the tiny piece of bloodied shirt that he'd cut off and stuck in his pocket. "How about I canvas the Sea Side residents and see if any of them have noticed anything suspicious lately?"

John smiled. "Good thought. Since we have zero leads, both the chief and the mayor are having extreme panic attacks. Especially with the Easter surf festival in two weeks."

Scott got up and said, "Christ, I totally forgot about that. Bet the sponsors are having fits, too."

"That's an understatement. Anyway, let's go pound pavement. Unless you need some help, I want to talk to Wendy Stephens again. She was pretty out of it yesterday."

"Can't blame her. Hell, wonder if she's still in town..." Scott looked at his boss. "Okay, let's hit the streets."

## Saturday, March 24 - 10AM

Kaitlyn Prentice was on a serious high. Aside from the joint she and her friends had shared in the confines of her car, she was basking in the glow of the sun, sand, and surf.

As a politician's daughter, Kaitlyn always felt like she was under a public microscope. Here, on the beach, she was just another young girl out for a good time. Grinning from ear to ear, she chatted with all the guys who stopped by her "spot" to say hello...and ogle her huge breasts that she'd done little to conceal.

After a geeky nerd had gotten her "not interested" message, Kaitlyn noticed an extremely handsome man sitting not far away, silently watching. Figuring he was a bit older—therefore, more mature—than most of the crowd, she gave him a rueful smile and a shrug. As if to say, "What can I do? I know I'm beautiful."

Luki Hasan smiled back and winked.

* * * * *

Scott went by to check on Erin and the dogs before he began the painstaking chore of knocking on doors. He'd also taken an official statement from her, knowing that would be the easiest one he got from the Sea Side residents.

*Thank God, this is a ritzy place and there are only twenty condos*, Scott thought as he walked down the emergency stairs. Plus, he realized he had to ask fairly general questions so as not to alarm anyone...or to alert the suspect he was investigating.

After no responses until he got to the fifth floor, Scott was getting frustrated. Wondering if this was a waste of time, he nevertheless continued to ask those he found at home if they'd noticed anything suspicious lately. Told them he was just following procedure because of Sea Side's close proximity to the recent murder scenes. He got absolutely nowhere with the few he talked to until he reached the second floor, where a very old lady invited him in. Lenore Rosenberg, after all, had a lot to say.

* * * * *

Hasan had found the perfect place to dispose of his gore-covered gloves, wash his hands and knife, and otherwise clean up before heading to the condo: the

Banana River. As this waterway was lined with a myriad of access ramps, Luki had discovered a semi-hidden path not far from the pier, one lined with weeds as tall as he was that suited his purposes just fine. This time, he'd left a body there, too.

But no way was he going to toss his only trophy, the blood-stained sweatshirt. He'd put it in the garbage bag he kept under the bed with the two others he'd stashed, as the smell was a great comfort to him. He'd also take great pleasure in keeping this slut's fluids since she thought she was so high and mighty. Even as he slashed her to ribbons, she kept on mewling something about her daddy being fucking important. As if he fucking cared.

Checking the time, Luki decided to swing by the next fast-food drive-through he saw. Having skimped on meals for the last few days, he was suddenly famished so a rare hamburger dripping its juices down his chin was something he now craved more than chopping up another whore.

*  *  *  *  *

Sitting on the edge of his seat, devouring Lenore's words with every fiber of his being, Scott was jolted out of focus by the buzzing of his cell phone. John was calling.

"Excuse me a moment, Mrs. Rosenberg," he said. "I really need to take this."

"Of course, Detective McBride." Lenore flicked her fingers towards the kitchen. "Take it in there. I'm not going anywhere."

Gone for a mere minute, Scott returned to the chair by the window and told the elderly woman he'd have to be leaving soon. A press conference was scheduled and his presence was required. But, if it was okay with her, he'd return later in the afternoon to finish their talk.

Lenore beamed and assured the young detective that was not a problem. That she was very glad someone had shown up who had the same concerns she did about "that weird new guy." That maybe they could have a glass of brandy together.....

.....Checking his surroundings, Luki hurried toward the lobby and stopped cold. For there, in a second-floor window, he saw the guy who owned the dog, chatting in earnest with some old bitch. On high alert, he darted through the door and raced up the stairs, not wanting to be seen waiting for the elevator. His heart pounding faster than his steps, his only thought was that he was running out of time.

## Saturday, March 24 - 1PM

Hank Harris, the mayor of Cocoa Beach, stood in front of the cameras sweating bullets. Alongside him, the chief of police looked just as nervous; behind him, Scott and John stared grimly at the media and the gathering crowd.

After the usual platitudes that law enforcement was doing everything within their power to apprehend the perpetrator of the recent murders, Harris turned to Patterson and introduced him, inviting him to add his comments. John reiterated what the mayor had said, thanked everyone for their patience, and turned away before the news crews could pepper him with questions he had no answers for.

Scott followed him and thought that, on a scale of one to ten, this particular press conference was a big fat zero.

* * * * *

Sitting in John's office, Scott grabbed a cup of coffee for both of them. "Well, that went well," he said.

John sighed. "I tried to talk the idiot out of it but you know politicians. But, on the bright side, we may have a bit of a lead."

Scott was all ears. "Yeah? And it is?"

"Well, the lab tech had already typed the blood from the two victims. Then she did the piece of shirt you brought in this morning and there was a match."

"I knew it!" Scott almost yelped.

"Hold on now." John picked up the lab report from his desk and handed it to Scott. "It seems that Christy Anderson is AB-negative, which is fairly rare. And what the tech got off the shirt was the same." He hesitated and took a sip of coffee. "It's still a stretch, but your instincts were good, Scott. At least now we have a reason to give this guy a closer look."

"Well, after you hear what one of the Sea Side residents told me, we may be able to get a whole lot closer."

* * * * *

Hasan sat on his balcony, staring at nothing. The "dog guy" had him worried as he could not figure out what the man was doing. From the first time he'd seen him, Luki had him pegged as the redhead's lover. But now he was wondering if there was more to him than met the eye. *And what was with that fucking dog?*

Then, as the sun began its slow decline to the west, it dawned on him. The bastard might be a cop.

Since Luki had no idea of who was who in this stupid little town, he had no way of knowing anything about its police force. Fuck! Just what he needed. A yokel Dirty Harry wannabe hanging out right next door and getting suspicious at that.

*Calm down*, he told himself. Lana's revenge isn't over yet. One more...at least one more. And maybe this time he'd get an erection, something he'd never had before. Terrified of sex due to his father and his religion, Hasan had a dick as limp as a cooked noodle and that angered him, too. All everyone seemed to care about was sex and more sex. But look what it had done to Lana.

He slapped himself in the head to clear his mind. Got to get going soon before the beach empties. *Go, Luki, go.* He could almost hear his sister prodding him. And with that, Hasan showered, changed into clean clothes, and this time headed south on A1A to Minutemen Causeway.

\* \* \* \* \*

Billy Jarvis steered his bike down the shaded path to the river. An Iraq war veteran, he'd been homeless for ten years and he came to this secret spot at least once a week to troll for oysters. Something that made him extremely popular with his fellow "campers," as he provided enough food for a communal cookout.

Grabbing his rake and bag, Jarvis waded into the water, then stopped and stared. *What the hell is that yellow stuff floating around?* Baby-stepping his way closer, Billy Jarvis saw something that scared the shit out of him. Dropping his gear, he ran like a bat out of hell toward the highway.

\* \* \* \* \*

Scott smiled at Lenore as she served him a glass of brandy in a dainty china cup. Her official statement already recorded, he thought he'd stay and chat for a while, as the old woman was obviously lonely. That idea went out the window when his cell phone buzzed. It was John again...another body had just been found.

\* \* \* \* \*

Megan Morse flung her long, blond hair from side to side as the camera captured every move she made.

The 22-year-old model from Miami was doing a swimsuit photo shoot for a national sports publication and knew this could be the break she'd been waiting for. Megan flashed a winning smile at the photographer when he signaled "that's a wrap" and hoped her half-naked pictures would be decent enough to plaster across the magazine's cover.

Grabbing a towel and an iced tea, Megan sauntered down to the water. Knowing she was being ogled by everyone, man and woman alike, she loved the attention. Especially from a super-looking guy who stood ankle deep in the surf with a look of bemusement on his face.

Approaching him, she asked, "So, did you enjoy the show?"

"Sure did, darlin'. My name is Larry...and you are?" Luki Hasan knew he'd found his next conquest when an hour later he'd made a dinner date with Megan Morse.

## Saturday, March 24 - 7PM

John Patterson's face was ashen. It had taken no time at all to identify the latest victim as the daughter of Orlando's mayor, Dale Prentice, from a political flyer found in her purse. And the shit quickly hit the fan.

Kaitlyn's family had been immediately notified and her father chauffeured to Cocoa Beach, where he'd given an in-depth interview to the media. Consequently, the story was already plastered as "breaking news" across the entire central Florida area.

Patterson looked across his desk at Scott, who was looking at the ceiling. "Okay, boyo. I want you to go and park it at Sea Side until you see that Cadillac. Then run the plates." He rubbed his jaw. "Christ, this is the only viable lead we have so far, though I'm still wondering if we're barking up the wrong tree."

Although Scott was listening, he was having a lot of trouble getting the picture of Kaitlyn Prentice's corpse out of his mind. "Okay, I'm on it. But, shit, I sure as hell hope we find whoever is doing this soon because he's obviously escalating. I mean, that poor girl didn't even look human."

"I know," John muttered, lost in his own morbid recap of the body's condition. "Anyway, you get going, and I'm going to finish up with Kaitlyn's friends. Though it's probably a waste of time since I'm having no luck at all in getting a decent description other than well-built and good-looking." He grabbed his keys and said, "Which describes about half the men on the beach now, and there are thousands of them. Oh, by the way, I put in a call to the property manager. Had to leave a message."

Scott shook his head as he followed his boss out the door. "Let me know if you hear back. I'm going to do a quick check on Erin and get Jinx, too. She and I will sit in the Tahoe and watch. Maybe we'll get lucky."

Patterson replied with no enthusiasm at all, "Yeah. Maybe."

* * * * *

Erin picked up the pepper spray off the foyer table and ushered the dogs out to the elevator, well aware of Scott's worry. But Jinx and Bo had bodily functions to attend to, the nut next door be damned.

After a good fifteen minutes in the side yard, she was returning to her condo when she saw Scott pull up.

"Hey you! Now don't get mad. The dogs had to go!" Erin hurried over to the SUV.

Scott hugged her and said, "Babe, I just didn't want you to stray too far, that's all." Noticing the can of spray in her hand, he smiled. "Besides, I knew you'd protect yourself."

Erin watched as the two dogs happily greeted this man they loved...the man she loved, too. "So, what the hell is happening? I saw on the news they found another body?"

Scott leaned wearily against the Tahoe and said, "Yeah. And it was beyond brutal. So Jinx and I are going to spend the night in the parking lot." Hearing her name, the shepherd sat and stared at her master. "Aren't we, girl?" Jinx barked.

"You're what??" Erin looked at him like he'd lost it.

"There was a type-match from one of the victims and the blood on that piece of shirt you gave me, so we're gonna sit out here and wait for your new neighbor to come home. According to Mrs. Rosenberg on the second floor, he drives a black Cadillac, so shouldn't be too hard to spot. I'll get the tag number and run it for an ID," Scott explained while he put Jinx in the back seat.

"Damn, Scott. Since I've been stuck inside all day, I cooked your favorite dinner."

"I'm sorry, sweetheart, but that lasagna is gonna have to wait. Hey, why don't you freeze it, and we'll celebrate with that and a huge bottle of wine when this is all over? Sound like a plan?" Scott knew Erin was disappointed and he felt like shit. Which reminded him that he needed to stop by his own house soon and check on the place, including the small diamond ring he'd bought for—hopefully—his soon-to-be fiancee.

"That sounds great. I'll just make a sandwich for dinner. What about you?"

Scott jerked his head towards the back and said, "Can't you tell?" Erin looked in where Jinx was staring intently at a bag of groceries on the Tahoe's floor.

"Oh, I see. You're settled in for a while, I guess. Call me later, okay?" With that, she kissed him and patted Jinx. "You two be careful! I love you." She turned and walked Bo back to the front door.

Scott watched her leave with a heavy heart and prayed this vigil was worth the effort.

## Saturday, March 24 - 10PM

Dinner at Surf-n-Turf had been a stellar success. Over multiple margaritas, Luki regaled Megan with his exotic background and she'd sat in awe of this man who had nothing more on his mind than piercing her vapid eyes with his switch blade.

Now, pulling into the Sea Side parking lot, Luki noticed a Chevy Tahoe that looked out of place simply because it sat all by its lonesome two rows behind all the other vehicles.

He got out of the Cadillac and stood staring at the entrance, waiting for Megan's rental car to appear. Yet he was also checking out the SUV and his adrenaline kicked into overdrive when he saw movement inside. Since street lights were right overhead, a man and a dog were clearly outlined in the front seat.

*Motherfucker,* he thought as he smiled at the eager whore trotting in his direction. Scrambling for what to do next, Luki Hasan knew there would be no revenge for Lana tonight. But what to do with the slut now that she was here?

Megan reached him and said, "Oh, whoa, Larry! What

a gorgeous place! Can't wait to see the view from your balcony."

Luki grabbed her hand and led her towards the lobby. "Yes, my darlin', I think you'll enjoy it." Chewing the inside of his cheek, he jabbed the elevator button.

Opening the door to the penthouse, Luki had a brainstorm. Pulling his cell phone from his pocket, he looked at the screen, frowned, then said, "Damn!"

"What's wrong, Larry?"

"Talk about bad timing. We're going to have to cut this evening short. Got a text from my connections in Dubai so it looks like I'm going to be on the phone all night dealing with this. Time difference and all that."

Megan poofed her lips out into what she thought was a cute pout. "Oh, shit. I was sooo looking forward to some serious sex."

Luki tried to act disappointed but could only think about how soon he could get her out of his condo. "I'm really sorry, my love. But how about I pick you up at dawn? Maybe we can catch the sunrise from up here and then we'll spend the day taking care of each other." He winked and Megan smiled.

"Ooh. That sounds wonderful," she cooed.

Luki got the hotel's name and Megan's room number, then sent her on her way. His head starting to pound, he went to bed. And, soaked in sweat, he plotted his next move.

* * * * *

Scott sat at Erin's dining room table, papers strewn about like confetti, and took notes as he talked to his boss.

"Well, he took the girl up to his condo so I didn't know what the hell to do. I mean, I couldn't very well bust in on him for bringing a date home. But it was weird...about ten minutes later, the girl came out of the lobby and left in her car, headed south."

"Is that all ya got?" Patterson asked him.

"No, there's more," Scott said. "I ran the plates. A

2011 Cadillac Escalade registered to a Luki Hasan of Daytona Beach. DMV records show a 5'11' male, 27-years-old, born in Saudi, has a green card." He scrolled down on his laptop. "Couldn't get the girl's tags as she wheeled out of here too fast. But I do know she's driving a beige, late-model Sonata."

"That's my man," John said. "I still haven't heard back from the property manager so I'll try again in the morning. So is this Luki still at home or do you know?"

"We waited for an hour." Scott rubbed the dog's ears. "But no activity so I came up to Erin's. Figure he's in for the night. At least, I hope he is. Not a lot else we can do right now, is there?"

"Guess not. So we're back to pissing in the wind. Shit!" John looked at the clock and said, "But I will have one of the pier patrol cars cruise Sea Side every hour just in case."

"Good idea. Anyway, I'm going to eat something and then hit the hay. I'm bushed...but ya know something I just thought of? That old lady, Mrs. Rosenberg, told me she sits up half the night since she can't sleep. That's why she's noticed this guy's comings and goings. I'll check with her tomorrow just for the hell of it."

"Okay, Scott. Now, go get some sleep." John yawned into the phone. "I'm gonna do the same unless..."

"Yeah, unless." Scott yawned, too, then hung up.

# CHAPTER FOUR

## Sunday, March 25 - 7AM

Officer Jimmy Donahue woke up with a start and looked at his watch. Time to go home. He'd missed the 6:00AM run by that condo complex but figured since the vehicle had been in the same place all night that he probably hadn't missed anything at all. A cop for forty years, Donahue didn't really care much either. Retirement was a month away and, crossing the causeway to Merritt Island, his thoughts drifted to eating a big breakfast with his wife before going to early Mass.

* * * * *

Luki wiped off the switch blade while viewing the gory piece of trash on the bed.

Megan's head was almost severed. Her breasts were, too. But, this time, Hasan had left the face intact...other than the word "whore" etched from left to right across the model's prominent cheekbones. Thoroughly disgusted by the sight, he hadn't felt like ramming his knife up her ass. So, instead, he'd just sliced off *those* cheeks and laid them on top of her flopping boobs.

Satisfied, and as sated as his impotence would allow, Hasan removed his sweatshirt and gloves, then stuffed them into one of Megan's carryalls. As an afterthought, he grabbed her purse.

Naked from the waist up, Luki drove back to the Sea Side complex. Leaving the bags in the Escalade, he put the knife in his pocket and scurried down to the beach. He'd rinse off in the water while trying to look like any other guy going for a casual sunrise walk along the shore.

Sensing that his revenge was over, Hasan wanted to savor the events of the last few days before he returned to the condo, retrieved his meager belongings, and got the hell out of town...and this God-forsaken country.

\* \* \* \* \*

Lenore Rosenberg woke with a start and looked out the bay window. There he was again! Now he had no shirt on. She noted the time and decided she'd call that nice Detective McBride and tell him what she'd seen.

\* \* \* \* \*

Scott forgot he had his cell phone set on ring, so when Springsteen's "Born in the USA" blared, he knocked over his coffee cup in surprise, Jinx started barking, then so did Bo, and Erin just shook her head and grinned.

"Yo! McBride here." He looked sheepishly at Erin and mouthed an apology as she began to clean up the mess.

"Uh, hello, Detective McBride. This is Lenore Rosenberg, the lady you interviewed. Remember?"

Scott got up and started pacing. "Of course, I remember you. Is everything all right? I mean, it's awfully early..."

"Oh, dear, I'm sorry. Did I wake you?" Lenore was suddenly feeling stupid for calling.

"No, no, it's fine. Do you need me to come to your place? I can be there in no time."

Lenore smiled to herself as she knew exactly where the handsome detective was. "Actually, Detective, if you'll go out on the balcony and look up and down the beach, you may see the subject of this call."

Scott hesitated. "Um, I'm not sure what you mean..."

Lenore interrupted him, her voice filled with warmth. "It's quite all right, Detective. As you know, I see everything that goes on around here so it would be rather hard to miss you and your beautiful dog going upstairs and not coming down." She added, "Personally, I think it's wonderful."

Scott grinned at the woman's perceptive candor. "Thanks, Mrs. Rosenberg. I appreciate that. And, now,

I'm doing just what you suggested. In the distance, I do see a guy walking in the water."

Lenore asked, "Is he shirtless? Or can you tell?"

"Shirtless? Can't be sure. It's still a little dark, and he's pretty far down."

"Well, let me fill you in while you watch." And Lenore Rosenberg proceeded to relate Luki Hasan's departure from the condo at precisely 5:15, his return at precisely 6:48.

Scott thanked the woman and hung up, scowling. He glanced at the time and noted it was ten after seven. The sun was just starting to show itself. And so was the wind. The only thought that crossed his mind was that the seas were going to get very rough very soon.

* * * * *

Rob Vance had owned and operated the Sand Dunes since 1985. Tucked in between the high-rise hotels that now loomed over the beach, his establishment was nevertheless considered a great place to stay as the ten suites offered small fully-equipped kitchens within each one. And many tourists enjoyed the personal attention Vance doled out, so he never had a problem with vacancies.

Doing his morning inspection, he walked around the U-shaped building not expecting to find much out of the ordinary as it was early Sunday. Yet he caught a glimpse of something definitely not right. Checking his clipboard, Vance noted who was staying in the end unit. A model from Miami and her door was blown wide open by the brisk breeze. As he reached the woman's room, he peeked in. Gagging, Vance stumbled back to the office and dialed 911.

* * * * *

Scott leaned on the balcony enjoying the fabulous view as much as any cop on alert could. But the wind was whipping up some decent waves that reminded him he hadn't been surfing in months.

Shoving that thought aside, he continued to watch the lone figure meandering slowly down the beach. Not sure if he should call John right away, his ringing phone took the decision out of his hands.

"Oh, no," is all he said when he saw it was his boss on the other end.

"Oh, yes," Patterson replied. "Motel manager down south found a dead body in one of his units. It's a young woman from Miami. Name of Megan Morse. No ID in the room but get this. There is a beige Sonata sitting right outside her door. I'm getting a search warrant as we speak."

Scott kept his eyes focused on the guy walking the beach. "Okay, John. I'm fairly certain I have Hasan in my sights." He related the info Lenore had provided, then asked, "So what do you want me to do?"

"I think we have enough to bring him in for questioning. You want to handle it alone or do you want backup?"

Scott thought a minute, then replied, "Why not send a patrol car with two officers up here. Tell them to wait in the parking lot and to be on the lookout for Hasan. I'm going to grab my cuffs and Taser from the truck just in case I run into a problem. But I'll have Jinx with me so…"

"Sounds like a plan," John said. "I'll meet you at the station whenever I get done here. But, Scott, be careful. If Hasan is indeed the perp, he has absolutely nothing to lose now."

"Will do, John. See ya in a bit."

* * * * *

Lenore Rosenberg found the old binoculars her Bernie had used in his bird-watching days, grabbed her cane, and went out on her balcony. She dusted off the sand from the rarely-used patio chair, sat down, and scanned the beach.

## Sunday, March 25 - 8AM

Two patrol cars entered the Sea Side parking lot just as Scott locked the Tahoe and headed towards the back of the complex. He gave them a thumbs up and, with Jinx on her leash, walked down to the dunes. Squatting, he fingered the baggie he'd placed in his T-shirt pocket and, as quietly as possible, opened the zip-lock just enough to make it easier for him to pull out its contents if need be.

Noticing Lenore sitting on her balcony—and Erin perched on hers—Scott put a finger to his lips in a 'be quiet' signal, then placed Jinx in a "down-stay" position. Seconds later, he saw Hasan turn back toward the condos.

\* \* \* \* \*

As Luki neared the complex, he saw someone sitting beside the beach access path. And the closer he got, he saw that it was the blond guy and his goddamn dog! *Fuck, now what?*

Still walking, he nevertheless slowed his pace as he tried to figure out the best thing to do. Maybe he should just act nonchalant, like nothing was amiss. Even go on the offense. And that's just what he'd decided to do when he saw the man rise and head in his direction.

\* \* \* \* \*

The old binoculars were working well so Lenore Rosenberg saw the furious expression on the weirdo's face as if he were right next to her. Reaching behind a potted plant, she grabbed the air horn she kept there to scare away coons.

\* \* \* \* \*

"Yo, Mr. Hasan," Scott called out, tightening his grip on Jinx's leash and commanding her to shush. "You are Luki Hasan, correct?"

Luki sneered and said, "Oh, it's you and your fucking dog again. And why is it any of your business who I am?"

Scott stopped within five feet of Hasan and said, "Sir, my name is Scott McBride and I'm a detective with the Cocoa Beach Police. I need you to come down to the station and answer a few questions regarding some recent unpleasant activities that have occurred since your arrival. So, you can come with me peacefully or, if not, I'm afraid I'll have to place you under arrest as a prime suspect."

Her nose twitching furiously, Jinx strained at the leash, a menacing growl low in her throat. And Scott knew then the situation was going to get out of control...fast.

Luki Hasan did the first thing that entered his mind. In an abrupt about-face, he ran pell-mell towards the ocean. Scott couldn't believe what the stupid shit was doing but he knew the "game over" was in his pocket.

Removing the blood-scented cloth and tossing it in the air, Scott released Jinx and commanded her to "find it." Needing no added incentive, Jinx shot off like a bullet after the fleeing man at the very same time that Lenore Rosenberg stood on wobbly legs and blew the air horn...over and over and over.

\* \* \* \* \*

Hasan zig-zagged in the knee-deep surf, heading back the way he'd come yet fully prepared to dive into the whitecaps and swim parallel to the shore until he reached the pier. But a God-awful sound pierced his ears and he pulled out his switch blade as a huge black-and-silver blur knocked him into the waves.

\* \* \* \* \*

Stunned at the events unfolding below her, yet trained to act in a heartbeat to life-threatening situations, Erin turned and ran through the penthouse, then down the stairs with a speed born of sheer protectiveness. Her loved ones were in mortal danger.....

.....The two cops waiting in the parking lot heard what sounded like an air-raid siren and, as one, emerged from their cars and ran towards the beach, guns drawn.

\* \* \* \* \*

Hasan felt an excruciating pain in his calf as he struggled to right himself. The fucking dog had a grip on his leg but, terrified and enraged, Luki managed to twist himself around and stab the beast with every ounce of strength he possessed, burying the blade deep into the animal's neck.

Taser in hand, Scott reached the pair just as Jinx collapsed. Writhing in the water, blood pooling around her head, she was starting to sink. Without a second thought, Scott pulled her to shore.

\* \* \* \* \*

Officers Joe Maxwell and Ryan Brady followed the redhead, who was screaming at the top of her lungs. All three converged on the man holding the wounded dog in his arms, his hand wrapped around the hilt of the protruding knife trying to stem the flow of blood. Scott looked up at them with tears in his eyes and simply said, "Kill that motherfucker!!".....

.....Lenore Rosenberg placed the binoculars and the air horn on the table beside her chair. She'd dialed 911 when she saw the shirtless son-of-a-bitch stab the dog. Hearing the sirens blaring behind her, there was nothing more she could do except try to pinpoint for the inevitable search parties exactly where Luki Hasan had disappeared into the sea.

# EPILOGUE

## Monday, March 26 - 7AM

The fisherman leaned on the pier's railing and dropped his line into the water. Simply hoping to get in a little quiet time before the beach started filling up with spring breakers, he yawned and watched the sun start its spectacular rise in the east.

Not really expecting to catch anything, he perked up when his rod bowed with a giant tug and he started reeling in as fast as he could. Seeing part of a bloody torso dangling from his hook, he staggered and puked all over his feet.

## Monday, March 26 - Noon

*We have breaking news at the top of the hour. The mangled body of Luki Hasan, the man accused of committing the recent atrocious murders of young women in Cocoa Beach, was recovered this morning. According to police, sharks had torn him apart and were most likely attracted by the gaping wound in his calf that a heroic ex-Military Working Dog inflicted yesterday morning when authorities trapped Hasan on the beach behind the Sea Side Condominiums.*

*Ironically, the remains of Hasan's body were discovered floating beside the pilings of the Cocoa Beach Pier where his first victim was also found. Stay tuned for further developments...*

## Monday, March 26 - 2PM

Scott had just stepped out of the shower when he heard his phone ringing.

"McBride here," he said.

"Hey, buddy," John Patterson spoke softly to his friend and colleague. "Just wanted to tell you that forensics got a set of fingerprints from the model's purse and compared them to those on file for Hasan. They match." He took a deep breath. "We also showed his license and green card photos to Wendy Stephens and she positively identified him as the guy Christy Anderson went off with. So I think we can call this case closed."

Scott listened intently and simply said, "Thanks for the info, John. Glad to hear the asshole was finally ID'd."

"Okay, that's all for now. I'll see ya Wednesday, right?"

"Yep, I'll be there with bells on."

Patterson started to hang up, but not before he asked the dreaded question. "Scott, I'm not sure how to say this. But Jinx. Is she...?"

His query went unanswered as McBride had already disconnected.

## Monday, March 26 - 3PM

The old woman's aging face lit up in girlish glee when she saw the dozen roses clutched in the young man's hand.

"These are for you, Mrs. Rosenberg. And, believe me, these flowers will never be enough to express my gratitude for all your help. If it wasn't for your information, no telling what would've happened." Scott smiled down at her and wiggled his eyebrows. "And I absolutely loved the air horn."

Lenore grinned. "You can borrow it any time, my dear."

## Monday, March 26 - 9PM

The full moon hovered over the ocean like a giant white ball suspended in space, its stark brilliance intensified by a stiff breeze that carried the clouds out to sea.

Sitting on the balcony, the table cleared of the remnants of an overdue lasagna dinner, Erin glanced at

Scott who seemed lost in deep thought.

"Earth to Detective McBride." She couldn't help but laugh. "Where'd you go, sweetie? Moonwalking?"

"Not at all. Just thinking how happy I am." He reached down and gently scratched around Jinx's bandaged neck. "I mean, what a difference a day makes, huh? Yesterday, I thought I'd lost one of the most precious things in my life. Today, thanks to you, I'm joyous."

"Joyous, huh?" Erin held up her left hand and watched the diamond glitter in the moonlight. "Hope you say that fifty years from now."

Scott smiled at his future wife, then at the two dogs snoring at their feet. "Seriously, Erin. I have to say the females really saved the day. Mrs. Rosenberg and her impromptu air raid. You and your medical knowledge. And, of course..." He knelt on the floor and cradled his injured pet's massive head.

Looking into the dog's sleepy eyes, he said, "You knew all along, didn't you, girl? That dumb son-of-a-bitch was outclassed, outsmarted, outmaneuvered..." He paused, took a deep breath, then whispered in her ear, "and totally jinxed."

### -END-

# About the Author of *Jinxed*

**Rebecca Stroud:** As an ardent animal lover, I have been involved with all creatures great and small for over thirty years, both hands-on and through my writing/activism. I am a former reporter/columnist; a former SPCA employee and wildlife sanctuary volunteer; and a present thorn in the side of anyone who abuses those who cannot defend themselves (be they human or animal).

And although I am now a full-time author, writing the gamut from short stories to suspense fiction, you can count on finding a dog in every work I produce.

I currently live in Florida with my wonderful husband and my adored—and very old—border collie mix. Suffice it to say, both are a handful, but I wouldn't trade either of them for the crown jewels.

You can find my books at major online retailers. They are:

**Devil's Moon**

**Do Unto Others**

**Zellwood: A Dog Story**

**A Three-Dog Night**

**The Animal Advocate**

If you'd like to reach me, my email address is: RebeccaStroud@aol.com (but please do put an 'identifier' in the subject line or else the messages go straight to ye olde spam-can).

\* \* \* \* \* \* \* \* \* \*

**All my work is dedicated to my beloved husband who, without a doubt, is the best thing that ever happened to me.**

\* \* \* \* \* \* \* \* \* \*